# A SUMMER SOUNDTRACK FOR FALLING IN love

## ARDEN POWELL

**RIPTIDE PUBLISHING**

Riptide Publishing
PO Box 1537
Burnsville, NC 28714
www.riptidepublishing.com

A Summer Soundtrack for Falling in Love

Cover art: Shayne Leighton, parliamentbookdesign.wordpress.com
Editor: Carole-ann Galloway
Layout: L.C. Chase, lcchase.com/design.htm

ISBN: 978-1-62649-853-2

First edition
October, 2018

Also available in ebook:
ISBN: 978-1-62649-852-5

# A SUMMER SOUNDTRACK FOR FALLING IN love

ARDEN POWELL

RIPTIDE PUBLISHING

*For all the bands I've ever loved.*

# TABLE OF CONTENTS

# THE CHOKECHERRIES' SUMMER TOUR SCHEDULE
## NEW YORK TO PURPLE SAGE

June 12: Hershey, PA—Hersheypark Stadium
June 13: Camden, NJ—BB&T Pavilion
June 14: Newark, NJ—Prudential Center
June 15: Charlottesville, VA—John Paul Jones Arena
June 17: Grand Rapids, MI—Van Andel Arena
June 18: Indianapolis, IN—Bankers Life Fieldhouse
June 20: Orlando, FL—Amway Center
June 21: Sunrise, FL—BB&T Center
June 22: Tampa, FL—Amalie Arena
June 23: Birmingham, AL—Legacy Arena
June 24: New Orleans, LA—Smoothie King Center
June 25: Dallas, TX—American Airlines Center
June 26: The Woodlands, TX—Cynthia Woods Mitchell Pavilion
June 27: Austin, TX—Austin360 Amphitheater
June 29: Phoenix, AZ—Talking Stick Resort Arena
June 30: Salt Lake City, UT—Vivint Smart Home Arena
July 1-6: Purple Sage Music Fest, NV

# CHAPTER ONE
## NEW YORK, NEW YORK

K ris Golding wasn't the kind of person to fly across the country
without a plan. His was foolproof, or at least fool resistant—but,
like most plans, was quickly crushed by circumstances outside his
control. When his plane took off from Kansas, he was content in the
knowledge that he had a job and a couch, if not an apartment, waiting
for him. By the time he touched down in New York, everything had
gone terribly wrong.

"What do you mean she kicked you out?" he asked his cousin as
patiently as he could. The cell connection was choppy as he stepped
off the bus in Manhattan after two hours on public transport.

"Well it's her place, right?" Marty said, his voice wheedling over
the line. "It's her name on the lease. So when she found out about me
and Maria, she called it quits. Threw all my stuff out in a garbage bag
on the street."

"Wait, who's Maria?"

"Somebody I work with at the club."

"The club where you said you had a job lined up for me," Kris
clarified.

"Yeah, man, but I got fired today."

"What? Why?"

"Cuz Maria, she's the owner's girl—"

Kris held the phone away from his ear to keep from throwing it
into traffic. He took a deep breath before returning it to hearing range.

"So I don't have a job," he said, cutting off whatever his cousin had
been saying. "And your boss won't introduce me to his music-industry
guys."

"I'm sorry, man, the timing, it's just—"

"And I don't have a place to stay."

Marty made a helpless noise.

"Great. That's amazing. Thanks."

"Hey, I'm in the same boat, okay? You could be a little more sympathetic."

Kris ended the call and shoved his phone back into his pocket.

"Well fuck," he said, to no one in particular. He slung his duffel bag of worldly goods over his shoulder, his guitar case secure on his back, and set off into the streets of New York to figure out what to do next.

The misfortune of his situation didn't detract from New York's beauty, even as his nerves started to gnaw at him. The whole city looked glittering and pulsing with possibility—the place where dreams came true. The buildings loomed high, scraping the clouds in endless panels of polished glass. Sure, everything was huge and impressively daunting, but Kris hadn't come all the way out here to admit defeat, no matter how intimidating the city proved.

He had two hundred dollars in his bank account and a pocketful of loose change. It was barely enough to buy a plane ticket home, but his parents would spring him one if he asked. He would work in his dad's garage to pay them back, and he'd have to keep his tail between his legs for the rest of his life because the one time he'd tried to get out and make something of himself, he'd come crawling back barely six hours later. His parents could be as supportive as they liked, but it wouldn't change the fact that he'd tried and failed. And then there was his brother, Brad, who had told him New York was a bad idea.

*"What's wrong with Kansas?"* Brad had demanded. *"You can make an honest living here. All those big-shot music-industry guys you look up to, they've never done a real day's work in their lives. There's nothing but freaks in that line of work, Kris. You're better off steering clear."*

Kris couldn't bear Brad's smug face if he went back defeated.

If he had to be homeless, at least the weather was good. The June air was warm, the bits of sky he could see between the buildings were blue, and the sun was aggressively bright, like it had something to prove. There were a few hours left before sunset, and even if it cooled down overnight, he had a coat in his bag. He could weather it. He had enough money to stay at a hostel, but only for a night, and he was loath to spend more than he had to. Two hundred dollars and change wouldn't stretch far. No, he would sleep on a bench, and scour the streets for any hiring signs. He could work retail or fast food; he could find a shelter or a friendly couch to crash on until he'd saved enough for a place of his own. He wasn't going to wind up freezing to death on a street corner, gnawed on by rats, as soon as the season changed. He was going to get a job, and he would be fine.

It wasn't a great plan, but it was something.

He started walking.

One problem in applying for jobs was that they wanted an address on the application form. The bigger stores did background checks Kris couldn't pass without a permanent residence, and if they didn't, they weren't hiring anyway. The smaller shops didn't offer more than a few hours a week, and unless he wanted to juggle three conflicting schedules, he'd never make enough to feed himself, let alone get an apartment. His desperation mounted as store after store turned him away, leaving his stomach a knot of anxiety and his palms itching with sweat.

He ended up on a bench at the edge of Central Park watching the pigeons. They were fearless in the way rural birds never were, flashing their colors and strutting back and forth. They quickly determined that he had nothing of value to offer, and ignored him in favor of accosting passing pedestrians for crumbs. Rejected by one of the lowest of the city's inhabitants—though a step up from the rats—Kris again weighed his options.

He still couldn't go home.

Instead, he texted his parents to tell them he'd landed safely, and he'd call them in a few days once he got settled. He was safe, after all; he might be close to panic, but they didn't have to be. He was an adult and he could look after himself. In theory, anyway. He had a bottle of water from the plane, an apple, and a granola bar. His nerves were like a guitar string wound up too tight and liable to snap at any second, and that put a damper on his appetite; what he had would last him till morning.

He settled in for a night on the bench. It wasn't the most comfortable place he'd ever been, but he couldn't say it was the worst, either. He didn't want to lie down in case someone recognized him for a vagrant and called the cops. If he looked like he was just resting a moment, or waiting for someone, he should be fine. He was dressed well enough. No one could tell that he didn't have anywhere else to go.

He crunched through his apple, more for something to do than out of hunger. It tasted sour, but it kept him awake. The sky slipped into pink as the sun sank behind the buildings, lighting them up in a warm glow as it passed. Kris couldn't hate the city. He had chosen New York partly because his cousin was here—working for a guy who had so many connections in the music industry that Marty had sworn he could set Kris up with a gig in no time—but mostly because it was as far from rural Kansas as he could imagine. He loved his parents and he loved his town, but it had been stifling. He didn't want to work in his dad's garage until he was sixty. He might not know exactly what he did want to do with his life, but he was determined to find out.

So far he was finding out that park benches were uncomfortable, and city pigeons were more intimidating than any bird had the right to be.

As the sun went down and the crowds thinned, Kris wrapped himself in his coat and prepared for a long night. The smaller shops locked up for the night as the streets finally emptied. The moon blinked out between the buildings but the stars stayed hidden behind the haze of clouds and the solid blocks of skyscrapers. He paced for a bit, exploring the park with a measured gait, his hands in his pockets as he tried to keep his blood moving. When he couldn't stop his feet from dragging or his eyes from closing, he found another bench and huddled down to roost again.

It didn't get cold, exactly, but it got cool, and the hours dragged into eternity and back. He drifted off once or twice, but the park was never fully deserted and he didn't trust that he'd wake up to find his bags still on him. He wouldn't particularly miss his clothes if the duffel bag got stolen, but his guitar—he couldn't bear the thought of losing that, even if Marty had lost him his chance at a career with it.

He watched the sun rise from the wrong side of the morning for the first time since he was a teenager. The sky lightened in strips: silver, then pale yellow, before making room for blue. The pigeons cooed and rustled their wings, waking one by one and then all at once, and the subways rumbled underground, a constant churning noise.

Straightening, he stretched his back until it gave a satisfying *crack*, and shuffled to his feet. The coffee he bought from a street vendor was black and bitter, and he was ready to shoot the caffeine straight into his veins if he had to. He was tired in a way that made everything feel thin and slightly unreal, like the world was hidden behind a film he could see through, but couldn't quite part.

After his first swallow, he crossed out of the park to the nearest café, busy enough in the morning rush that he could slip into the washroom unnoticed. As he splashed cold water over his face, he hoped he didn't look too haggard. He could stretch it another day before needing to shave; his stubble always took a while to show through, and he was fair enough that it never gave him much of a five-o'clock shadow anyway. Coffee in hand, he returned to his bench, sipping the drink and trying to make it last.

Today he would find somewhere to work. Twenty hours a week in retail might not be his dream of making a living off his music, but it would be better than nothing. He wasn't going to sleep on the bench again.

The pigeons looked skeptical.

He flipped them off and resumed drinking his coffee. The caffeine hit him like a ton of bricks, slamming into him all at once and setting his heart kicking behind his ribs. He took a deep breath and flexed his fingers. It was a drastic way to start the morning, but he was definitely awake now. The film separating him from reality peeled back and left him blinking into the sun like a newborn fawn, all wobbly-legged and uncertain.

*Find a job*, he told himself. *Take the first one you can. This isn't rock-bottom. This isn't even close.*

All he had to do was wait for the stores to come back to life. Most would probably open around nine—it was just past dawn. He had a few hours to kill. The coffee place across the road wasn't hiring, but maybe he could find a record shop or a music store that needed help.

He took out his guitar.

He couldn't say why he did it. There was no conscious thought behind the action. It was like the hand of some divine entity had reached down from the clouds and prodded him, right between the eyes, and said, *Hey, you. Play me something.* Music had always been like that for him, talking to him the way gods spoke to prophets: in the pure, undiluted language of the universe.

His guitar was a big acoustic thing, the wood polished until it glowed warm and gold. He'd bought it from a pawnshop for fifty bucks when he was thirteen; it had taken him all year to save up his allowances for it. In high school, he'd used to dream about his band making it big and playing in Madison Square Garden. It had been a couple of guys from his year and his little sister on drums. It fell apart before graduation and he'd put that particular dream aside, but he'd thought he could try his hand as a session musician, if nothing else. All he needed was one lucky break to get his foot in the door. He wouldn't call himself a prodigy, but he was good, and even if he'd never left Kansas to seek his fortune in the industry, he would have kept playing for himself.

As he tuned his guitar by ear, he ghosted his fingers over the frets, and gave it a strum. The chords rang out clear and true, and he drew in a deep breath as his nerves started to knit themselves together again.

Back home he had played in front of live audiences, albeit small ones—barbeques or house parties or just sitting out on the porch with his family in the summer evenings, strumming out chords overtop of the crickets. He had never busked before, though; his hometown was too small for it, and he'd never been as desperate for quick money as he was now. Easing into a bluegrass riff, half-remembered and half-invented, he kept his eyes down as he played. The song petered out after a few minutes, finding its natural ending like bluegrass always did, and he let the city eke back into his consciousness.

Someone tossed a crumpled bill into the case at his feet, and he smiled reflexively at the young woman who vanished back into the crowded street. He took a swig from his coffee and adjusted the guitar in his lap. Maybe one more song wouldn't hurt. One more song, and then he would start looking for music shops in the area.

By 9 a.m. he had thirty dollars in his case and a steady stream of attention from the park's passersby. By ten he had as much as he would have made from a day's work at any minimum-wage gig. His fingers ached and he was so hungry his stomach nearly drowned out the music with its complaints, but no one had yelled at him for loitering, and the pigeons hadn't tried to make away with his money. He couldn't stop smiling.

He laid his guitar down in the nest of bills and loose coins and closed his case. The little gathering he'd attracted gradually wandered off, one or two people pressing a last offering into his hand as they left. It was only when the path was clear that he noticed the one man who had yet to depart, leaning against the broad trunk of a tree, his arms crossed as he watched Kris unabashedly.

Kris tucked his last few bills in his pocket, raised his brows, and met the man's gaze head-on. In response, the man peeled himself from the tree and approached. He was tall, dark, and handsome, almost ridiculously so, with legs that went on for miles, and a wild mane of deep brown hair that stopped just above his shoulders. He was dressed all in black, chic rather than goth, his shirt open at the collar to reveal a hint of tattoos against the brown skin of his chest.

"Hi there," the man said. He slung his hands in his pockets and smiled, bright and easy. "I was watching you play—you're amazing."

"Thanks," Kris said. "It wasn't a planned performance, but these things happen."

"Do you mind if I sit? I'm Rayne. Rayne Bakshi." Rayne offered a hand. He wore a ring on nearly every finger, and when Kris took it, his grip was warm and firm. He had a little mercury tattoo on the base of his left thumb.

"I was about to go find some food, but sure," Kris said. His stomach whined but he ignored it. There was something about the man that demanded his full attention, and a tingly feeling swept through Kris's veins, suggesting he was perched on the edge of something momentous. He didn't get that feeling very often; it felt careless to disregard it, especially in so strange a time as this. "I'm Kris."

Rayne grinned and slid onto the bench beside Kris. "I'll be quick," he promised. "I wanted to ask you about your music, if you have a second."

"Okay," Kris said. Up close, he could make out a smattering of freckles across Rayne's nose.

"You've been out here for hours. Are you a busker?"

"I'm between jobs," Kris said. "Technically."

"Are you a professional musician?"

"Not exactly. I was a mechanic. The stars didn't align when I tried to change tracks, so now I'm . . . whatever will have me, I guess. It's kind of a long story."

"But you'd like to be? A professional musician, I mean. I happen to need a guitarist, and here you are, so."

Kris stared at him. Rayne stared back. His eyes were the color of sea glass, a perfectly clear, pale green, startlingly light against the rest of his features. His eyelashes were unreasonably long. His face held no trace of insincerity; Kris must have misheard him.

"Sorry?"

"Also a long story. Do you like burgers? There's this great place a few blocks over—it's a bit early, but let me buy you brunch, and we'll talk."

"Sure," Kris said slowly.

"No pressure," Rayne assured him. "But the food is really good."

Kris's stomach howled like a coyote, right on cue. "Burgers sound great."

He wasn't one to turn down a free meal, especially not now with his money situation being what it was, but more than that, he was intrigued. Hope sparked in his chest; maybe he hadn't lost his chance after all.

Kris let Rayne carry his duffel bag, counting on him not to make a run for it. Rayne kept up a steady stream of chatter as they walked, which Kris, sleep-deprived and overcaffeinated, mostly tuned out. It didn't seem to matter to Rayne whether Kris joined in; he was perfectly capable of carrying the conversation by himself, which Kris appreciated. As the streets grew busier, Rayne slipped through the crowds like a fish, with Kris floundering in his wake.

When Rayne had said "burger place," Kris had not pictured anything like the restaurant Rayne took him to. It was long, with ambient lighting and private booths lining the walls. The entire back wall was an aquarium; the fish inside shimmered and flickered back and forth, lit up in purple and green. It was classier than any burger joint Kris had ever seen, and he faltered as he walked in. The rest of his body was preoccupied with getting fed, and didn't care about his insecurities. Rayne seemed oblivious on all counts, and led him to a secluded booth without letting up his one-sided conversation.

Kris slunk in after him, trying to avoid eye contact with the staff. At the table, he stuttered as he read over the menu before settling on an innocuous-sounding cheeseburger and fries, and tried not to look at the cost. Unless they hand-reared the cows themselves, there was no reason for the prices to be so high. Rayne ordered a veggie burger with a salad, and returned the menus to the waitress with a smile that had the girl blushing and scurrying to the kitchen.

"So I have this band," Rayne said, twirling his straw between his fingers. "And due to unfortunate circumstances involving a lot of heroin and some even worse life choices, our guitarist is out of commission."

"I'm sorry," Kris said.

"Don't be. His mom had to call us to explain that he's in rehab—a week before we leave for tour. Don't get me wrong," Rayne added, "I'm glad he's getting help, but his timing leaves a lot to be desired. Anyway." He took a sip of his water. "Don't do heroin."

"Right," Kris said. "No, that wasn't high on my list. When you say band—"

"The Chokecherries," Rayne said, as if that clarified anything.

It sounded vaguely familiar, but not enough to bet on.

"We've been auditioning people for the past six days, but no one's worked out yet. The label's threatening to send a session musician on tour with us, which would be fine, but only as a last resort. We're a band; we should have chemistry, you know?"

"Right," Kris agreed. "Of course. How popular exactly is your band?"

The waitress arrived with their plates, blushing furiously again and unable to meet Rayne's eye. Rayne smiled like he was used to it, thanking her before she fled the scene. Rayne was attractive enough to cause that kind of reaction anyway, but Kris suspected he might actually be famous. Kris filed that away to deal with after eating. His cheeseburger was huge, nearly the size of the plate, and his mouth flooded with drool the second he smelled it. He chomped down a fry before returning his attention to Rayne, who looked amused.

"We're international," Rayne said. "Where are you from?"

Kris's breath caught for a second before he swallowed. International was a lot bigger than Marty's club owner could have offered. "Kansas. I don't think I know The Chokecherries."

Rayne took a bite of his burger. He didn't seem in the least offended. "Do you want to?"

"I'll be honest with you: I don't have a lot else going on right now."

Rayne flicked through his phone for a second before handing it to Kris, who reluctantly set his burger aside. There was a video on screen, waiting for him to press Play.

"We have two albums out now," Rayne said. "Our second went platinum; we're heading out on tour the day after tomorrow. The shows are already sold out. All we need is a guitarist."

Kris frowned and pressed Play. He could tell the music was good right away: the production quality was high, the guitar slick, and the bass throbbing. The band was dressed in leather jackets, torn jeans, and bright T-shirts, caught halfway between punk and impossible glamour. Their instruments caught the studio lights and flashed them around; their hair gleamed; and their makeup demanded attention. But it was the vocals that stood out above everything else, twining through the music, perfectly on key. Kris couldn't catch any hint of auto-tune on the track, but no one had that kind of range anymore, not since Mercury. The Rayne in the video closed his kohl-lined eyes and purred into the mike, his fingers wrapping around the stand as he sang about a satisfaction just out of reach.

"That drumbeat is really familiar," Kris said. "I think my sister listens to you."

"Then she has good taste. So? Are you interested?"

As the video ended and the screen went dark, Kris put the phone back on the table. The Chokecherries were a far cry from his old high school band, in aesthetic and musical talent both. They looked like a pantheon of young gods, and Kris was wearing a flannel shirt and worn-out converse sneakers. They also sounded different than any contemporary band he'd heard in a long time, seductive and aggressive all at once. Rayne sat across the table, watching him with an impossibly hopeful expression.

"I feel like this is a weird lucid dream or something," Kris said. "Maybe I fell asleep out there after all."

"What can I say to convince you you're awake?" Rayne asked. "Actually—what can I say to convince you to play guitar for us, too?"

"For real?"

"I watched you play for an hour this morning. You're miles beyond anyone we've auditioned so far." Rayne leaned forward, his hands folded before him on the table. He looked so earnest that Kris squirmed under the attention, and then immediately pretended he hadn't. "You've got talent, Kris. Real, raw talent, the kind most people practice lifetimes to get close to. Whatever you want, I can give you—just audition for my band."

"Whatever I want," Kris echoed dumbly. His day couldn't be more surreal if one of the fish leaped out from the tank and offered him three wishes.

"Fame? You got it. Money? I promise, we will get you a really nice contract. You want to travel? Meet your favorite band? Whoever it is, we can swing it, I guarantee." Rayne drummed his fingers against the table. His rings glinted in the low light of the restaurant. His nails were painted black, matte and immaculate. "Whatever it takes to get you to drop everything else, I will make sure you get it."

Kris's head spun and he held up one hand. Rayne's mouth snapped shut instantly, and Rayne waited, all ears, for Kris's bargain.

"You pretty much had me at the burger," Kris said. "Even if I had something else to drop, this is— You're serious? You want me in your band?"

Rayne broke into a broad grin. "I can keep buying you burgers, if that's all it takes. I can buy you a burger every single day. Ultimately, it's up to our manager to accept new members, so this isn't a legally binding arrangement just yet, but I think you could be the one."

"You might have to switch it up with pizza like, once a week or so. I wouldn't want to get sick of them." Kris ate another fry to give his heart a chance to return to normal speed. "You don't even know me, though. You just saw me playing on a bench. I could be anybody."

"I can tell you're not a junkie; I've gotten pretty good at reading those signs, unfortunately. Am I wrong?"

"No, I'm not into drugs."

"Are you an ax murderer?"

"No."

"Cultist?"

"No."

"Republican?"

"God, no."

"Then I'm not going to worry too much," Rayne said. "Tell you what—we've got a private show tonight, before we hit the road. If you're interested, come meet the rest of the band, audition and charm our manager, play with us, then sleep on it. Okay?"

"About that," Kris said, carefully studying the sesame seeds on his burger bun. "Sleeping on it."

"I know it's short notice, but it's just a little show. We're only playing covers, so you don't even have to learn our songs."

"No, I mean, I'm kind of technically homeless? At the moment? So I don't really have anywhere . . . to sleep. As it were." Kris bit his lip and glanced at Rayne.

Rayne looked at him for a long moment, his expression intrigued. "You did say it was a long story," he said eventually.

"On the plus side, it doesn't involve heroin?" Kris offered. He tried to drink his water too quickly and nearly choked.

"How about we finish eating and you tell me all about it," Rayne suggested.

Kris shoved the rest of the burger in his mouth and nodded. "So I have this cousin . . ."

# CHAPTER TWO
## NONE OF THESE PEOPLE
## ARE CANNIBALS

"I've never auditioned for a band before," Kris said. "I played with some guys in high school, but we were just messing around. You guys are legit."

"Yeah, but unless you try to murder our manager or start spouting conspiracy theories about the music industry to the people who sign our checks, you'll be fine." They were sitting side by side in the back of a sleek black cab that matched Rayne's outfit as if it had been hand-picked for that reason. He smiled reassuringly at Kris from across the seat. "Just play like you were doing back in the park, okay? You've got this."

Kris nodded. His stomach twisted itself into knots and set itself on fire. He fidgeted, lacing his fingers together and undoing them again. Rayne reached over and patted his knee. The touch sent sparks zinging up and down Kris's leg, and while it did nothing to loosen the Gordian knot inside him, he tried to leach a little comfort from it anyway.

He hadn't been this nervous when he'd planned to audition for that club owner, but there was something distinctly different between that imagined scenario and going to meet an actual international band. Kris didn't know The Chokecherries; he wasn't suddenly terrified of meeting his idols. This was just a bunch of musicians getting together to play some music—and if they didn't like him, he'd go back to sleeping on the streets and begging for loose change to keep from starving to death. Or, somewhat less drastically, he'd go back home to live with his parents again. It was a totally no-pressure deal. Rayne had only met him an hour ago, and he believed in him. Kris could do this.

"You look like you expect them to eat you alive," Rayne said. "They probably won't. Being a cannibal is on that same list as ax murderer and Republican, you know. Breathe."

Kris nodded and curled around Rayne's borrowed phone. Tucking his earbuds in, he skimmed through the music collection. He passed playlists of foreign music, their titles long and with more syllables than he was used to, as well as lists of more familiar punk and indie bands, before he found The Chokecherries. As they headed out of Manhattan to the studio in Queens, he focused on memorizing their singles. Kris watched every video, running through the playlist from start to finish, studying the faces until he could recognize all the band members at a glance. Rayne stood out first and foremost, with dark makeup on his eyes and glitter on his cheekbones, his nails black as he played with the mike cord. There was something dangerous about his stage persona that Kris couldn't see in real life—something dark and predatory that made Kris's stomach flip, half-excited and half-terrified. Rayne could be an entirely different species, he was so far removed from anyone back home. Beside him, Rayne drummed his fingers against the door in a soundless beat.

The rest of the band was just as captivating. A Japanese girl with ashy hair played keyboards, her eyes and lips and nails all painted gold, her expression never wavering as her hands flew over the keys. On drums, a black dreadlocked man sat shirtless, tattoos dancing over his body as he moved like they were alive. Bass was taken by a slight, dark-haired figure nearly vibrating with energy, wielding the instrument like a weapon. And last—there: the former guitarist who had landed Kris the opportunity in the first place. He was tall and lean, almost gaunt. Kris couldn't tell he was a junkie just from looking at him, but makeup could cover a multitude of sins. The man kept his eyes down, either rapt in the music or a million miles away.

Kris's gaze flickered back and forth between the Rayne on screen and the one beside him, trying to reconcile the two. It was disorienting, but no more so than the rest of Kris's time in New York so far. He could roll with it.

The songs slipped from sultry to sexual to aggressively upbeat and back again, and no matter what Rayne did with his voice, Kris wanted more. He didn't try to focus on the guitar just yet. Instead, he let the music wash over and through him as he tried to figure out what the band was all about.

They weren't going to eat him alive. They weren't. Rayne wouldn't let them.

Kris took a deep breath, closed his eyes, and let himself imagine being someone famous. He rekindled his old fantasy and pictured a sold-out crowd at Madison Square Garden, the heat from the stage lights, a roar of adulation—nothing between him and the oblivion of a million screaming fans but his guitar.

He opened his eyes and tugged one earbud out to dangle around his neck. "Rayne? I don't have an electric guitar."

Rayne glanced over. "You can play one though, right?"

"Sure, but I can't afford one unless your record label wants to give me an advance on signing."

"Oh, don't worry about that. I'll get you one this afternoon."

Kris's mouth went dry. "Business expenses?"

"It's all budgeted in," Rayne assured him. "Don't worry about a thing. I got you."

The studio was a little building with a burly security guy at the door, who seemed to be doing his best to come across as a more intimidating feature of the brickwork. He nodded to Rayne and looked Kris up and down with an impressively impassive expression. Kris waved.

"This is Butch," Rayne said. "He's our guard dog."

"Hi, Butch," Kris said.

Butch sighed. "Get inside, Bakshi. They're waiting on this big surprise you said you had."

"Please don't say that's me," Kris whispered as Butch held the door for them.

"That's you! Hey guys, look what I've got!"

The Chokecherries turned their heads as one.

"Is it a guitarist?" the bassist asked.

"Got it in one! Everybody, this is Kris. Kris, this is everybody."

The band let out a chorus of hellos as they crowded near, inquisitive and smiling. Rayne caught Kris's hand and tugged him over to meet them halfway.

"This is Maki, Stef, Lenny, and Brian," Rayne introduced. "Maki on keyboards, Stef on bass, and Len on drums. Brian's our manager. Guys, Kris is going to audition for guitar. I picked him up off the street and promised him none of you are cannibals."

"Hey," Kris greeted. He offered them an awkward wave, his other hand still trapped in Rayne's, which no one was commenting on. "For the record, I never actually thought anyone was a cannibal, but it's nice to know for sure."

The band was less intimidating in real life than they were in the videos. They were dressed casually, hair down, without the flashy stage makeup. Stef wore a pair of thick-framed hipster glasses and a beanie. Everyone was in jeans and T-shirts. Only Brian, the manager, looked skeptical, his arms crossed as he eyed Kris over the tops of his glasses.

"You picked him up off the street," Brian said. "Rayne . . ."

"He just arrived in the city! Listen to him play before you judge me for adopting strays."

Brian sighed and dropped his arms. "It's not strays I'm worried about, it's getting involved with another Fink. Kris? You want to play us something?"

"Fink?" Kris asked.

"The last guy," Rayne supplied.

"Right."

Kris slipped away from Rayne, missing his warmth immediately—there was comfort in having his hand held, but he needed to focus—and took his guitar out. He slung the strap over his shoulder, fiddled with the tuning one more time just to have something to do, and shifted on his feet.

"So what do you want to hear?"

"Whatever you want," Rayne said.

"Anything but 'Wonderwall,'" Stef said. "If you play 'Wonderwall' I'm vetoing Rayne's vote to bring you in."

"You don't have veto power," Rayne said, "and we're only pretending this is a democracy."

"Ignore them," Brian cut in. He had a patient, long-suffering air about him that must have come from wrangling rock stars all day. "Play anything."

Kris nodded, blew out his breath, and played.

As he played, everything else stopped. He didn't worry about money or employment or how his future hung on this one audition: there was nothing in his head but the music. His hands flew over the frets, the strings biting into his fingertips with every touch, and the music swelled to fill the studio with a rich, heavy sound.

"That's ours!" Rayne exclaimed as Kris moved into the chorus. "Did you learn that in the car ride over?"

"It's not perfect," Kris said, letting the notes peter out. "I didn't have time to memorize it; there are bits I had to make up as I went along."

"But you got all that by ear in forty minutes," Rayne said.

Kris shrugged. "I guess?" he offered sheepishly.

He transitioned to a seventies medley of Bowie, Queen, and T. Rex, and Rayne flung his arm around Brian's shoulders, beaming ear to ear. "We can keep him, right?"

"He's not high and he's not jonesing," Brian said reluctantly. "I can tell that much just from looking. Kid? You got any bad habits we should know about? Anything likely to interfere with the band?"

Kris shook his head, hugging his guitar like a shield.

"You know I wouldn't take that kind of risk this close to the tour," Rayne said. "We're desperate, not suicidal. I've got a good feeling about him, Brian."

Brian grunted. "Kris? You want in?"

"Please," Kris said. "Not to guilt-trip you or anything, but the alternative is moving back in with my parents and embracing my Midwest heritage. Or living under a bridge somewhere. Just so you know."

Brian winced. "Let's try to avoid that. Here's what I'll do." Everyone else quieted. "We'll take you on for a trial period. We've got sixteen shows between New York and the Nevada festival. If you make it through all that without a hitch, we'll talk about signing you on for good. But you make one wrong move, and I've got a session musician on speed dial who already knows all the tracks, and is just waiting to jump in and cover for us. All right?"

"Okay," Kris said quickly. "I'll be on my best behavior, one hundred percent. No wrong moves."

Brian seemed skeptical, but he nodded. "I'll get a contract drawn up tying you to the tour as far as Nevada."

Kris's heart skipped giddily and he tried not to let it show.

"Everybody on board?" Rayne asked.

"The kid can play," Lenny acknowledged.

"Of course we're on board," Maki said.

"You'd pitch a fit if we weren't," Stef concluded.

"They're all thrilled to have you here," Rayne said, fixing the band with a stern look. "Right?"

"Yeah, we're just fucking with you," Stef said. "You sound great. Not that Fink was a tough act to follow, but whatever."

Maki shook her head. "Fink was always a mess. I'm surprised he lasted this long."

"He could play guitar but he was no prodigy," Stef agreed. "And all that fucking heroin was a pain."

"You shouldn't speak ill of the dead," Rayne said mildly.

"He's not dead; he's in rehab."

"Yeah, but he's dead to me. So, Kris—no drugs."

"No, of course not," Kris promised. He glanced at Brian. "Uh. Weed?"

"Doesn't count," they all said in unison.

"No hard drugs," Rayne amended. "Weed and party drugs are okay. Partake responsibly."

"I've never done anything besides weed."

"He's cute," Maki said decisively, and just like that, Kris was accepted into the fold.

"I'll pay you back for it as soon as I can," Kris said.

They stood on the sidewalk in front of the music store. The neon letters in the window read *OPEN*, and the display was full of bright, shiny new instruments Kris didn't have a chance in hell of affording anytime soon.

"Shut up and let me buy you a guitar," Rayne said pleasantly.

Inside, the store was low-lit but spacious. Aisles of cords, cables, speakers, and amps filled the front half of the room, giving way to keyboards as they moved farther in. Rayne steered him to the left side near the back where, tucked away in a little nook, the electric guitars and basses were covering every inch of the three walls. They were glossy and bright and came in every size, shape, and color, and Kris's eyes glazed over with want just looking at them.

Rayne nudged his shoulder. "Find one you like."

"Any one?"

They both glanced at the double-necked beast on the back wall. It had to weigh more than Kris.

"Maybe not that one," Rayne amended. "Anything else."

Kris stepped into the nook with the sensation of stepping into a whole new world. He reached out to touch the nearest guitar. Rayne waited in the main body of the store, letting him explore on his own, for which Kris was grateful. The one-eighty degree spin his life had taken since landing in New York was still catching up to him, as dizzying as a hurricane and keeping him off-balance. Right now, looking at the wall of guitars and knowing he was going to take one of them home—or out of the store, anyway, wherever "home" was—he was nearly in tears.

He checked the nearest price tag and swallowed. His acoustic had cost him fifty bucks. These were significantly more.

"Pick one up, try it out," Rayne said. "Play me something."

Kris forced his attention off the numbers and onto the guitars. He landed on a Squier Mini Strat in the back corner, and had lifted it from its hook before he was aware of his actions. The body was a dark cherry red, wood grains showing through black near the base. Rayne hummed in approval. The Fender was smaller than the others—Kris was short and needed a guitar with a shorter neck to match. He knelt down, balancing it across his lap, and gave it a strum. Unplugged, the sound was faint, but the notes were true. He closed his eyes and plucked out a scale, skipping up and down the frets.

"You like it?" Rayne asked. "Plug her in and play me a song."

There was an amp waiting in the corner beside a stool and a pair of headphones. Kris plugged in and spun out a riff to match the Green Day song on the overhead speakers, and Rayne grinned in return. The guitar felt warm and alive under his hands. He liked the look and the feel of it—it was just the money niggling at him.

"You want to try any others?" Rayne asked.

"This one's talking to me."

The longer Kris sat with it, the more attached he got. He played until Rayne wandered off to look at something, and as soon as his back was turned, Kris snuck a peek at the price. It wasn't the most expensive guitar on the wall; maybe it was even the cheapest. That didn't make it affordable.

The cherry-red finish glinted up at him.

"You sure you don't want to get me a used one somewhere?" Kris asked, calling Rayne back.

"You looked at the price, didn't you?"

"Maybe."

"You make it hard for people to buy you stuff, you know that?" Rayne said. "You like it, right? Best out of all the ones they've got?"

"Yeah, but—"

"No buts." Rayne nudged him until he stood. "You're in the band; you need a guitar. I promise, the label can afford a decent instrument or two."

Kris shifted, cradling the guitar in his arms like a baby, and relented.

Rayne grinned. "You'll get used to the whole rock-star thing. Wait till we hit LA. You're allowed to be a diva there. Hell, you're expected to be."

"I'm from Kansas. We don't have divas or rock stars there. We have wheat. And cows."

"Yeah, you look like a cowboy kind of guy." Rayne held out his arm, beckoning Kris in. Kris stepped up and Rayne caught him around the shoulders, steering him out of the nook. "Come on. We've got a show tonight."

They ended up at the register with the guitar, a hard case, a strap, and a pack of extra strings—Rayne said that Fink had left behind his old amplifier, and Kris was more than welcome to inherit it.

"Hey, Rayne," the cashier greeted them. "Find everything okay?"

"This is baby's first electric guitar," Rayne said, ruffling Kris's hair.

"Your boy's got good taste," she said, ringing up the instrument. "You guys have fun?"

"I think I'm in shock," Kris said. "Should I wait outside while you pay for this?"

"Don't be dumb," Rayne replied as the girl punched the numbers in. "After this I'm buying you coffee—one of those fancy ones with the ridiculous names and ten hundred toppings."

"Thanks," Kris said helplessly.

"Get used to it, babe. You're living in the fast lane now."

The total flashed up on the register, and Kris broke out in a sweat and had to look away. Rayne paid with his business account without batting an eye, and Kris was only allowed to carry the stuff to their car after fighting Rayne for it first. Butch, who'd been waiting patiently behind the wheel of the '66 Mustang, put the top down and drove them around the block to the nearest coffee shop. Kris bolted from the car, vaulting over the door before Rayne had undone his seat belt, and flung himself into the shop, adamant that he would get in line and pay before Rayne could.

The barista spelled both their names wrong, and Rayne laughed at him the entire drive back to the studio. Somehow, that didn't stop Kris from enjoying his drink, though he suspected the caffeine was going to fry his nerves. They could get fried—the important thing was staying awake to play the show.

"You good?" Rayne asked as they pulled back into the studio lot, twisting in his seat to look back at Kris. Butch killed the engine and disembarked, warning them not to linger too long.

Kris rolled his cup between his hands and breathed. "Yeah, I'm okay. I'm just trying to wrap my head around everything. I feel like I left Kansas in the real world, and I landed in some parallel dimension where everything is just . . ." He met Rayne's gaze. "Wild. Unbelievable. And good? But like." He let the condensation from the cup drip over his fingers. Rayne smiled encouragingly. "I have no idea what I'm doing," Kris finished.

"I didn't give you a lot of time to think about it—" Rayne began, but Kris cut him off with a shake of his head.

"I want this," he said firmly. "This could be the best thing that's ever happened to me. You met me a few hours ago, and you've already bought me a guitar, man! This isn't how real life works. I should be working twenty hours a week as a cashier making minimum wage in some crappy convenience store, not—" He gestured up and down to Rayne.

"The guitar suits you," Rayne said. "You look good with it."

"It outclasses me by a mile."

"You wouldn't have picked it if you thought it wouldn't work for you, and you wouldn't have blown that audition out of the water if you weren't meant for this."

"I want it to suit me," Kris said. "I think it could, but . . . maybe a version of me that doesn't exist yet."

"It will," Rayne promised. "Maybe you think I'm nuts for offering you all this when I barely know you, but listen—I have a good instinct for people. When I saw you in the park, even before I heard you play, I knew you were worth taking a chance on. You're pure potential right now, and we're going to shape you into something incredible. Besides, Brian won't let you fuck up too badly."

Kris thought about the little red guitar in the trunk of the Mustang and tried to imagine himself onstage with The Chokecherries, in leather and makeup and too much glitter, playing for a crowd of thousands—his old dream, glimmering on the brink of coming true. His head spun at the thought of it.

"That," Rayne said. "Whatever you were thinking right there. That's what we're going to make you into."

"I'm in." Kris's mouth was dry and his heart beating too fast. "Just tell me what to do."

# CHAPTER THREE
## THE AFTER-PARTY

Rayne described the show as "intimate," but the venue looked plenty big to Kris. The set list had twelve tracks, all covers the band had chosen once it became apparent Fink wasn't coming back and they couldn't train a new guitarist on their original material in time. Kris knew all the songs and could play most of them; those he couldn't, he was confident he could fake. Bowie, the Rolling Stones, Nirvana—they were so deeply ingrained in Kris's mind he could play them in his sleep. He'd cut his teeth on The White Stripes' song, learning to play back in middle school.

"You're going straight from Britney Spears to Nine Inch Nails?" he asked.

"Have to keep them guessing," Rayne said. "They'll love it."

It was already 5 p.m. The show was slated to start at eight. Kris was running on caffeine and not much else, and he hadn't played with a real live band in ten years. Brian walked him through all the equipment as the others warmed up. The tech was familiar, albeit fancier and more expensive than Kris was used to, but muscle memory kicked in and he managed well enough, even if he felt like a kid pretending to be a grown-up.

"You're fine," Brian determined. "We'll get you in better shape by the time we hit the road, but you'll do for now."

"Right." Kris took a deep breath. "I've got this."

"Ready?" Rayne asked.

Kris shifted his guitar around until it felt like part of his body and nodded. "Okay. Go."

He kept to himself at first, concentrating on the music and the equipment and learning how the different players fit together.

The Chokecherries were so familiar with one another they could communicate without words, and Kris felt left behind—like he was stuck on the ground trying to understand the beauty of a flock of birds. Maki and Lenny were the easiest to pin down; they stayed by their stations, Lenny emanating quiet ease while Maki seemed effortlessly cool, keeping to herself until she needed to trade sarcastic asides with Stef. Stef, meanwhile, took up every inch of space they could manage, strutting back and forth, their hair falling in their face as they thrashed their bass around with a palpable aggression.

And then there was Rayne.

He stayed near his mike stand, giving directions and suggestions between tracks, sometimes pacing, but with nowhere near the energy Kris had seen in the videos. Rather than making the rehearsal feel dull in comparison to them, the air was thick with anticipation, like the room was waiting for the tiger to burst from its cage.

By the time they had run through every track, it was one hour till showtime. They tucked themselves away backstage in a single dressing room, waiting for the audience to pile in.

"It's a going-away show," Rayne said. "Mostly friends and family. It's really small; a few hundred people, tops. We're not even dressing up for it."

Kris nodded and pretended he wasn't being eaten alive by nerves. The others were all comfortably settled in their preshow rituals, and he didn't want to interrupt to demand reassurances. He knew the songs, could use the equipment, and the rehearsal had gone fine. Rayne believed in him. Kris swallowed his anxiety, wiped his palms on his jeans, and smiled. It felt shaky, but no one questioned it. He spent the last hour as a ball of nervous energy, pacing backstage, tuning his guitar, trying to sit, drinking too much water and then running to the bathroom every five minutes. He could hear the venue starting to fill, a low thrum of voices and bodies behind the curtain, waiting for the band.

He left his flannel shirt folded over the back of the dressing room couch and hoped he didn't look too out of place. The Chokecherries were exotic even in plain clothes, and Kris wondered if he might have preferred taking the stage for the first time behind a mask of makeup and high fashion.

"You good?" Rayne asked brightly.

"Yeah," Kris croaked, holding his guitar in a death grip.

"It's going to be great." Rayne slung an arm around Kris's neck and toppled him off-balance into a hug. "They're going to love you."

"Right. No, totally. I'm not even nervous."

Rayne flashed him one last smile before the voices reached a crescendo and he lunged forward to take the stage. The sudden well of screams—a few hundred, but god, the noise—was the last thing Kris heard before he followed Rayne into the blinding lights.

Kris couldn't remember a single detail about the show once it was over. As soon as Rayne was done with the introductions—"The Chokecherries" left a rich taste in Kris's mouth: sweet as honey, and just a little bit dirty—and they launched into their first song, his mind went blank and all that was left was the music. It passed like a fever dream: a rush of sound and color that was over as quickly as it had begun. He remembered the feel of the strings under his fingers, and the way the floor vibrated with the heartbeat of the drums, but little else. He couldn't have answered to his own name, but he knew Rayne's. The crowd chanted it like a prayer.

He returned to himself when he staggered backstage, disoriented and high on adrenaline. Setting his guitar on the couch, he dropped down beside it like his strings had been cut. His ears were ringing and his knees were weak. He'd never felt more alive in his life.

Coming in after him, Rayne was flushed and bright-eyed, his hair damp with sweat. He looked ecstatic.

"Did I do good?" Kris felt slightly drunk, like all the stress had *whoosh*ed out of him during the show, and champagne bubbles had sprung up to take its place.

"Baby, you did great," Rayne said, hauling Kris to his feet to pass him around to the rest of the band like a party favor.

They all clapped him on the back and ruffled his hair, obviously exhausted and pleased with themselves. Lenny handed him a beer from the minifridge, and Kris cracked it open as they cheered him on. The audience had seemed to love the set and he hadn't messed anything up too badly—not that he could remember, anyway—but it was the band's approval he needed. He caught Rayne's eye amid the group, and Rayne smiled like a cat. Kris let out the breath he'd been holding all evening. He wasn't going to starve to death on the streets. He was going to play festivals and tour the world with a platinum-selling glam-punk band. It wasn't his Madison Square Garden fantasy, but it was better, because it was real.

They went straight from the show to a party at Rayne's penthouse in SoHo. Butch drove the band in a long black limo, slipping in and out of traffic as they left the venue behind. Sandwiched between Rayne and Stef, Kris wondered whether the never-ending somersault in his stomach was going to level out soon. It didn't seem inclined to, but then, maybe it was his body's way of telling him to stop drinking coffee and start considering solid food again sometime soon.

Instead he was going to give it more alcohol.

Rayne's penthouse was bigger than any house in Kris's hometown, with floor-to-ceiling windows and a balcony overlooking the city. Stairs led to an open-concept loft where the bedrooms were housed, and framed art pieces colored the walls. An Indian Buddha statue sat on a table in one corner, gleaming gold and surrounded by leafy houseplants.

A black girl with a huge halo of hair greeted them at the door. She had a bright smile and, like Rayne, was dressed to the nines, jewelry glinting at her throat and fingers.

"Angel, this is Kris, our new guitarist," Rayne said, putting his arm around her and kissing her cheek as they crossed the threshold en masse. "Kris, this is Angel. She's my best girl, and she's coming on tour with us."

"Nice to meet you," Kris said.

Angel offered her hand for a shake. Her nails were long and painted with glitter, and she smelled like vanilla and sugar cookies.

"He's a little bit drunk," Rayne said.

"No, I'm not." He was, a little. He'd made peace with his lightweight tendencies years ago.

"There's food and drinks in the kitchen," Rayne directed. "More people are going to show up within the hour, so if you want to eat, get in there."

He shepherded Kris through to the kitchen with one hand on the small of his back, and Kris, pleasantly buzzed, let himself be steered. There was something reassuring about knowing he would never get lost in New York, because Rayne would never let him out of arm's reach.

The kitchen island was piled high with trays of nachos, pizza, and fruit and vegetable platters. Bowls of chips and dips lined the counters, with bottles of soda and booze and empty cups standing sentinel behind them. Kris grabbed a paper plate and piled it high. He hoped getting some food in him would take the edge off the tipsiness, but suspected it was half excitement.

He spent the next three hours in a daze of company, food, and booze. Midnight ticked past and the party grew from the band to friends of the band, and friends of friends, and relatives Kris couldn't keep track of. The girls were all flawlessly made up, charming and dazzlingly sharp, and the men all looked like models, nearly as made up as the girls. Rayne's social circle wasn't only model-beautiful, but beautifully androgynous too. Everyone wore designer clothes; even the punks looked groomed. Kris, used to faded denim and sneakers so old the soles were worn through, drank more and talked faster to keep up.

He could play the hell out of a guitar, but surrounded by all these glittering socialites, all stars or stars in the making, he felt like a moth in the company of butterflies. His hair was a nondescript brown, his eyes much the same. His mom called them hazel, but she was being generous. He was small, skinny—*"pocket-sized,"* one of his old girlfriends had joked. Definitely nothing that would stand out in a crowd.

Just after 1 a.m., he escaped to the balcony, desperate for some fresh air to clear his head, and ensconced himself on the porch swing nestled in amid a throng of plants.

"Hey," said Angel, approaching with a drink in her hand. "How you doing?"

"Hi." Whatever her perfume was, it was intoxicating. "I'm good. I'm fine. I haven't slept in forty-two hours, but that's cool."

"Rayne said he found you on a street corner this morning. This your first time at a dig like this?"

"This is my first time for a lot of things," Kris said. "I'm breaking personal records for how many firsts I've had today. Do you want to sit?"

Angel slid onto the swing beside him and balanced her drink in her lap.

"Rayne said you're going on tour with them?" Kris didn't want to jinx it and say *us* without signing a contract first.

"I do makeup and wardrobe. Rayne says it's my job to make everybody pretty."

"Everybody looks pretty pretty already, from where I'm standing."

Kris could tell when a guy was attractive, though he could never say that kind of thing back home. There, they took pride in their ruggedness, like moisturizer was an affront to their masculinity, and they'd rather die than get called *pretty*. Here the men preened like peacocks, and Rayne out-peacocked them all, with his earrings, heeled boots, and glittering makeup: the kind of beautiful Kris had never seen before but wanted to see a lot more of.

Angel hummed knowingly and took a drink.

"You going to make me all fancy for the shows too?"

"Yep," Angel said.

"Clothes and makeup and glitter and everything," he clarified.

"The whole shebang. You good with that?"

He thought about it. He didn't know how he'd look, dolled up like the rest of the band was in their videos. Would he even recognize himself in the mirror?

Maybe it was time for a change.

Then again, he was a few drinks past tipsy.

"Sure." He shrugged easily. "Sounds fun; why not?"

"You'll be fine," she agreed.

"He didn't find me on a street corner, though. That sounds so trashy. I was on a park bench."

"Ah, you're right. That's much more respectable."

She bumped their shoulders together with a teasing smile, and Kris was almost drunk enough to think kissing her would be a good idea. The one sober part of his brain holding the fort cleared its metaphorical throat and suggested that if they were all going to be touring together, making a move on Rayne's self-described best girl wouldn't be the smartest move.

"You're really pretty," his mouth said, with zero input from his brain.

"Thanks." She was still smiling. "You're pretty cute yourself."

"I told you so." Rayne came out through the back door, his boots clicking against the balcony floor. "People told me you guys had hidden away out here. I came to make sure you were still having a good time."

"I needed some air," Kris said, smiling up at him. Rayne was as pretty as Angel, and just as kissable. Kris bet he knew how to moisturize.

"He was trying to decide whether to kiss me," Angel explained.

"Whoops. Did I interrupt?" Rayne asked with a teasing grin.

"I wasn't," Kris said, and tamped down the urge to admit he would consider kissing Rayne too. "I definitely was not. Also, I'm drunk."

"You are," Rayne said. "You want to come back inside? Maki's making these mixed drinks that are, like, ninety percent sugar—they're amazing. You have to try one."

The sober part of his brain, rapidly drowning in alcohol, shook its head. "I should probably call it quits, actually. Try to get some sleep before morning." Kris froze. "Um."

"Shit, I'm sorry, I never thought about where to put you tonight," Rayne said. "I should have got you a hotel or something. I've got rooms upstairs if you want to crash here."

"Is that okay? I didn't even think— I'm still all jet-lagged and weird."

"Don't worry about it." He coaxed Kris to his feet, collecting his empty beer can from him as he went. "Go get some sleep."

"Thanks." Standing brought Kris a fresh wave of dizziness, and with it, the realization that he was drunker than he thought. "Bye, Angel. Night, Rayne."

"You can think about kissing me next time," Angel said with a wink.

"Nope," Kris said. "Drunk brain. No kissing anybody."

"Good night, Kris," Rayne said, laughing. "Don't hurt yourself."

Kris gave them a sloppy salute before heading back into the warm buzz of the party. He waved to everyone he recognized as he passed them and then headed up the stairs to the loft, one hand on the rail for balance. Upstairs was quieter, unspokenly off-limits to the partygoers, and Kris shimmied into the first bedroom he saw, flopping face-first onto the mattress without bothering to remove his shoes, which dangled over the end of the bed. As long as he left them hovering in the air like that, he wouldn't feel rude.

It was a good party, and he liked Rayne's friends, even if they outpaced and outclassed him. Maybe he could sleep for an hour and then rejoin them, or at least help clean up after. But then, maybe Rayne was rich enough to have a maid. Maybe Butch did cleaning on top of security and chauffeuring.

Preoccupied by thoughts of rock stars and limousines, Kris tipped from drowsiness into sleep between one breath and the next.

He blinked awake, groggy and disoriented, when someone entered the room. The clock on the bedside table glowed soft and red, the numbers informing him it was 4:13 a.m. His mouth felt like something had curled up and died in it.

"Ughh?" he said.

"Sorry. I didn't think—"

"Rayne?" Kris lifted his head and tried to find a face in the shadows. Everything looked blue and fuzzy. "Party over? Meant to come back downstairs. Sorry."

"It's okay. Go back to sleep, Kris."

"Am I in your bed?"

"I'll take one of the guest rooms."

Kris frowned. That wasn't right. But before he could protest, Rayne was gone again, the door pulled shut behind him. Kris dropped back to the pillow and back into sleep, unconscious before Rayne's footsteps had faded.

He woke with the dawn, feeling less zombie-ish than he had at four, but not by much. He shuffled down the hall in search of the bathroom, mentally noting which room was Rayne's so he wouldn't make the same mistake twice. After, he headed downstairs, where he found the remnants of the party scattered over tables and counters, though the guests themselves must have left sometime in the night.

He shrugged and found a garbage bag to shift greasy paper plates and food scraps into, moving from room to room as the sun rose. He helped himself to leftover pizza as he went, the cheese congealed but to his slightly hungover self, perfect. The remaining booze he capped and set aside, not looking at it straight on in case his stomach decided to object.

Keeping busy stopped his brain from overthinking things, like how he'd wanted to kiss Rayne the night before. Sober, he had more important things to dwell on. They were leaving for the tour the next day, and Kris still needed to sign a contract and learn the songs. Could he afford an apartment in New York after the tour was over? Would he even want to stay in the city?

He found a broom tucked away beside the fridge and started sweeping the kitchen, fanning out to the living room and then the balcony, just in case. That was where Rayne found him—Rayne, sporting an incredible show of bedhead and, judging by his bright eyes and easy smile, apparently unaffected by the previous night's events.

"Hey, Kris," Rayne said around a yawn. "Are you sweeping my balcony?"

"Maybe."

"Okay, cool. You want breakfast? Coffee? You can help yourself to anything in the fridge."

"I had pizza, but coffee would be amazing."

Rayne's nose scrunched up. "The pizza that was sitting out all night?"

Kris shrugged. It wouldn't kill him.

They returned to the kitchen, and Rayne got the coffee started—the machine was huge and chrome and insanely complicated—and Kris leaned against the counter as the smell filled the kitchen and made his mouth water.

"Sleep well?" Rayne asked.

"Like a rock. Sorry I took your bed. I wasn't really on top of my game last night."

"I noticed," Rayne said, smiling easily. "It's fine. Did you have fun at the party?"

"It was great, but I won't remember half those people's names."

"That's okay. Barely any are coming on tour with us."

"About that . . ."

Rayne stilled. "You're not changing your mind, are you? Because that's not allowed."

"No! Not at all. I just— The contract?"

Rayne relaxed, though he looked faintly alarmed around the eyes. "It doesn't tie you to anything further than the festival, but you do have to promise you won't leave us hanging in the middle of nowhere without a guitarist. And Brian's reserving the right to kick you out at the first sign of trouble, just in case."

"Right," Kris said. "It's just, I've never signed a contract before. Should I get a lawyer to look it over?"

"Do you have a lawyer?"

"No?"

"The label's lawyers will explain everything," Rayne promised. "No tricks, no mind games. You play guitar, and they give you money. Speaking of!" He dug into his jeans' pocket— They were plastered on so tight that Kris didn't think they could fit anything in there at all, but Rayne proved him wrong and pulled out a wad of bills wrapped in an elastic band. "Here's your cut from the show last night." He handed it to Kris with a grin. "I wasn't sure about your banking situation what with the whole, you know, sleeping on the street, so I thought cash would be safer."

"I have a bank account," Kris said faintly. "This is, like, two hundred dollars."

"You should probably deposit it, then. We can stop and do that on the way."

"The way to what?"

"Business first, and then the fun stuff. Drink up and get changed, babe. We're going to make you famous."

# CHAPTER FOUR
## THE START OF SOMETHING NEW

The trick to surviving a day of shopping with a friend, Kris had learned years ago, was to let that friend do whatever they wanted. Back home it had been his girlfriend, and all he'd had to do was stand around, tell her she looked good, and hold her bags.

Shopping with Rayne and Angel promised to be considerably more interactive. They walked from Rayne's apartment into the heart of SoHo, where block after block of shops crowded the streets, all connected by roads thronged with pedestrians who had no apparent regard for the cars or bikes trying to eke their way through. Butch promised to come by later with the car to collect their bags, and Kris mentally prepared himself for a day of walking, shopping, and spending more money than he could imagine on clothes.

"We'll start you with jeans and a tee," Rayne said, leading him into their first store, a tiny boutique with a green storefront, ironically called The Emporium.

"I have jeans and tees," Kris said.

"You do."

"Is there something wrong with them?"

"No! Of course not."

"You can tell me if there is. I know I'm not up to your fancy rock star standards yet. That's why we're here, right?"

"We're shopping for clothes that are a little more fitted," Angel said, in an admirable attempt at diplomacy. "And black."

Kris glanced down at the jeans he was wearing. They were a basic straight-leg denim wash. "You want a pair that'll make my ass look good?" he guessed. "Because I hate to break it to you, but I don't really have one."

"We'll work something out," Rayne assured him.

After trying on five different pairs of jeans, Kris was feeling weirdly smug about it.

"Okay," Rayne said. "You really don't have an ass."

Kris turned around like he was trying to see himself better in the mirror, but he was actually just flaunting his complete lack of assets. "I don't know; you want to keep trying? I heard that girls have these padded butts they wear under their pants to make themselves bigger. You want to get me one of those?"

"You're the worst," Rayne said. "You're like a couple of toothpicks propping up a pipe cleaner. You're tiny."

"I'm pocket-sized."

Kris did like the jeans, though. They clung to his legs and made him seem even smaller, somehow; the back pockets were embellished with sequins and stones in little looping patterns. The stitches up the side seams were lighter than the fabric of the pants.

"Hey," he said. "Are these girls' jeans?"

Rayne and Angel glanced at each other.

"They fit better, don't they?" Angel asked.

Kris looked back in the mirror. They really did. He actually had thighs and calves in them instead of the skinny, shapeless sticks his men's-style jeans gave him.

"Huh," he said. "Okay. What else they got in the girls' section?"

They left The Emporium with him wearing one outfit and carrying two additional pairs of jeans and an armful of tops: tees, tanks, and what Kris was resolutely refusing to think of as blouses. They were silky and kind of see-through, sure, but he had to draw the line somewhere.

When he said it out loud, Angel flatly replied, "They're blouses. The sooner you make peace with that, the sooner we can move on."

Kris wrinkled his nose.

"You said you liked them," Rayne pointed out. "You want to take them back? We can do it right now. We're not even at the car yet."

"I do like them. They're flattering."

They were, but half of that was Rayne telling him they looked good on him. Kris had found himself preening under the attention, and though the trying on and taking off of outfits had been exhausting, not to mention stiflingly hot, there was something about being dressed up to fit Rayne's whims that had given him a little thrill. Rayne hadn't been shy about expressing his appreciation, either, raking his gaze over Kris or stepping into Kris's space to adjust some part of the outfit to his liking. Angel had been quieter, but Kris had figured out how to read her easily enough. She might not say as much out loud, but her opinions resided in her eyebrows and in the shape of her mouth, and she'd seemed pleased with the results so far.

Still.

"I feel like a kid playing dress-up," he said, scrutinizing his reflection in the car window. From the neck down, he could slip into any one of The Chokecherries' videos and feel at home. From the neck up, he was still a nobody from his dusty little hometown. If he came out of this shopping excursion looking half as put together as either Rayne or Angel, he'd be surprised.

"We'll get you there," Angel said. "Now, about your hair . . ." It was just dark enough to escape being called mousy, but too light to make a statement. "You mind if I change it up?" she asked. "Dye it, cut it?"

"There's not a lot here to cut."

"I'll make it work."

He shrugged. "Knock yourself out, then. I'm in your hands."

They tossed the bags in the trunk and headed for their next stop. Rayne detoured and got smoothies from a trendy little café where everything was vegan, organic, and obscenely expensive, and they drank them as they walked.

"Now you need your statement pieces," Rayne explained around his straw. "At least one really good jacket, some boots, some belts. Something with bling. Do you like scarves?"

Kris had never worn a scarf except in winter, but that probably wasn't what Rayne meant.

"I'm open to scarves." Kris was open to anything. He liked the attention, which he had expected, but he also liked being dressed up like a mannequin, which he hadn't. When Rayne and Angel led him into the second shop and took him through the women's section, it felt illicit; his stomach flipped with nerves, and he kept glancing around to see if the shop assistants were looking at him. They weren't. He clearly wasn't even a blip on their radar.

"You're enjoying this more than I thought you would," Rayne said.

"A guy can't shop?"

Rayne held his hands up in surrender. "I'm just saying!"

Kris picked up something sparkly and gold, covered in tassels and sequins. He was pretty sure it was a scarf.

"So, jackets," he said. "If they're not denim or leather I'm kind of lost."

"We can do leather! Come over here."

Rayne dragged him into another room in the store, where rack after rack of jackets and coats filled the floor.

"You don't want anything too heavy or it'll look like it's eating you."

Kris was barely five six; he knew all too well the limits of his wardrobe options. He wandered through the racks, letting his attention drift until a little black piece with too many gold zippers and buckles to make any sense caught his eye. The leather was impossibly soft, the metal impossibly bright. He shrugged it over his shoulders and let it settle, searching out his reflection in one of the mirrors along the walls.

"Picture that, but with blond hair and eyeliner," Angel said.

Kris could see it. His heart thudded harder and he tugged at the cuffs. They came down to his knuckles, the zipper tags jingling.

"This one," he said.

"You don't want to try anything else?" Rayne asked.

"Nope. This is it."

He handed it to Rayne, who glanced at the tag before adding it to the pile. "Vegan leather, nice. Points for you. Lunch break and then go find you some shoes?"

"I've got shoes."

"You could have new ones."

"These are comfy."

They were so worn in they had no choice but to be comfortable. He wasn't opposed to getting new shoes, but he had never seen the point if his current ones were still functional. Although these were practically slippers now.

"I will buy you the exact same pair if you really want to stick with Converse," Rayne said, "but the ones you're wearing won't survive the tour."

Kris wiggled his toes in them. "Fine. But they have to be high-tops."

Rayne hauled their loot to the counter, and Kris watched the assistant ring it up. There was the jacket, a collection of scarves, one covered in skulls, and a sequined top that Kris honestly wasn't sure how to wear, but which Rayne had assured him would look amazing.

"You're getting better at not panicking about the money," Rayne observed as the assistant wrapped the items in tissue paper.

"I've figured out that panicking won't stop you from spending it, so I've decided not to bother."

"Smart move."

They loaded the bags into the car, the trunk getting full, and went in search of a place for lunch. The sun was warm on Kris's face, the breeze ruffled his hair, and Rayne and Angel walked on either side of him, jostling into him occasionally. Sometimes Rayne's hand brushed his, and it sent electric tingles up and down Kris's arm.

Physical intimacy wasn't done in Kris's hometown. It was reserved as an expression between couples, and anything outside of courtship was put down as an accident. Guys didn't hug; there was no such thing as a casual touch outside of a romantic relationship. So Kris had filled that void with his family and the girls he dated, or wanted to date, until he hadn't realized there was a void at all. Rayne didn't work like that. He simultaneously dragged that void out into the open and set about filling it before Kris could say *culture shock*. Kris could get used to it. It had only been two days, and he would already miss it if it stopped.

Rayne took them to an Indian café and laughed at Kris when he tried to make sense of the menu. He didn't recognize half the words, never mind the dishes. He finally gave up, ordered an iced tea, and let Rayne recommend him something. He never found out what it was, but it was colorful and tasted good, so he couldn't complain. Rayne told him about the cities he was most excited to play in, their opening band, and the next tattoo he was going to get. Angel talked about the band's fashion, the club she owned, and where they were playing in her hometown of New Orleans. Kris watched them, ate his food, and basked in the warmth and the company.

"One night ago I was sleeping on a bench," he said suddenly, sliding into a gap in the conversation.

They both looked at him.

"Sorry," he said. "I wasn't going anywhere with that. It just hit me."

"The world works in mysterious ways," Rayne said.

The second realization hit him like a brick to the face. "I need to learn two albums' worth of songs before our first show."

"Total faith in you," Rayne assured him, though he seemed slightly worried. "You've already got a couple of them down. As long as you know the tune you can make the rest up as you go, right?"

"You want me to fake the riffs? Won't people notice?"

"Not fake them so much as improvise. It's a tour—the fans will expect it to sound a little different from the albums."

"Yeah. No, I can—I can totally do that." Kris nodded and tried to laugh. It wasn't very convincing.

"Let's get him some shoes and head back," Angel said, clearing her plate. "Before the boy has a nervous breakdown."

"It's not a breakdown," Kris said. "I just need a minute." He held up his fingers to measure the smidgeon of a minute he was taking. "Just to get my bearings."

"You're good though, right?" Rayne checked. "You still want this?"

"I'm good," Kris promised. He could absolutely learn two albums in twenty-four hours.

Bleach, he learned, stung like a bitch. He bit his lip to keep from squirming as Angel wrapped the top of his head in plastic to let the stuff set. It burned his scalp, digging in like fire ants, and he hated it.

"You'll get used to it," she said, seemingly unconcerned about how his entire head was aflame. "After the first few times you won't even feel it anymore."

"Uh-huh," he said, not believing a word of her lies. Her hair was all natural. She was clearly much smarter than he was. He turned the box over in his hands, rereading the warnings for the tenth time. "You sure this won't blind me or anything?"

"As long as you don't rub it in your eyes."

"I wasn't planning to."

They were in Rayne's penthouse, crowded into the bathroom-cum-salon on the lower level. Angel had apparently converted it herself: bright bare bulbs shone in stripes around the mirror, which took up nearly an entire wall; another wall was packed with neat little shelves housing every kind and color of makeup, dye, and polish under the sun. It was glamorous, hyperfeminine, streamlined to the point of peak efficiency, and reminded Kris of some weird science fiction spaceship. It was incredible, and he was scared to touch any of it.

"Are you bringing all this on tour with you?" he asked.

"Only the basics," she said. "Everyone's got their own style figured out except for you, so I can narrow it down to the bare essentials."

"How do I figure out my style?"

"We'll start with where you're comfortable and go from there. Lenny just wears a bit of eyeliner; Maki spends up to an hour in the chair before a show. I'll make sure you look good, but you don't have to wear anything you don't want."

Kris caught Rayne's eye in the mirror. "No, I'm down to, like, experiment."

"I'm guessing you never tried this back in Kansas," Angel said.

"I never tried a lot of things in Kansas."

In the mirror, Rayne's lips curved in a slow smile. Kris grinned to himself and dropped his gaze. "In for a penny, right? I want you to make me pretty."

He stayed at Rayne's place again that night. The next morning they would leave for the tour, heading across the country toward Nevada for the Purple Sage Music Fest, a six-day desert festival, playing sold-out arenas along the way. Rayne brushed aside Kris's offer of finding a hotel, saying it would be more convenient for everyone if he just stayed where he was. One less trip for Butch to make in the morning when he collected everyone. Kris caved without more than a token protest. A hotel room sounded lonely after two days of constant company.

That evening, as the sun started to slip below the horizon, he spread his belongings over the guest room bed and looked at the trappings of a life that wasn't yet his. The little red Fender lay on top, gleaming up at him. It was even brighter and more beautiful by itself, without the competition from the hundred other guitars in the shop, and Kris loved it with his entire heart. He was bringing his acoustic too; he couldn't bear leaving it behind after all these years, even if he wouldn't play it onstage. Folded neatly in a borrowed suitcase were his new stage clothes. He got a buzz just from looking at them, like they had the power to turn him into someone new, and he couldn't wait to find out who that person was.

His phone buzzed with an incoming text from his mom. *Kris, have just heard from your cousin. PLEASE CALL US.*

He winced, moved the guitar aside to perch on the edge of the bed, and video-called home. It connected immediately and his parents and younger sister, Cass, stuttered into frame. He was relieved to see that Brad, his older brother, was absent—while his parents were remarkably open-minded for small-town folks, Brad had leaned increasingly to the right ever since falling in with the wrong crowd at community college, and there was no way he'd be pleased about Kris wearing girls' jeans or joining a glam band, no matter how punk it was.

"Hi, everybody," he said. "So, I've got news."

"Kris," his mom said. "Kris, your aunt called and told us about Marty. What happened? Why didn't you come home?"

"I didn't want to give up that quickly, but it worked out! I was just going to call you and tell you the news."

"Good news?" his dad asked.

"Really good news." He felt shaky, balancing on the precipice of saying it out loud for the first time to someone else. "I've got a job and a place to stay, at least for now. The money's good, and I'm excited for it."

"What job?" his dad pressed.

"Um, I joined a band . . ."

Cassie gave an excited squeak.

"A real band," he added. "We're leaving for tour tomorrow—I signed a contract and everything. It's totally professional."

"What band?" Cass asked.

"The Chokecherries?"

She let out an inarticulate yell and leaped from the couch, pacing with barely contained energy. "Like, as a roadie?" she demanded.

"As their guitarist."

She made a noise like a pterodactyl.

"Do you know them, sweetie?" his mom asked.

"They're huge," Cass gushed. "Kris, you met them? You met Rayne Bakshi?"

"Yeah," Kris said. "Rayne's really nice. I'm staying at his penthouse. And I like their music. This is basically the best thing that could've happened to me."

"You're staying at Rayne Bakshi's penthouse."

"He's in the next room; don't make this weird."

"I have a poster of him in my bedroom," Cassie said. "I learned drums playing along to their songs. Oh my god."

"Hang on," his dad said. "You signed a contract?"

"It's totally legit," Kris assured him. "They had lawyers walk me through it and everything. They were really professional. There was a limo."

"And you're getting paid?" his mom checked.

Kris could still see the amount dancing behind his eyelids every time he blinked. There were a lot of zeroes. "I'm getting paid. It's good money, Mom. I'm going to be okay. I'll send you the tour schedule when I figure it out—we're going west to this Nevada festival first with a few stops on the way, and then heading back east again."

"You're going to be a rock star," Cassie stressed.

"I came here hoping to land a session gig or something, do a few anonymous backing tracks, but this is so much better than anything Marty's boss could have set me up with. It fell into my lap right when I needed it most, and it would be crazy stupid to turn it down, you know?"

"Rayne Bakshi fell into your lap," Cassie said. "Oh my god, Kris."

"We're happy for you," his mom promised, "but you'll be careful, won't you? You hear stories about rock bands, and life on the road . . ."

"Heroin," Cassie coughed.

"I'll be fine, Mom. We're all adults."

"I know you are! I just worry."

"You don't have to anymore. I've got a contract and a full-blown benefactor and a job I think I'm going to love. If you need to worry, worry about my idiot cousin who got himself kicked out and fired in a single move."

His parents sighed in unison.

"Marty was never a bright kid," his dad said. "I'm glad you didn't end up staying with him."

"Same. Rayne has a really nice place, you know. There's a balcony."

"Of course there's a balcony. Send me pictures," Cassie said.

"I'm not sending you pictures of his apartment, you little stalker."

"Okay, that was a bit stalkerish," she conceded. "Send me a picture of him instead? Take a selfie! Is he still in the next room?"

"He's probably busy; leave him alone. Anyway, I'm sure you'll see videos from the tour."

"I will," Cassie said. "I'll show them to you guys," she added to their parents. "Now that Kris is with The Chokecherries, you have to see everything they've ever done."

Their parents visibly steeled themselves, but nodded.

"Listen, I'm going to go to bed," Kris said. "We're heading out first thing, and I've had a really long couple of days. I'll text lots, okay?"

"Skype when you can," his mom said. "It's nice to see your face. Did you do something with your hair?"

"Maybe? Love you! Bye!"

He ended the call and stretched out on the bed on top of all his new clothes, his phone held against his heart, and he stared up at the ceiling as the day's last light chased itself over the walls and down below the horizon. After finishing community college, he had worked in his dad's garage, and the years had passed without him noticing. It wasn't until Cassie had decided she was going away to get a bachelor's degree out of state—the first of all the Goldings, to their parents' pride and joy—that Kris had realized he could leave too. Now Cassie was almost done college and Kris was twenty-five, and he felt like he had a whole decade of misspent youth to catch up on. Joining a band and crossing the country on a sold-out tour sounded like a solid way to start. He couldn't stop smiling.

# CHAPTER FIVE
## A KISS AND A PROPOSITION

The Chokecherries shared a tour bus while a second bus housing their opening act, Passionfruit, would join them at their first show in Pennsylvania. The bus was a tight fit, but overall roomier than Kris had expected, with a bathroom at the back and a fridge at the front. There were eight bunks and a couch crammed in, leaving little leg space, but Kris didn't take up much room.

"The international leg of the tour is all flying," Rayne said, "so I really fought for the buses while we stayed in the States. It's a classic, you know? I wanted that experience."

"I get it," Kris said. "It makes it more about the journey than the destination."

Rayne beamed. "Exactly!"

Hersheypark Stadium was only a few hours away, and though the whole band and crew were buzzing with energy, Kris toppled straight into nerves. Despite going to bed early the night before, he'd stayed awake for hours fantasizing about the tour, and now he was ready to crash. He sat on the couch, his back pressed to the window, and listened to The Chokecherries' albums on repeat, struggling to keep up on his guitar. The others gave him space, careful not to interrupt, though he must have been driving them nuts. After the third hour, Rayne finally dropped into the seat beside him, and Kris tugged his earbuds out.

"How's it going?" Rayne asked.

"I don't want to fuck up in front of twenty thousand people." The words rushed out in a single panicked breath.

"You played our New York show fine. Pretend it's like that again."

"Yeah, no, I was scared shitless then too," Kris admitted. "I just didn't say anything. And that was only playing covers, but now it's your music, and I might be freaking out a tiny bit."

"Do you think you're going to fuck up?"

Kris shrugged and gnawed his lip.

"I probably will," Rayne offered. "I mess up lyrics all the time. If anyone asks, I say I did it on purpose, but I don't actually notice. Stef fucked up a bass solo on our first tour."

"Epically fucked," Stef agreed from the other side of the bus. "I was so high I couldn't remember what song we were doing, so I did a Flea cover instead. It was awesome."

"I just want to make a good impression," Kris said. "I thought the nerves would go away now that I've done it once, but I think they've gotten worse."

Rayne put his arm around Kris's shoulders, and Kris leaned into him, careful not to stick him with the neck of the guitar. Rayne was warm and solid and his hair smelled good.

"Believe me when I say you're going to kick ass onstage tonight. You're a natural performer, Kris. You might not realize it yet, but you will."

Rayne said it with a conviction Kris didn't know how to fight, and besides, he wanted to believe it. He turned, leaned his back against Rayne's shoulder, and popped his earbuds back in, returning to track one of their set list as he hefted his guitar back into place. He could do this. Talking about his nerves hadn't made them go away, but Rayne's confidence was hard to resist.

By the time they rolled into the venue, the borrowed confidence wasn't good enough anymore, and the butterflies in Kris's stomach were ready to eat him alive. His legs shook a little as he disembarked onto solid ground. Rayne intervened as the second bus pulled up behind them, dragging Kris over to meet Passionfruit before he could get any more worked up.

"Angel introduced us during last year's festival circuit," he explained, "and we just knew we had to do something together. These guys have incredible energy onstage; you have to see them play. They're insane in all the best ways."

Passionfruit was a four-man band, and they spilled out of their bus to greet The Chokecherries like long-lost friends, the one at the forefront pulling Angel into a hug before even saying hello.

"New guitarist, Kris," Rayne said. "Kris, Billie—and Jay, Hatchwork, and Knocks. Vocals, guitar, bass, and drums, in that order."

"Hey," the band chorused.

"Hi," Billie said, detaching from Angel's side.

He was ghostly pale, with messy black hair and smudges of maybe makeup, or maybe signs of exhaustion under his eyes, and he had the softest voice Kris had ever heard. Jay was Métis and sporting a devil's lock and a mischievous spark in his eye; Hatchwork wore an impressively waxed auburn moustache; and Knocks was skinny, dark, and had a head of curls that would give Rayne a run for his money. The others disbanded almost immediately after introductions, wandering off in different directions to explore the venue, until only Billie remained.

"You ready for this?" he asked.

"Haven't decided yet," Kris said. "Might sit and panic about it a bit longer."

"That's a valid option," Billie agreed.

"No one's panicking," Rayne said. "We're going straight into rehearsal, and by the time we're done, he'll be raring to go."

"Or that," Kris said.

"Cool," Billie said. "I should go find Jay before he sets something on fire. See you around!"

Kris stared after him. "Fire?"

"Honestly, it's best not to ask," Rayne said. "Come on, come get your stuff set up."

Rehearsal went as well as Kris could hope. He fucked up a few times, but so did everyone else. Playing a Chokecherries' set felt different from playing covers: the energy was tighter, almost crackling in the air, so sharp Kris could taste it. The butterflies in his stomach spiraled faster in synchronized loops, threatening to choke him, but he swallowed them down and played like his life depended on it. When Rayne finally called a break for lunch and the others dispersed for snacks and water, Kris stayed where he was, his fingers clenched around the neck of his guitar.

"You're doing great," Rayne said. "You want food?"

"Actually great, or you're just saying that so I'll stop freaking out?"

"I can't mean both at once?" Rayne prodded him until Kris relented and lifted the guitar from around his shoulders. "Eat," Rayne ordered. "Or drink some water, at least. The doors open at seven; we take the stage at nine."

It was 1 p.m. Kris tried to remember the last time he'd had a full night's sleep: before the flight, for sure. Maybe he should get another coffee.

"Jay's got energy drinks," Rayne said, as if reading his mind, "but they might kill you. Imbibe with caution."

"Caution. Roger that."

"I want to run through this one more time during sound check at five," Rayne said, "and Angel wants you in her chair by six."

Kris swallowed and nodded.

"Don't play your fingers to the bone before then, okay?"

Rayne put his hand on Kris's shoulder and ran it down Kris's arm in a long stroke, leaving tingles trailing in his wake. Kris leaned into it, desperate for any reassurance he could get, and Rayne didn't hesitate before pulling him into a hug.

"I get it," Kris said into Rayne's shoulder. "Why you guys are so touchy-feely. It's because you're all on the verge of a mental breakdown at any second, isn't it? I thought you were all, like, in touch with your emotions and stuff, but you're actually just hella stressed all the time."

Rayne huffed out a laugh and rubbed circles between Kris's shoulder blades, and Kris went boneless against him, practically purring.

"You'll get used to it," Rayne said. "The preshow nerves never go away completely, but you'll find ways to manage them. Or you'll get a therapist and a nice antianxiety prescription. Either way, you'll play the shows and you'll be fine."

"Can I keep getting hugs in the meantime?" Kris asked.

Rayne squeezed him tighter. "For sure. Anytime you need one, you come find me."

"Your hugs are really great." Kris dug his chin into Rayne's shoulder—he had to stand on his toes to reach it—and from there he nuzzled into Rayne's mane of hair. Rayne's shampoo was citrusy, but his cologne smelled like sandalwood and peppermint. Kris breathed in deep to carry it with him through the show. "Macho guys never hug other guys. They're missing out."

"Yeah, they are," Rayne said, and ruffled his fingers through Kris's hair. "You're tiny and pretty and you play guitar like a fucking prodigy. You want to fling yourself into my arms, you do it. That's a sacrifice I can make."

"Take one for the team," Kris mumbled.

Rayne pushed him back far enough to look him in the eye. "By the end of the night, you're going to be a rock star, and you're going to love it."

"Promise?"

"Cross my heart, babe. You're going to have it all."

Kris went to find Angel later in the afternoon. She was holding court in the Passionfruit dressing room, engrossed in a conversation about eye shadow brands with Billie. Both seemed to be taking it very seriously. Kris knocked on the doorframe and leaned in. "Am I interrupting?"

"Billie's a makeup aficionado too," Angel said. "This is Kris's first time getting done up," she added to Billie. "He's never tried before."

"Oh cool," Billie said. "You'll love it. I started doing mine in high school—emo phase, you know." He shrugged self-deprecatingly. "One of those things you never really shake."

"Did you need something?" Angel asked.

"No, I'm just having a tiny breakdown about the show tonight, so I thought I'd come hang out here." Kris scuffed his toe across the floor. "I mean, if that's okay. I can go somewhere else if you're busy. I'm looking for a distraction."

"I can go get Jay," Billie offered. "He's, like, a walking distraction."

"Setting stuff on fire?" Kris asked.

Billie frowned. "Not on purpose. He's accident prone, and the accidents don't always follow the laws of physics, so I've found it's best to prepare for the worst possible outcome and err on the side of caution." He paused. "Actually, I should go find him." He slid from his chair, passed Kris, and departed with a backward wave.

"Billie and I were roommates in art school," Angel said. "He's a doll. That's where I learned that the best way for me to deal with stress is to do makeup, and since you came to me, that's my suggestion. Get your makeup done. You'd have to do it in another hour or two anyway, so you might as well."

"Sure, why not. Beats pacing for another hour, right? And if I practice any more, my fingers are going to fall off."

"That would suck," she agreed. She gestured for him to follow her to The Chokecherries' room, where Kris hopped up into the chair and folded his hands in his lap.

"Close your eyes and let me work some magic on you. You'll feel better in no time."

Kris obeyed. The dressing room setup was wildly different from her salon at Rayne's: still brightly lit with a huge mirror, but not nearly as streamlined or personalized. It didn't seem to make any difference to Angel; she could probably work in the dark and it would come out great. Her hands were steady against his face, wielding brushes and pencils and other, more exotic instruments Kris couldn't identify. He kept his eyes shut the whole time, and as she worked, she chatted—about her club in New Orleans, how she met Billie and Jay in art school, and how Billie was the first person she'd ever come out as trans to, and about her plans for after the tour. Her words washed over Kris like a stream, and he gradually relaxed, muscle by muscle. He didn't have to talk back—he tried a few times, and she told him to stop moving his face—but he hummed here and there, just to show he was still paying attention.

After maybe half an hour, her talking lulled for a second and he twitched.

"Okay," she said. "Open your eyes."

Kris blinked and stared into the mirror reflecting a face he couldn't recognize. It looked bewildered but very, very pretty.

Over his shoulder, Angel smiled. "What do you think?"

Kris opened his mouth and all that came out was "Wow."

"Good wow?"

His lips were dark red, like oxblood; his eyes were done up with smoky eye shadow in jewel tones, and rimmed with thick black kohl. The mascara made his lashes feel like spider legs. He blinked, his reflection blinked back, and the fact that it was really him slammed into him. The makeup didn't have the exaggerated contours of drag, and he didn't look like a girl, but he didn't look much like a boy anymore either. He was caught somewhere between the binaries in a space he hadn't realized existed, and it thrilled him to his core.

"It's really drastic in the light," Angel said, "but onstage it'll be amazing. Just wait till the others see you."

"Wait, don't bring anyone in yet," Kris said. "I want a minute to admire myself first."

He looked like some hedonist's wet dream from the seventies, androgynous and fey.

"You do that," she said. "I'm going to do your hair."

He still wasn't used to the blond. It was so pale it was nearly white, and next to the makeup it made him seem ghostly. Angel had buzzed the sides short back in New York, and now she fluffed it up along the top, teasing it with hairspray before easing wax along the roots and the bangs. It wasn't long enough to really style, but Angel promised she could work magic with anything as long as it sat still, so Kris waited, making faces in the mirror until he could recognize himself again. Angel fixed his hair up like a cockatoo's ruff and stood back with her hands on her hips.

"Rayne is going to drop dead when he sees you."

"In a good way?"

"In the best way," she promised.

Kris grinned. A pleased little blush spread over his cheeks, visible even through the makeup, but he didn't care. Angel had been right—the routine and the attention had calmed him, and now that he had a mask in place, he felt ready to take on anything. He changed into his stage clothes, feeling heady and invincible, and from there went backstage for sound check and one last rehearsal.

It didn't take long for Rayne to notice him. Kris kept his head down and his attention trained on his guitar. He didn't stop when he heard Rayne's boots clicking over the floor behind him, and he didn't stop when Rayne circled around to stand in front of him and stare, either.

"It's good, right?" Kris asked, aiming for confidence and falling just short.

"Fuck, Kris."

He glanced up.

Rayne was studying him in open appreciation, from the outfit to the makeup and hair and back again. Kris licked his lips self-consciously and came away with the bitter taste of lipstick on his tongue.

"Gorgeous," Rayne proclaimed, though he seemed like he wanted to say something more.

Kris fidgeted with his guitar and ducked his head, infinitely pleased. His face was hot.

"You're going to inspire a thousand crises of teenage sexuality," Rayne said, slinging his arm around Kris's shoulders.

"Just what I always wanted," Kris deadpanned. "My mom will be so proud."

"She should be. You ready?"

"I don't know."

"Close enough. I still get nervous before a show. Like I've got a live wire running through me. It's good." Rayne nodded, seemingly more to himself than to Kris. Kris nodded along anyway.

Passionfruit, Kris learned, was not just an opening act. They weren't worried about converting The Chokecherries' fans to their music; they brought their own fans who screamed for them and knew all their lyrics, and Passionfruit whipped them into a frenzy. Kris watched from the side, burning with secondhand adrenaline. They were half-feral and completely unrecognizable from when Kris had first met them. Billie was unstoppable. Whether Jay was slamming into him like a battering ram or the crowd was surging up against security to mount the barrier, he never missed a note, singing his throat raw.

"The crowd looks ready to riot," Kris said.

Rayne laughed. "You didn't get many punk bands out your way, huh?"

"We were more of a country town. Banjos and shit."

"That's terrifying," Rayne said mildly. "You ready?"

Onstage, Passionfruit didn't wind down so much as drop abruptly out of their last song. Billie said something about love and respect—the crowd screamed—the drum kit crashed—and the band came staggering backstage as the lights went dark. They were all soaked in sweat but their smiles were incandescent; The Chokecherries hugged or patted them as they passed.

"Twenty minutes," Rayne said in Kris's ear.

The crew nipped out to turn the stage over for them, clearing away things the fans had thrown—pamphlets and flowers and the occasional item of intimate clothing—and wiping up the spilled water. Kris vibrated with restrained energy as the crowd chanted in a low rumble of anticipation, waiting to overflow. His blood felt like mercury in his veins.

Something must have shown in his expression because Rayne said, "Come here," and drew him into an embrace, tucking him in close so Kris couldn't protest.

Kris pressed his face against the ridges of Rayne's jacket buckles, careful not to disturb his makeup, and breathed in. Rayne smelled warm, like spices, and his jacket was clean and leathery.

"You've got this," Rayne said. "They're going to love you."

"Promise?"

"Promise. I do, so they have to, because I'm not getting rid of you anytime soon."

One by one, the rest of the band slipped onto the stage until it was only Rayne and Kris left behind. The crowd sounded insatiable. Lenny kicked up the drums to a roar of screams, and Stef opened with a slinky bass line minutes later. By the time Maki set the keyboard in motion the roar was deafening—twenty-seven thousand voices all demanding Rayne.

"Your turn," Rayne said.

His eyes were dark in the dim lights, and Kris could feel his heart skipping through their clothes. Kris gave him one last squeeze for luck before ducking through the curtain and taking the stage.

It was blinding. The noise was unreal, even through his earpieces; the stage pulsed under his feet with every beat. He could barely see the crowd through the stage lights—they were a sea of dark shapes, no faces, only voices. He took his position on stage left, planted his feet, and tried to breathe. The music helped. He matched his breaths to the rhythm of the bass and struck up the chords to the intro as the screams reached a crescendo, and he knew Rayne was coming.

They charged into the intro song as Rayne took the stage, the crowd falling back as soon as he started to sing. By the time they reached the chorus, the pace was blistering, the crowd manic, and Kris's nerves were seared away under the onslaught. He felt bare—no insecurities, no fears, no stress. It was like he belonged on the stage, like he'd been born there, and there was nowhere else in the universe he should be instead.

The intro finished with a flourish and the crowd roared as Rayne grinned and took the mike from its stand.

"Hi, guys," he said, then waited for the cries to die down again. "It's great to be back. A lot's changed in the past two years—maybe you heard we got a new guitarist? Well, maybe not. We've been keeping him a secret."

Kris twanged out a few chords in response and Rayne laughed. A ripple ran through the crowd.

"I like him," Rayne continued. "I hope you guys do too. But first, let me introduce the more familiar faces. On bass, we have Stef Morganstern."

Stef thumbed out something dark and sexual as Rayne swayed to the beat, center stage.

"On drums, Lenny Lawson."

Every beat brought Kris closer to his own introduction, and his heart lodged in his throat, nervous and tight. The butterflies in his stomach were so intense he thought their hurricane might carry him away.

"On keyboards, the lovely Maki Ito."

Maki played a little scale, so sharp it had teeth.

"And finally, on guitar." Rayne turned to him. The lights lit him up from behind like he was haloed. "Our brand-new member, Kris Golding!"

Kris launched into his solo like he was throwing himself off a cliff. His hand stayed steady on the strings, though he couldn't remember a single note they'd practiced together. He flew into an improvisation, barely knowing what the next note might be, and above it all, the crowd screamed their greeting.

"Now you know," Rayne said, "this is his first time touring. In fact, this is the very first show over a hundred people that he's ever played. So I want you to give him a lot of love, okay? Give him as much love as you can." He let them scream themselves hoarse a minute longer before continuing. "And obviously I'm Rayne Bakshi, and we are The Chokecherries."

If Kris hadn't taped the set list to the floor in front of him, he would have been lost. As it was, he swam through the next few songs back-to-back with barely a pause to catch his breath. How Rayne did it, he didn't know. Kris only got lost once, stumbling for a second at the start of the third track, but if anyone noticed they didn't say. He invented a melody when he had to; it was too early to rely on muscle memory. But even when he couldn't remember the name of the song they were playing, the words to the next verse, or exactly how his solo was meant to go, he breathed in the thick air, crackling with energy, and reveled in it.

There was nothing better than sweating through his shirt under the volcanic glow of the lights, basking in the attention of twenty-seven thousand fans, all screaming Rayne's words back to him. He lost himself in the rhythm, concentrating on playing. Rayne was on fire, and the crowd was wild, swelling and crashing like a wave against the barrier. Kris looked up in time to see Rayne prowling over and a reckless feeling surged through him, his fingers never slowing against the strings. When Rayne was close enough to touch, Kris wondered what he was doing, but that wonder stuttered out in a split second as Rayne closed the gap, curling his hand behind Kris's neck to draw their mouths together.

Kris shut his eyes and saw red, a flood of heat that started in his lips and surged through him like a bolt of lightning. Every atom in his body sang, and when he inhaled, all he could smell was Rayne: peppermint and citrus and sandalwood and sweat. His knees buckled and he keened, leaning into Rayne for balance, his guitar the only thing stopping him from melting into the embrace.

He opened his eyes when Rayne let go, dazed and dizzy, and Rayne smiled like a promise before turning back to the crowd. Kris fumbled a note before regaining his wits. His legs were still weak; he locked his knees and braced himself to keep from falling. Across the stage he caught Stef's gaze. Stef winked and blew him a kiss.

Kris dropped his eyes back to his guitar, staring at his own hands like he was twelve and just learning to play. The rest of the show passed in a blur of colored lights and heat and a beat so throbbing that Kris could barely tell whether it was the bass, the drums, or his own pulse. As they crashed into their final track, Kris felt drunk from success. The last note from Stef's bass ripped through the air, and he staggered offstage to untangle himself from his guitar and dump a bottle of water over his head. Rayne collided with him like a freight train, wrapping his arms around Kris's chest from behind and pressing his face into Kris's neck. Kris sagged back against him like he'd been waiting for it all his life.

"Encore in five," Rayne announced, his hands trailing over Kris's shoulders as he withdrew.

Kris paced backstage, running his fingers through his hair. The water had done nothing to the spray; whatever Angel used, it was impervious to the elements and kept Kris's hair in place like a crown. When Rayne finally called them back to the stage, Kris felt more jittery than before, but stepping under those lights and hearing the roar of the crowd let him breathe again.

"We were perfect," Rayne said.

They shed their instruments and most of their clothes backstage, downing water like they were dying. Kris peeled his shirt off, not caring who was watching, and all the while Rayne circled them like a shark, unable to keep his hands off anyone for too long.

"You like your first show?" Stef asked.

"Perfect," Kris echoed, panting through his grin.

Rayne grinned back, catching his hand and tangling their fingers together, and for a second Kris thought Rayne was going to kiss him again. His enthusiasm was infectious, and so was his skin hunger. Kris launched himself at him, and Rayne wrapped his arms around Kris's middle, lifting him off the floor. Burying his face in Rayne's neck, Kris laughed.

"I'm in a band," he said, breathless as soon as his feet touched the ground. "I'm touring in a band. I'm going to be famous."

"As soon as those videos go online, you will be," Stef said. "You're Rayne Bakshi's new boy toy."

"There are worse things to be," Rayne said.

He still hadn't let go, though Kris was standing on his own two feet again. They kept their arms wrapped around each other, leaning in. Kris was trapped in orbit and wildly, excruciatingly happy. He felt so high coming offstage he thought his heart might burst straight from his chest—he understood why so many bands got caught up in drugs and booze and parties trying to sustain the sensation. He shivered at the memory of the kiss, his lips burning as he raised his hand to brush his fingers over them. Rayne just pulled him closer, one hand mussing through Kris's hair as the other planted itself warmly over his heart.

"Yeah, there are worse things," Kris agreed.

The band eventually separated, wandering off to find food or drinks or a bathroom, and Kris headed for the bus, needing to lie down before he fell over. His phone buzzed with a text before he even left the venue.

Cass: *OMG YOU DOG.*

It took him a solid minute to realize that of course his sister would have been scouring the internet for concert footage, and of course there would be a lot to find. He had kissed Rayne in front of twenty-seven thousand people—or rather, Rayne had kissed him, and he'd kissed back.

His parents were going to see that footage.

*Oops?* he replied.

She called him less than a second later.

"Hi, Cassie."

"That show looked so good!" she yelled. He held the phone away from his ear. "You looked amazing—holy shit, I couldn't recognize you at first! If I hadn't known it was you, I never would have guessed."

"Thanks?" he hazarded.

"So good," she stressed. "Amazing. Was it good? Did you like it?"

"The show?"

"No, dumbass—yes, the show! I'm not actually going to grill you about the kiss," she added. "If it was anyone else up there, I'd say it was hot, but as my brother, you made it weird."

He decided not to dig into that. "The show was mind-blowing," he said instead. "It was everything I ever wanted. You have no idea, Cass, it was . . . everything."

"I bet," she said wistfully. "Shit man, I'm so happy for you. Mom and Dad watched the video, by the way. You should've seen their faces."

"Uh, maybe not."

"No, you should have! They're going to call you next, you know, so you should call them first. They seem cool with it. I told them it was a performance thing. Fan service, you know? Lots of guys get freaky onstage for attention. Anyway, the video was pretty crappy; it was too low-res for them to get really scandalized."

"That's good?" Kris offered, hesitantly.

"Was it scandalous, though?"

Kris thought about the hot press of Rayne's lips on his, the brush of his hair against Kris's face. "I don't know. It happened so quickly."

"Did he slip you the tongue?"

"I thought you weren't grilling me about this."

She crowed in triumph.

"No!" he said. "No, he didn't! Or—I don't think he did. Or I did." They both paused.

"I told you he was hot," Cass said.

Kris sighed. "Bye, Cass. I'll text you later, 'kay?"

"Bye, Kris! Give my love to Rayne!" She ended the call with a wet smacking noise and, from what Kris could tell, zero shame.

He texted his parents rather than call them, a quick note that he was heading out with the band and he'd call in the morning. Then, like a complete coward, he turned his phone off and hoped his brother wouldn't find the footage along with the rest of his family.

As far as Kris's hometown was concerned, he was straight. He'd never kissed a man before Rayne, and he'd definitely never done more than that. He might have thought about it with different people over the years, but since he liked girls and girls liked him, he'd seen no reason to push himself into uncharted territory that would have gotten his teeth kicked in in certain parts of town. That, and everyone knew some distant relative or friend of a friend who'd been disowned for getting involved with the wrong sex. Though Kris couldn't imagine his parents doing anything like that, he couldn't help but heed the warnings.

So he knew bisexuality was a thing, and that it almost definitely applied to him, but he'd never had the chance to take it for a test run, as it were, back in Kansas.

Being on tour with The Chokecherries was providing ample opportunity.

Anyone could see Rayne was attractive. Girls wanted him and men wanted to be him, and maybe there was a little crossover between the two. Kris wasn't entirely sure on which side of the line he fell— though he had suspected it ran to the former, even before they'd kissed—but he had the chance to find out, and that was more than most people could say.

He shook his head. His post-show nap would have to wait; he needed to see Rayne.

Kris found him lounging on the couch in their dressing room, sharing a smoke with Angel. Rayne was still dressed for the stage, black from head to toe, with rhinestones on his boots and glitter in his hair.

"Want a hit before Butch drags us back to the bus?" Rayne asked, offering the pipe. It was glass, handblown, with a multitude of colors swirling around from stem to bowl.

Kris accepted it and took a drag. The weed helped bolster his courage. "Thanks. Can I talk to you for a sec?"

"Yeah, of course." Rayne blinked, then visibly pulled himself together. "Oh—are we cool? I should have asked earlier. I get carried away sometimes, and boundaries, you know, blur." He raked his hand through his hair, looking sheepish. "Do I need to apologize?"

"For offending my delicate sensibilities?"

"Or something," Rayne agreed.

Kris's lips tingled in memory of the kiss, and his gaze dropped to Rayne's for a second of its own accord. Angel glanced back and forth between them, cleared her throat, and stood. "I'm going to go find Billie and the guys," she said. "You guys just . . . have a chat." She patted Kris on the chest as she left.

Kris took another hit as he considered how to best approach this. However interested Kris might be, Rayne was the one keeping him in the band and off the street, and getting involved with the boss seemed like a monumentally bad idea—especially with Brian threatening to watch for the slightest reason to kick him out of the band. Anyway, it wasn't as if Rayne had kissed him and Kris had fallen instantly in love. He needed to draw a line, make sure they were both clear about where it lay, and then be careful not to cross it.

"The thing is, I like girls," Kris said. "I've only ever been with them."

"Okay," Rayne said slowly. "Are you trying to let me down gently or something?"

"I don't want any, like, misunderstandings," Kris said, sinking into the couch, his knee knocking into Rayne's as he handed the pipe back. "I'm not complaining, like, at all. I like kissing. I just want to make sure we're on the same page."

"That I'm not harboring any latent, pent-up desires for you?" Rayne asked, lifting the pipe to his lips again.

"Right. Exactly." Kris's insides burned at the thought. He doused them with the threat of being kicked out of the band if things turned sour.

"I don't know. Are you offering?" Rayne jostled Kris's shoulder as he grinned. "No. It was a lot of adrenaline, and it was our first show together, and I got a bit overexcited. But I make a point not to get involved with straight guys, so it won't happen again."

"Why would a straight guy get involved with another guy at all?" Kris asked blankly.

Rayne shrugged. "They want to prove how open-minded they are, or they want to experiment, or whatever. Doesn't matter. I won't do it. That way lies heartbreak and misery, believe me."

Kris opened his mouth with no idea what he was about to say. Before he could find out, Butch stuck his head around the corner, eyed them, and waved them over. "Bus time, guys. Up and at 'em."

"Hold that thought," Kris said to Rayne as they got up, each taking one more long drag on the pipe. He needed a minute to get his brain straightened out. That line he'd drawn looked a little shaky.

# CHAPTER SIX
## THE WHITE RABBIT

Kris thought about the kiss for the next hour, tucked away in his bunk as the bus trundled down the highway to New Jersey for their Camden and Newark shows. He lay on his back, his guitar across his ribs, strumming up and down the frets with no real intent. When, after sixty minutes of practicing riffs, he couldn't shake the memory of the kiss from his lips, he set his guitar aside and went to find Rayne. The weed was still curling through his thoughts, heavy and sweet, urging him to erase lines and push boundaries.

Rayne was stretched out along the couch in as private an alcove as there was on the bus, his boots propped up on one arm with his head on the other, looking like a giant cat, relaxed and languid.

"Hey," Kris said, testing the limits of his faculties, which were rapidly expanding in all directions. "So I was thinking about that kiss."

Rayne rolled his head to the side to glance at him. "What about it?"

Kris took a deep breath and let his words out in a rush. "You want to do that again?"

Rayne perked up, lifting his head.

"Onstage," Kris clarified. "For the show."

"As a regular thing?"

"Yeah, like, to amp up the tension and stuff. They'll eat that shit up. Or that's what my sister says, anyway. You said no straight guys, but I'm—" He cut himself off before he could out himself, and changed tracks. "I mean, if it's just for the show, that doesn't count, right?"

"Kissing," Rayne said.

"Or more. I'm not asking you to maul me out there, but I thought. I wouldn't mind?"

Rayne's eyebrows were up near his hairline. "Straight."

Kris shrugged. He didn't want to publicly commit to a label until he was a hundred percent sure of it, and if Rayne thought he was straight—ish—in the meantime, that kept things simple. That, and his Midwest upbringing left him cautious of announcing he was any variety of queer at all, even when he was surrounded by the most welcoming people he could imagine. He just needed the chance to figure out what he liked without the risk of anyone getting hurt, and if Rayne was into it . . .

"You'd let me do . . . anything?" Rayne asked.

"I'm pretty sure there are public decency laws and stuff, but anything legal, sure."

"Kris Golding," Rayne said, like he was savoring the taste. Kris liked how his name sounded in Rayne's mouth. "You're a bit of a wild card, aren't you?"

"Is that a yes?"

Rayne sat up, dropping his feet to the floor, and stood, tall and suddenly looming. Kris tilted his head back and waited, his breath caught in his throat, as Rayne moved his hand to Kris's hair. He went slowly enough that Kris could duck away if he wanted, but Kris didn't move. Rayne threaded his fingers through Kris's crown.

"You've never been the center of attention before," Rayne said in a low voice. "You sure you want that?"

"As your boy toy?" Kris asked, repeating Stef from earlier. "You worried people might think we're fucking?"

Rayne's grip tightened for a second. "No. Aren't you?"

Kris butted his head against Rayne's hand. "Nah. It's just kissing. We'll tell everyone it's for the show; it's not like I joined a band and suddenly turned gay. The fans will love it, my family will understand, and you can handle the press."

Rayne's eyes went dark, the green almost eclipsed by pupil.

"We don't have to." Kris bit his tongue, needling the tip with his teeth as he waited.

"Honestly? I'm wondering how far you'll let me push it."

Kris prodded him in the chest, under the collarbone where his chains and pendants started to tangle. "Probably pretty far. Try it and find out."

"Kissing," Rayne said.

Kris's lips buzzed with a phantom touch.

"Hair pulling?" Rayne tugged on a lock to demonstrate. Kris leaned with it, sparks zinging through his scalp.

"I'm going to grow it out. By the end of tour it'll be long enough to yank around for real."

Rayne's lips parted for a second. "Can I touch you?"

"You're touching me right now."

"For the show, brat."

"Sure," Kris said, and purposefully didn't ask what kind of touch Rayne meant. When Rayne touched him skin to skin, it burned like a furnace and sent him shivering all over in its wake. "You don't need to write up a contract, you know. You can just do whatever feels right. Whatever you think will work."

"Carte blanche." Rayne looked like he wanted to eat Kris alive.

"Yeah. That." Kris's mouth was desert-dry. He ran his tongue over his lips and Rayne's eyes went unfocused for a second before he seemed to snap back into himself and put space between them.

"God, you're something else. And I thought I might have upset you with that kiss."

"I'm pretty easygoing."

"I'm so lucky I found you."

"I'm the lucky one," Kris countered. "But we're cool?"

"We'll mess around onstage and put on a show," Rayne said. "No strings, no complications, no messy feelings."

That sounded perfect. Kris bumped their fists together. "Sounds good, man."

Rayne sat back down on the couch, smiling like this was an everyday transaction. Kris thought about lying down and trying to sleep as his skin buzzed from the memory of Rayne's lips on his with twenty-seven thousand people screaming for more. His thoughts were slow and rambling, the high still curling around his brain and making it hard to focus on anything but that kiss.

"You should find out where Angel gets her stuff," he said absently. "This is good shit."

"She knows what's up," Rayne agreed, tipping his head back and letting his eyes fall closed.

The days turned into a week as they went from New Jersey to Virginia, then Michigan, and Indiana; down to Florida for three shows, to Alabama for one, until they were thirteen days in and playing in New Orleans to twelve thousand people, and Kris had barely had time to catch his breath, let alone work out the details of his attraction to Rayne. In between shows, Rayne did press, giving interviews and sound bites for the flashing cameras, coy when they asked about his love life and honest when they wanted to talk music. Kris didn't know how he had the patience for it, but Rayne took the business side of his music seriously, and gave the press just enough intrigue to keep The Chokecherries in the public eye.

The band threw themselves into their shows without hesitation. They never played a crowd under ten thousand, and as soon as the people knew to expect Rayne and Kris's midshow kiss—they always had at least one, but as the shows went on the number climbed—they screamed and cheered for more. Kris had worried that with the booze and drugs out of their systems, he and Rayne would reconsider the discussion they'd had after Hershey. It was the most pointless worry Kris had ever had in his life. Rayne's daring only grew as the tour went on, kissing Kris harder, for longer, and more often, running his hands through Kris's hair, tugging on his shirt, playing with his belt while Kris tried not to miss a chord.

The fan sites swarmed with videos and theories. Cassie sent Kris links to fanfiction featuring his and Rayne's imagined backstage love life, which he quickly learned to avoid without opening, though the first one stuck with him. There was something unsettling about strangers speculating on the details of his nonexistent sex life, especially in such graphic detail—though he could admit it was hot, from under his blanket of embarrassment.

The more people reacted, the more Rayne pushed, until Kris was looking forward to Rayne's kisses as much as he looked forward to his solos, and their energy burned and crackled as they ramped it up with every show they played. After two weeks of near daily making out, and hugs and casual touches in between, Kris was so acclimatized to Rayne that he thought he might go into withdrawal if he went a day without him.

Luckily, that didn't seem likely—the fans and the press ate up the shows, and the rest of the band seemed delighted by the reaction. Kris was in heaven. By the time they played New Orleans, he felt like he could do this for the rest of his life.

As soon as they finished their set, Angel was waiting to whisk them offstage and back to the bus, cramming both bands in one, to see her club.

"Is it like a strip club?" Kris hazarded, glancing sideways at her to gauge her reaction to his guess.

"The White Rabbit's a burlesque club," she corrected, as Butch turned the engine over and pulled out onto the road. "We do strip shows, but not like you're thinking."

Kris's hometown had a bar where the girls dressed provocatively, but technically there was no stripping. Whatever went on in the back room was done under the table, and Kris had never asked about it. He'd only been once, and that at Brad's behest—it had taken him a week to shake the sleazy feeling and look his girlfriend in the eye again. Angel didn't seem capable of running a joint like that.

"So what's burlesque like?" he asked.

Angel just smiled, sphinxlike, and Rayne laughed. It didn't answer a thing, but Kris nestled in between them and watched the city stream by, all glowing neon and car taillights, and decided he didn't mind finding out firsthand.

"My godfather sold me the building for a fraction of its worth," Angel explained, "and I turned it into something completely new."

"It's a beautiful club," Rayne added. "Billie helped design it, right?"

"Yeah, you bought the place like a year after graduation?" Billie said. "And you asked me to help with bits. It was fun, like a giant installation project."

"That was before I met Rayne," Angel said.

"And she didn't introduce me to Billie and Passionfruit until last year, when we—Passionfruit and The Chokecherries—were both playing the same festival together, and Angel was touring with us as our makeup artist," Rayne said.

"Huh," Kris said. "Small world."

"Not too small, or we'd get bored," Angel said. "Here we are."

The bus slowed and pulled over to the side of the street. The White Rabbit was identified by a neon rabbit on a door that was otherwise unmarked, squeezed in between the brick walls of two other clubs. The rabbit glowed fat and white, neither inviting nor off-putting as Angel led them through the door, down the narrow stairs, and onward to greet the bouncer at the bottom. They slipped through without a cover charge, and the guard held the second door open for them as they entered the club beyond.

The White Rabbit was sumptuous, decadent, and sybaritic, like it had rolled out from an erotic Victorian fantasy. Leather couches lined the walls; the bar glittered with a hundred different kinds of alcohol in glass bottles and crystal decanters. The walls were a deep, rich red like bloodshed or rose petals, the ceiling was covered in tiny mirrors that winked in the changing light, and the place was full of the most beautiful people Kris had ever seen, dressed in leather or lace or lingerie or, in some cases, very little at all. On the stage at the back, someone hidden by huge ostrich plumes like a flapper pinup posed under a spotlight, nothing but long legs, pale skin, and high heels.

"They're expecting me to take the stage," Angel said. "Grab a seat and enjoy the show." She pressed a quick kiss to Rayne's jaw before darting away behind the stage to change.

"Drinks," Rayne said. "She'll say they're on the house, but we're not doing that. I've got this round."

Kris ordered something stiffer than his usual; it seemed like he was going to need it. They crowded around a couple of tables that had been saved for them near the stage, and Kris tried to figure out how to look at the other people in the room without being rude. Some of them wore masks and little else, making it impossible to meet their eyes. Kris settled on staring at their shoulders and trying not to blush. Rayne laughed at him, and Kris hid his face behind his drink.

When Angel took the stage, the music swelled and the conversation quieted. The beat was sultry and seductive, and she walked out in an enormous fur wrap that covered her from throat to thigh, her heels so high she was almost walking en pointe. She was like a showgirl from the Moulin Rouge, her mouth dark and pouty, her eyes glittering in the low lights of the club. Kris wondered again how he had stumbled out of his universe and into this one—it must have been here all along, just waiting for him to pull back the surface and take a peek.

Angel danced like every eye in the world was on her, and she knew how to give them exactly what they wanted. The fur came away inch by inch revealing a smooth expanse of dark-brown skin, interrupted by the crisscrossing straps of her lingerie, refusing to give away the whole picture at once. She caught Kris's eye, and his mouth went so dry he nearly choked on his own tongue. Rayne put his arm around Kris's shoulders and spoke in his ear, close enough to be heard over the music.

"Better than you expected?"

"Different," Kris agreed.

The music deepened, and Angel stepped from the stage, leaving her fur in a heap behind her. She wore a bra and garter set designed to look like flower petals, and Kris had never seen a more beautiful girl before in his life. She approached Jay, who sat nearest the stage, and curled her fingers under his chin as everyone jeered and wolf-whistled.

"I'd do this for Billie," she said, "but I know he's shy when he's not onstage." She sidled in closer until she was right over his lap, and Jay dropped his head back, laughing helplessly under her attention.

"I'm filming this and sending it to your fiancée," Billie cackled.

"She'll love it," Jay countered. "She'll just be mad she's not here in person."

Angel rolled her eyes without pausing in her dance. She swayed her hips, careful not to touch him, her arms crossed above her head as Jay clearly tried to work out where to put his hands without making it awkward. He eventually settled on tucking a folded bill into the top of her stocking. She kissed him on the cheek, leaving a rose-petal of lipstick behind, and stepped back, still moving to the beat.

"Who else wants to dance with me?"

Rayne looked at Kris, who squeaked.

"Oh, honey," Angel said, stepping closer on those impossible heels until she was near enough to smooth her hand through his hair. "You don't have to have a dance if you don't want one." She leaned in until her lips ghosted over his cheek, and his eyes fluttered shut of their own accord. "But if you change your mind, you let me know."

She left him and sauntered back to the stage, where the music swelled again and the lights flared to welcome her back. Kris's heart was beating a mile a minute now, and Rayne's arm stayed heavy around his shoulders.

"You know when you're a kid at a restaurant and someone tells the waiter it's your birthday?" Kris said.

"You think being offered a lap dance is as bad as having a roomful of strangers sing at you?"

"How red is my face right now? I feel like I'm burning up."

"It makes you look healthy," Rayne said.

Angel's number ended and despite Kris's embarrassment, he kept his eyes on her until she disappeared backstage, and the club exploded in applause.

"Let's get you another drink," Rayne decided.

Kris couldn't agree more.

He was buzzed but not drunk when Angel returned, wearing a silk robe over the lingerie, and shoes that, while still aggressively fashionable, seemed considerably less dangerous to walk in. With all the alcohol in his system, Kris had a harder time keeping his eyes from wandering; Angel caught on straightaway and smiled.

"Like what you see?" she asked. "You're allowed to look as long as we're both in the club. That's the whole point of me being onstage."

"You look . . . really nice," Kris stuttered, trying his hardest to stay polite.

She laughed and put her hand on his arm. "You're the sweetest thing."

"You'd never know I found him on the roadside like a kitten in a cardboard box," Rayne agreed. "Such a gentleman."

"Every time you tell this story, it gets worse," Kris complained, without meaning it. "I was busking!"

"You didn't have a permit."

"You need a permit to busk? That might be the first illegal thing I've ever done in my life. Besides the weed, I guess."

"Weed doesn't count."

"I'm sure it won't be the last thing, anyway," Angel said. "Next round is on the house, and, Rayne, don't even try to sneak the bartender your money. I see you. Let's get turned up."

Kris wasn't sure how he ended up dancing in between Rayne and Angel half an hour later. He wasn't drunk enough to excuse it, but between the post-show high, the exhaustion preceding it, and the giddiness that had followed him ever since meeting Rayne, he might as well be ten shots in. Rayne's hands were on Kris's hips as they moved in tandem to the music, a slow, rhythmic beat slinking out from the speakers. There was a bare inch of space between their bodies; little enough that he could feel Rayne's body heat through his clothes, but they didn't touch. Angel caught his eye and nudged him back to close the gap. Kris's shoulders met Rayne's chest as Rayne caught and held him there, lightly, so Kris could squirm away if he wanted—but he didn't move. He leaned back and let Rayne turn him around so they were face to face, and looked up to meet Rayne's eye.

"Hi," Rayne said.

In close quarters, surrounded by people, it would be second nature to reach up and kiss him. Kris fought the urge and slipped from Rayne's arms before he could do anything impulsive. No strings, no complications, and no causing trouble. "I'm going to get another drink."

Taking a deep breath, he headed for the bar, signaling for a refill of whatever he'd had last time. He slid onto a stool beside a stranger: tall and blond, not attached to either band, but clearly not a White Rabbit performer, either. The man was wholesomely handsome in a way that made him stand out among the club's sultrier inhabitants, and Kris gave him a smile before reaching for his wallet to pay for his drink.

"Hey, let me get that," the man said, smiling back and offering a few bills to the bartender. "I'm Tom."

"Kris. Thanks for the drink."

"Are you performing tonight?"

"Oh, I'm not— I'm in a band," Kris explained, stupidly proud of being able to say that. "We're just hanging out."

Kris was still wearing his makeup from the show, but doubted it had survived without smudging. Angel and the other burlesque performers were flawless, not a line or hair out of place. Maybe Tom was drunker than Kris.

"I've been coming here for the past few months," Tom was saying. "I haven't seen you before but I assumed—I thought you must be one of the dancers. You're very pretty."

"Thanks," Kris said again, preening a little. He liked being called pretty; no one ever had before he met Rayne. "So what do you do, Tom?"

"I'm in seminary school," Tom said brightly. "I want to be a youth pastor."

Kris blinked. "And you're hanging out in a burlesque club?"

Tom blushed and the freckles on his nose stood out. "I just wanted to see what it was like. I haven't taken any vows yet."

"Huh."

"There's beauty in everything," Tom said, clearly warming to his subject now that Kris hadn't run away screaming. "I don't want to preach about sin and shame; I want to appreciate God's work in everyone and everything." He looked into the depths of his glass. "I might be drunk."

"I'm not judging you, man," Kris said. "I think it's great that you've got an open mind."

"I don't want to condemn people," Tom said, "not when they haven't hurt anyone. Look at you—a nice young lady—just because we met in a place like this, doesn't mean—"

"Hang on," Kris said.

Tom blinked at him, his expression open and painfully sincere.

"Never mind," Kris said. The alcohol made it seem like too much effort to correct him, and besides, he was strangely flattered by the attention, however misguided. "Doesn't mean what?"

"That you're not blessed," Tom said. "Everyone in here—we're all blessed. Can I get you another drink?"

"Why not."

Kris was tucking into his second, something pink and sugary and with a significantly higher alcohol content than his usual, because girly drinks didn't fuck around, when Rayne joined them, flagging the bartender down.

"Making friends?" he asked Kris.

"This is Tom," Kris said. "He thinks I'm the prettiest girl in the whole club." Rayne raised one eyebrow and Kris shrugged. "What's up?"

"Brian," Rayne said, with uncharacteristic sourness. Kris made a concerned noise and Rayne waved him off. "Business stuff. Don't worry about it. I'm just not drunk enough for the conversation he wants to have. I'll tell you about it later." The bartender slid him his drink and Rayne took a gulp as he put his money down. He swallowed and smiled. "Seriously, don't worry. You two kids have fun getting acquainted. Nice to meet you, Tom." Rayne saluted them with his drink and slipped back onto the dance floor.

Kris watched him go, wondering if he should chase him down and press him for details, but Tom spoke before he could decide.

"Are you on tour?"

Kris shook Rayne's moodiness off. If it was due to business, he'd find out the cause sooner or later. "We're heading west to Nevada for the Purple Sage Music Fest. It's my first festival. It's my first lots of things." Two weeks into the tour didn't feel any realer than it had on the first day, and he smiled around his straw, bright and tipsily enthusiastic. "Have you ever been?"

"No, I've never done much either," Tom said.

"Well, if you have a pre-priesthood bucket list, add it. A lot of people have, like, spiritual awakenings at music events. Maybe you'll get something out of it."

"Maybe," Tom agreed, hesitantly. "I'd like to try as many spiritual experiences as I can."

"Isn't that blasphemous?"

"I don't think so. God is everywhere, after all." Tom examined his drink again. "I think He is, anyway."

"You're the one with the calling," Kris said with a shrug. "You must know better than most." Tom seemed reassured, and Kris swallowed the last of his drink and clapped him on the shoulder. "Come see us if you decide to head that way. I'm going to go find my friends."

He found Angel sitting on one of the long, low couches, her legs crossed and a drink in her hand as she looked around her club with the air of a queen surveying her castle. Rayne was beside her on the arm of the couch, and there was something uncharacteristically tense in the way he was holding himself that made Kris pause in his approach, and then hang back amid a throng of dancers.

"I haven't decided anything yet," Rayne was saying, "but I don't want Kris to hear it from anybody but me. Okay?"

Angel raised her hands. "I'm steering clear of all of this."

Rayne glanced around but apparently didn't catch sight of Kris, then slid down onto the couch cushions, put his arm around Angel's shoulders, and whispered directly into her ear. Intrigued, Kris snuck in nearer, having drunk too much to feel properly guilty about eavesdropping. Something was bothering Rayne, and if Kris was even tangentially involved, he wanted to know what it was. He took up residence behind a giant potted fern at the far end of the couch and tried not to feel overly ridiculous. He missed the first half of Rayne's whispered sentence, but caught "publicity stunt" near the end.

"Me and some guy at the festival," Rayne finished.

"What kind of stunt?" Angel whispered back.

Kris didn't catch what followed, but Angel gasped, and flashed a wicked smile that she quickly hid behind her hand. Rayne heaved a sigh. "I shouldn't be talking about this at all."

"Security breach." Angel nodded sagely.

"I should go."

"You do that. Get some sleep, and when you've got your head on straight, then you decide what to do about it. No decision-making when you're drunk. You got that?"

"Don't tell Kris."

Rayne swam back into the sea of dancers, and Angel shook her head at his retreating back. Kris, crouched on the floor in the shadows of the plant, tried to make sense of what he'd heard, but all he got for his troubles was a twist in his stomach that had more to do with Rayne keeping secrets than from the alcohol. It served him right for eavesdropping in the first place. He stood, careful not to disturb the leaves and give himself away, and circled around to approach Angel as if he hadn't been hiding amid her décor for the past two minutes. The whole thing left him feeling a bit like a scumbag.

Angel straightened when she caught sight of him and smiled, extending her free hand to beckon him in.

"Hi," Kris said. "Am I interrupting?"

"Of course not; I was just admiring the view. Come sit."

Kris sat gratefully, tipping sideways into Angel's shoulder. He stole a sip of her drink and she laughed. "Enjoying yourself?"

"I'm good. I like it here. In the club, with the band and everybody." He forced the million questions on the tip of his tongue to the back of his mind. He didn't want to think about secrets, not even business-related ones, not when he was so close to having everything he'd ever dreamed of. Shuffling down, he rested his head in her lap. "This okay?"

"Mm. You're an affectionate drunk, aren't you?"

"You're just really nice. And comfortable. What's owning a club like?"

"A lot of work. I love it, but some days it feels like this place is determined to fall apart around me."

"You can't tell from looking." Kris couldn't, anyway; the place was beautiful, and Angel had clearly poured every drop of love she had into it.

"Boy, this whole place is smoke and mirrors." She petted his hair, and he closed his eyes, drifting contentedly on a current of drunkenness. "I need a live-in repairman to keep on top of things. I wouldn't trade it for the world, though. Not for anything. What I should do is start managing it full-time again, get everything back on track."

"It must be nice to have somewhere to come home to. Somewhere that's all yours."

"Kansas isn't home for you?" she asked.

"Nah. Not my hometown, anyway. It's a good place to grow up, or a good place to retire, but there's nothing to do in between. I had to get out."

"Lucky thing Rayne found you."

"Lucky I met him. Lucky I met you too. Need you to keep making me pretty."

"Rayne seems to appreciate it."

Kris snorted and flicked her knee. "I appreciate it. I never got to play around with any of this stuff back home. I didn't have the guts. Now you're dressing me up in girls' clothes and makeup and I'm— Onstage, with the— It's fun. I wish I could have started years ago."

"Well, you're too old now," Angel said matter-of-factly. "Can't make up for lost time."

"I'm baby-faced."

"Over the hill. Ancient." She fluffed his hair. With all the spray in it, it stayed in whatever position she put it. Kris was counting down the days until it would be long enough for her to have some real fun styling. "Soon you'll go bald, and then what? Career, over."

"I'll get a wig. Rayne would get me a wig, right?"

"Honey, I think Rayne would get you anything you asked for."

Kris hummed, pleased. "Good." He poked her knee again. "He's a good kisser, you know."

"I figured. A couple hundred thousand people figured."

Kris grinned and turned to look up at the ceiling, where the mirrors glittered and winked above them. He remembered first meeting Angel; he'd been drunk then too, and had spent the night wondering if he should kiss her, or maybe kiss Rayne. In the end Rayne had made the choice for him, and he didn't regret how it had played out. He didn't regret anything about that night, or anything about the tour after. The constant travel and playing had left him exhausted, but the drinks had taken the edge off and left him boneless and content. Angel was warm beneath him, her fingers twining through his hair, and he was suddenly, intensely grateful for the turn his life had taken.

"You're a good friend, you know that?" he said. "Rayne's lucky to have you. You're just—you're a really a good person, and I'm glad I met you."

She laughed, and he felt it all the way through his body. "How much have you had to drink, hun?"

"Some," he admitted, "but it's still true."

"Well, thank you."

Their conversation paused for a second, and the questions Kris had tried to bury came tumbling back. He chewed on the inside of his lip before finally asking, "Do you know what's bugging Rayne? He was annoyed with Brian, but he wouldn't tell me what about. Did he talk to you about it?"

"It's business stuff, but it might turn out to be nothing. If it is something, he wanted to tell you himself. Nothing to worry your pretty little head over, in any case."

Even drunk, Kris was skeptical. "Promise?"

"You haven't been around long enough to see the business side of things," she said. "I promise: if it's really important, Rayne or Brian will call a meeting. This is just . . ." She shrugged. "Rayne likes to make a fuss once in a while. He's a diva at heart, you know. Then he'll get over it and move on."

Kris couldn't imagine Angel lying, so he took her at her word and let it slide. Rayne would tell him eventually, and in the meantime, he would pretend he'd never heard anything at all.

They lapsed back into silence, watching the dancers move over the floor like fish shimmering in a pond. They were beautiful, all leather and lace, and Kris wondered again how he had ended up in such a place, and why it had taken him so long to realize it was where he belonged.

"Angel?"

She blinked and looked down at him. "Hm?"

"When did you know you were trans?"

She paused. "That's a big question," she said eventually. "I didn't start calling myself trans till I was almost through art school, but I did drag for a while before that. I took baby steps to figure it out. Some people know and are out from the minute they're born, and others take a more scenic route, like me. There's no wrong way to do it."

"So you didn't just, like—" Kris wet his lips. He could still taste the sugar from his last drink on them. "You didn't just wake up one morning and start dressing in girls' clothes, and like . . ."

"Turn queer?"

"Yeah."

"I don't think it works like that." She smoothed his hair down again. "Why? You got something on your mind?"

"The clothes, and the makeup, and stuff. I like it. I like wearing it." He bit his lip and glanced up at her. "I can still be a boy if I do that, right?"

"The gender police aren't going to come arrest you because you like wearing skinny jeans, hun. If you want to be a boy, you're a boy." She tapped his nose. "Just like kissing Rayne onstage doesn't make you gay."

His ears burned, suddenly too hot under the club lights. "I still like girls," he blurted, trying to force his blush back before it gave him away.

"Sure you do," she replied, obviously fighting a smile. "You can still like girls and like kissing Rayne at the same time. They've even got a word for folks who like both. Hell, they've got a couple of words."

He poked her. "Stop making fun."

"I'm not, sweetie. I'm just saying."

"I don't know if I'm, you know. Ready. For those words yet."

He felt her hum more than he heard it. "I get that. Anything in particular holding you back?"

He shrugged ineffectually. "Not really? Where I grew up—Kansas isn't a great place for stuff like that. Experimenting, or coming out, or . . . any of it. I guess I'm still wrapping my head around things." He chewed on his lip for a minute before tipping his head back to look at her properly. "You won't tell anybody, right?"

"Course not. You can tell whoever you want when you're ready." She paused. "Rayne would be excited to hear it, though. Everybody would, but especially him. Just so you know."

"He's a good guy," Kris agreed. "I know he'd be supportive of whatever." He caught a glimpse of Angel rolling her eyes as he settled more comfortably. "What?"

"Nothing, hun."

He huffed and crossed his arms over his chest, still lying on his back with his head on her lap. He knew he looked ridiculous, but he didn't mind. "He's right, you know," he said, apropos of nothing. "The not-a-priest-yet over there." He waved to the bar.

"Tom? He's been coming here a few months now. He's a good regular. What's he say?"

Kris smiled. He could feel his blush lingering over his nose; it felt like he was glowing. "That we're blessed. That we're all blessed."

# CHAPTER SEVEN
## JIAO FANG AND
## THE SNAKE TATTOO

They rolled into Texas at ten the next morning, a solid ten hours before their Dallas show. While the majority of Passionfruit and The Chokecherries seemed happy to bury themselves in their bunks and take the time to sleep in, Rayne was out the door as soon as the bus stopped moving. Kris followed him, blinking in the sudden sun. Whatever had been bothering Rayne at the club seemed to have dissipated overnight, which Kris hoped meant Angel had been right about it being an overreaction. In the meantime Kris, though still curious, was happy to let it go.

"My tattoo artist from LA has a guest spot at one of the parlors here this week, and I've got an appointment," Rayne said, fairly buzzing with energy.

Kris was aware of a certain internet faction's obsession with Rayne's tattoos. He'd just never seen more than two in person in any detail before. He knew the mercury sign on Rayne's left thumb and the burst of rose blooms on the side of his neck, but the others remained hidden, only caught in stolen glimpses when Rayne changed backstage. The pictures on the internet didn't do them justice, and anyway, Kris was trying to feel as little like a stalker as possible.

Cassie, who emailed him scanned magazine spreads, wasn't helping.

"What are you getting?" Kris asked.

"A snake. She sent me the drawing a month ago, and I've been freaking out ever since. It's going to be amazing. Do you want to come?"

"Yes. Can I? I've never been to a tattoo parlor before."

"It's going to take the whole day," Rayne warned. "It's a long session."

"If I get bored I'll go walk around, or I'll have a nap in the corner," Kris said. "No big deal. I want to see."

They walked to the tattoo parlor, Rayne insisting it was just far enough to stretch their legs, while Kris was happy to tag along and soak up the sun. The only thing to identify the place was a koi fish painted on the door; there was no sign or window or anything else to indicate the nature of the building. Rayne pushed through the door and led Kris up a narrow staircase wallpapered in art, over the landing, and into the shop above. A long black couch sat in front of the reception desk and framed art hung on the walls. The buzz of tattoo guns filled the air as a handful of artists worked at their stations, scattered around the room.

"Rayne!"

The woman who greeted them was maybe forty, with spiky black hair and inked art covering every inch of exposed skin below her jaw.

"Hey, Jiao," Rayne said with a wave. "This is Kris; he's just here for company. Kris, this is Jiao Fang, my artist."

"Nice to meet you, Kris," Jiao said. "Come over here, take a look at the final design."

She led them to her station in the back corner. The two walls were covered floor to ceiling in art: pencil sketches, charcoal, watercolor, ink—Kris's mouth dropped open at the sheer skill of it. There were dragons and phoenixes and flowers, unidentifiable monsters, fish, knights, and portraits drawn with such delicate attention to detail that he couldn't fathom the time they must have taken. He could understand Rayne's devotion to Jiao; if he were going to have a drawing tattooed on his body forever, he would want it from someone as skilled as her.

Jiao fished a drawing from her desk drawer and handed it to Rayne. It was marked with a faint grid, but on top of the lines was a thick, coiled serpent, its scales immaculately rendered, flashing its fangs as it reached back for its own tail.

"This is what I sent you earlier," Jiao said. "If you're happy with it, we're all set."

"It's perfect," Rayne breathed. "I love it." He beckoned Kris over. "Isn't it perfect? Jiao's done every tattoo I have. She's the best there is."

"I believe it," Kris said.

Jiao smiled and retrieved the drawing. "I'll transfer it to the tattoo paper and we'll be ready in a minute." She headed off in the direction of the printer to do just that, leaving Kris and Rayne alone.

"Where are you putting it?" Kris asked.

"My arm. It'll start here"—Rayne pointed to his shoulder, right where it met his chest—"and wrap around down to my elbow."

"That's huge. Won't it hurt?"

"Yeah, but in a good way."

Kris's eyebrows lifted of their own accord.

"What? You don't think there's different kinds of hurt? This is worth it because you get to walk away with something amazing at the end. It's not like you're suffering for no reason."

"Uh-huh, sure."

Rayne waved him off. "Get one yourself and you'll see what I mean."

Kris looked back at the wall of art. He'd never really considered it before, but then, he'd never considered a lot of things before The Chokecherries. Not seriously considered, anyway. His eyes were smudged from yesterday's makeup, his nails were painted black, and he had left home for the big city and joined a rock band he'd never heard of before. It occurred to him that he was the perfect candidate for a spontaneous tattoo.

"Huh," was all he said aloud.

Before Kris could elaborate, Rayne took his shirt off and Kris lost his train of thought entirely. He could see Rayne's tattoos.

Rayne had two birds perched on his chest, one near either shoulder. The left wore a crown, and the right had an arrow through its heart. Under his throat, running parallel to his collarbone, was an old-fashioned key. His right shoulder was capped with flowers, the same roses that crawled up the side of his neck to sit under his jaw, always half hidden by his hair, opposite where the snake's tail would start. The tattoos were all blackwork, and all recognizably Jiao's. Kris wanted Rayne to turn around to see if he had any more on his back. Maybe there were others below the waist of his jeans.

He swallowed.

"Like them?" Rayne asked, his tongue poking out between his teeth.

"They're beautiful," Kris replied, and Rayne's eyes softened and lost their teasing edge.

"Thanks. I've got these ones too."

He turned; between his shoulder blades was a mandala like the sun, and when he lifted his hair there was a second mandala hidden along his hairline, peeking out down the back of his neck, like the fan of a peacock's tail. Kris inched closer to get a better look. The ink was older there, but it was still Jiao's work.

"The one on my neck was my first," Rayne said, dropping his hair and turning back. "I had an undercut then; it's a full mandala, but I grew my hair out and you can't see the top half anymore. It's supposed to be—"

"A peacock," Kris finished. "I can tell. It suits you," he added. "They all do."

Rayne preened but whatever he was about to say was cut short by Jiao's return. The snake was printed on transfer paper, the design in reverse, and she smoothed it over Rayne's arm bit by bit, adjusting the angles as she went, starting at his chest and working her way down. When she removed the last of the paper, the snake coiled blue around Rayne's arm with not a scale out of place. Rayne twisted around to see it from all angles as Jiao held up a mirror, waiting patiently as he examined every inch of it.

"Okay, I'm set," he finally announced, sliding onto the chair. Jiao took up her position at his side, snapping her gloves into place, and her gun buzzed to life. Kris pulled a nearby stool closer and settled in to watch.

Whatever Rayne said about the pain, it didn't show on his face. His hair fanned out over the chair's headrest, and he chatted back and forth with Jiao and Kris like he was out for coffee, rather than getting a tiny needle dragged repeatedly over his skin. Kris winced for him, but couldn't look away. The fingers of Jiao's gloves turned black with ink as she wiped away the excess, moving slowly and methodically over her design. The snake came to life under her hands one scale at a time, and Kris stared, transfixed. Rayne didn't watch. Occasionally something else leaked over his skin besides ink, and Kris leaned in closer, intrigued.

"Is that blood?" he asked.

"Yep." Jiao swiped it away with her cloth. "Inner bicep has thin skin. He'll bleed more here."

"Sounds fun."

"It's not that bad right now," Rayne said, "but I guarantee I'll be bitching about it tomorrow."

"Adrenaline," Jiao said wisely. "He likes it though. I gave him his first piece six years ago, when I opened my shop in LA. He's been coming back ever since."

The black ink was smoky and rich against the brown of Rayne's skin, and Kris wanted to touch the healed ones, just to see if they were as smooth and indistinguishable as they seemed.

Maybe later he could ask.

"Benji is free this afternoon," Jiao said, "if you're interested in a small piece. Her appointment canceled, so she left the slot open for walk-ins." She didn't look away from her work.

"No pressure," Rayne said. "Your first tattoo, you should know for sure."

Kris wet his lips. "Isn't your first tattoo supposed to be something meaningful? Because I'm feeling pretty impulsive here."

"Tattoos can be whatever you want," Jiao said. "Get one if you want one. You should be sure you want it, but it's only ink." She shrugged. "Not the end of the world."

Kris was saved from answering when his phone buzzed with an incoming call from his brother. "I'm going to take this." He patted Rayne's knee. "You keep at it, champ."

He crossed to the emptier side of the parlor and sank onto the couch. "Hey, Bradley."

"Hey, Kris. Sorry I didn't call earlier. I heard you joined a band."

"Yeah, I did. It's going great. How's work?"

"Good, good," Brad said absently. "Listen—I've seen some of the concert footage."

Kris picked at his nail polish and waited.

"You doing okay?" Brad asked. "Mom and Dad told me how plans fell through with Marty; you must have been really stressed trying to find something. I get if you just grabbed the first thing that came your way, but there are always other options, you know? You can always come home."

"I like the band, Brad."

"I know you like playing guitar, but you're a country kid, Kris. This—what you're doing onstage—you know that's not you, right?"

"Pretty sure it is," Kris said, a thread of annoyance winding through him. "And I never played country. I played bluegrass."

"I'm worried about you."

"Well, don't be," Kris shot back. "I'm happy. I'm having a great time."

"They've got you dressing up and wearing makeup like some kind of a—"

"Bradley," Kris warned.

Brad let out his breath. It came across as a crackle of static over the line. "You can do better than this. Don't change into something you're not just to fit in."

Kris ended the call, his fingers shaking, and shoved his phone back into his pocket with more force than was necessary. A girl with short rainbow hair was sitting at an empty station, flipping through her phone and pretending not to hear to his conversation.

Kris raked his hands through his hair before approaching her. "Hey, are you Benji?"

"That's me."

He smiled, still shaky. "Can I make one of those walk-in appointments Jiao was talking about? I think I need a tattoo after all."

Benji walked him through the paperwork, and he scribbled his signature swearing he wasn't drunk and wouldn't blame them for any complications or change of heart later on, and she led him to her chair, sat him down, and handed him a thick portfolio of flash designs.

"They've all got their prices marked, or if you want something not in the book, we can make a deal," she said. "Did you have anything particular in mind?"

Kris flipped through the pages of artwork. There were death's-head moths, skeletons, hearts, and daggers—all the classics, all with their original spin. The art was flawless. He chewed on his lip as he thought it over, his heart racing. "Can I just get a star?" he finally asked.

"Like an outline?"

"Yeah, just a five point star, right here." He pointed to the inside of his left wrist, just below the joint.

"Sure," Benji said. "Our base charge is eighty bucks, and a star should only take a couple of minutes. I won't charge you more than that."

He handed her the portfolio back and tried to calm his heartbeat. She pulled a marker out, took his wrist, and drew a perfect freehand star on his skin, the lines straight and the points sharp. "Like this?"

He examined it. His pulse still felt like it was going to burst out of his skin, but he nodded and tried not to grin like an idiot. "Yes, please. Do that."

She donned her gloves, fitted a new needle to her gun, and he gave her his wrist. The first bite of the needle didn't hurt as much as he'd expected, but he still went tense from it. It felt like a hard, biting drag against his skin, but Benji's hands were steady, and he was more excited than uncomfortable. She paused to wipe away the ink and he watched a bright-red drop of blood well up in its wake.

"So it's like scarring, right? That's why it bleeds?"

"It needs to go deep enough for the ink to set permanently," Benji said. "It's technically an open wound until it scabs over; that's why aftercare is so important."

"Gross."

"Yeah," she agreed, and wiped the last of the ink away with a smile. "But not gross enough to stop people. You're all done."

His wrist now sported a perfect five-point star. The lines looked puffy and tender.

"I'll wrap it up for you, and then you can pay Alicia at the front desk. All good?"

"Perfect. So perfect, thank you so much."

She covered the tattoo in a plastic medical film that stuck to his skin, explaining what she was doing as she worked. He nodded along, unable to take his eyes off his wrist.

"Alicia will give you a pamphlet with everything written down," Benji added at the end, "but it's pretty easy. Leave this on for twenty-four hours, and then replace it whenever it gets dirty over the next week." She handed him a few sheets of the medical product, already cut to fit his tattoo, the plastic waiting to be peeled from its paper backing.

"This isn't plastic wrap from the kitchen," she warned. "They're not interchangeable. This stuff is breathable and antibacterial, and using regular plastic wrap will leave you open to infection. Okay?"

Kris nodded emphatically. "Special medical wrap, no kitchen supplies. Got it."

"After a week, you can leave it uncovered. Keep it clean and moisturized, and you're good to go. A little one like this should be healed in no time."

After paying at the desk, which was decorated with sugar skulls and tiny statues of samurai warriors, Kris wandered back to Rayne and Jiao. The snake didn't have a head yet, but it was coming along.

"You got one!" Rayne said, clearly torn between delight and accusation. "I wanted to watch."

Kris thrust his wrist out, bursting with pride. The star was blurry under the ink and the blood, which collected in the wrap's creases, but he didn't care how gory it looked. It was perfect.

"Nice," Rayne said. "You decided, just like that?"

"It's my body," Kris said. "I get to do whatever I want with it, right?"

"Course," Rayne agreed, but he caught Kris's hand and held it. "You good?" He glanced at Kris's phone, which was sticking out of his shallow pocket.

"I'm fine," Kris promised. "It was dumb family stuff. Your snake is awesome though—you still bleeding?"

"He'll keep bleeding till I'm done," Jiao said.

Rayne gave a dismissive wave. "Who cares about that. Did yours hurt? Your first tattoo on the inside of your wrist—that's brave."

"Nah, it's only little. And this plastic stuff is really cool. I thought I was going to get all wrapped in gauze or something, but now I can keep an eye on it the entire time."

"It's the same wrapping they use on burn victims," Jiao said. "It's less work for you than cleaning and moisturizing it every day as it heals. You leave it on for a few days, and when you peel it off, you're all done."

"Burn victims," Kris said. "Don't they use baby foreskins in that stuff?"

Rayne froze. They looked at each other.

"They have amazing medical properties," Jiao said with a shrug. "Try not to think about it."

Kris glanced down at the plastic film. Underneath, the excess ink blotted and welled. "Yeah, you know what? Pretend I never asked." He patted Rayne's knee reassuringly. "Just pretend I never said anything at all."

"Right," Rayne said faintly.

"I've been using that stuff on you for years," Jiao said. "Don't be childish."

Kris sniggered and Rayne smacked him. He deserved it.

It took another hour for Jiao to finish the snake. Rayne talked less as time passed, the discomfort finally catching up to him, but Kris stayed by his side until it was done. His own wrist started to sting as the adrenaline wore off, but Rayne was right: it was the good kind of pain. It felt like commitment. No matter what happened on tour, or where he ended up after, he had a piece of it under his skin now, and even if he never wore makeup or girls' jeans or dyed his hair again, his star would stay with him. He rubbed his thumb along the perimeter of the wrap and smiled to himself as Jiao's gun buzzed away, etching the snake into Rayne's arm. Soon the snake and the star would both be healed, smooth and indistinguishable to the touch, and when they were hidden under shirts and jackets, no one else would know they were there.

# CHAPTER EIGHT
## A HOTEL, A BED, A DREAM

They had three back-to-back shows in Texas, and each show ratcheted the sexual tension between them up another notch. The night after their tattoos, Rayne set himself on Kris like a dog on a rabbit, and twelve thousand people screamed their approval. Dizzy from the taste of fame, Kris couldn't tell whether it was the roar of the crowd or Rayne's lips on his that had his blood pumping so hard, but he didn't question it. It was good—the lurch of his stomach, the weakness in his knees, the way he saw stars when he closed his eyes, listening to Rayne's voice soar above the music. Every show, Rayne pulled his hair and petted his chest and stalked him, intent and predatory, radiating want. The crowd's screams always reached their crescendo when they kissed, almost as loud as when they played their encore, and Kris, breathless and drunk on the music and the smell of Rayne's cologne, lapped it up like he was starving.

He knew how they looked together. Cassie sent him the videos afterward: the same kiss from a hundred different angles, the reverent gasps and shrieks from a thousand different mouths. Backstage after the shows, Kris's whole body tingled with phantom touches. He could remember every brush of Rayne's skin against his own—hand to hand, or at his throat, against his scalp, inside his collar and down his chest, a slow, dragging tease—

He was more of an exhibitionist than he had thought, but then, the stage was the stage. If he wasn't up there for the attention, what was the point?

"Just don't get arrested," Brian said, when it became evident that their public petting was only going to get heavier. "Keep all your private bits private. If this leads to public indecency charges, that's on your head, Kris. You're still on a trial run here. And Rayne? You know what happened last time, and none of us want a repeat of that mess."

"That's not happening again," Rayne said firmly. "I have this under control."

Brian seemed skeptical. "And what we talked about in New Orleans—"

"I know," Rayne said. "I said I'd tell you when I decided."

Kris looked between the two of them, not wanting to get on anyone's bad side by asking for clarification.

Brian sighed and waved them away. "Fine, okay. Other than that, go nuts."

Passionfruit joined in on their antics immediately following Brian's reluctant blessing.

"Don't you guys have fiancées?" Kris asked before the first of their newly sexually charged shows.

"Yeah, and they've both given their very enthusiastic permission." Jay held up his phone; on the screen was a text message that consisted of nothing but exclamation marks, followed by a second one that read *GOD YES SEND PICS.*

"Huh," Kris said. "Well, whatever works, right?"

"Just a couple of straight guys being dudes," Billie agreed, fixing his makeup with a handheld mirror. "Do you think red eye shadow is too much?"

"What is this, 2005?" Jay asked.

"Too late, I'm doing it anyway."

Passionfruit approached their new stage play with the same aggression they poured into their music: raw and desperate, as compared to Rayne's simmering sensuality. Still, it seemed to work for them. Jay and Billie dragged each other around the stage, hands fisted in one another's hair, and Billie dropped to his knees to scream his lyrics out to Jay's guitar from below.

Kris watched from the side. He couldn't deny it was hot, in a feral way. Whatever chemistry Jay and Billie had before—and he was pretty sure Billie had been joking when he'd said they were both straight—it came boiling over now, frothing at the mouth and leaving the crowd hoarse with lust. The band came backstage invariably soaked with sweat and brimming with energy. Jay thumped Kris appreciatively on the chest as he passed.

"Great idea, man. The best."

"It really adds something to the performance," Billie added, watching Jay strip off his sodden shirt and upend an entire bottle of water over his head.

"Happy to help," Kris said. "Hope the girlfriends like it."

"They'll be so jealous they can't see it in person," Jay said.

Kris nodded and elected not to pry any further.

The thing about life on the road, Kris decided sixteen days in, was that it was fucking exhausting. When he stole naps during the day the bus rocked him to sleep like he was a toddler, and at night he passed out cold, impervious to every outside stimulus, from snoring to traffic to blown tires, but he never seemed any better rested. The bunk wreaked havoc on his back, and he longed for a single night without his mattress moving under him. When Brian announced after their Austin show—two stops away from Purple Sage—that they were staying in a hotel, Kris nearly cried from sheer relief. A real bed, in a real room—he was going to sleep for twelve hours straight and there wasn't a force in the entire universe that could stop him.

"So, there's been a slight mix-up," Brian said apologetically that night.

"Please tell me we have a room."

Everyone else had already shuffled off to their respective suites for the night; it was only Kris and Rayne left in the hotel lobby with Brian.

"You do," Brian said. "But you're sharing."

"Not a problem," Kris said quickly. "No problem at all."

"There's only one bed."

Kris glanced at Rayne.

"They can bring up a cot though, can't they?" Rayne said.

"I'm not sleeping on a cot," Kris said. "I might as well stay on the bus."

Rayne, the diva, gave him a look that said he was most certainly not sleeping on any cot either.

"Forget it. I don't care. We can share a bed, right, Rayne?"

"It's queen-sized," Brian said, seeming like he wanted to crawl straight into his own bed, and damn their sleeping arrangements.

Kris poked Rayne in the arm, careful that it wasn't the tattooed one. "Your call, big shot. Are we sharing or not?"

"We can share," Rayne said. "As long as I can lay down within the next ten minutes, I really don't care."

"Make it sound like such a chore," Kris grumbled. Rayne reeled him into a sideways hug, and Kris dropped the act, ducking his head with a grin and hugging him back.

"Good. Perfect. Here's your key; we're checking out at eight. Don't be late." Brian dropped the key in Rayne's palm and departed without a backward glance. Kris couldn't blame him. He and Butch had been taking turns driving, and if Kris was tired, they must be nearly comatose.

"Dibs on the shower," Rayne said, pushing Kris toward the elevator.

Reaching their floor a minute later, Kris stumbled along, dragging his bag down the corridor. As soon as they arrived at the room, he face-planted into the pillow. He melted into the mattress as Rayne started the shower; the pipes rattled and the suite filled with the familiar hum of running water. Kris rolled onto his back and stared at the ceiling, absently listening to Rayne move in the bathroom, the spray shifting as he stepped into the stream. Kris had never lived this closely with anyone before, not even his own family. Touring was like living on top of one another for every minute of the day, a constant crush of forced intimacy, yet it felt good: there was always someone in touching distance, always someone to talk to, no matter the hour. Kris had taken to it like he'd been waiting all his life.

He understood how it could be overwhelming. Maki disappeared on a regular basis, slipping away to rebuild her personal space without a dozen eyes on her. Stef wore noise-canceling headphones nearly constantly unless they were onstage. Sometimes Kris needed room to breathe too, but he found reassurance in never being alone. He was so comfortable with his bandmates already, and Rayne in particular, like he'd known him a million years.

When Rayne came out from the bathroom, Kris was flicking through his phone, looking at conversations he'd had with people months ago, old acquaintances he'd never deleted from his contacts, even after leaving Kansas and assuming he'd never see them again. He felt like a different person now. Would any of them recognize him anymore?

"Your turn," Rayne said.

He wore nothing but a towel slung low around his hips, inviting Kris's attention. Rayne didn't seem to know how to be shy, not about his body or anything else. Kris took the bait and whistled as leeringly as he could while pretending to be unaffected. Rayne laughed.

It was hard not to look, though, and Kris didn't fight the urge for long. Rayne was broad-shouldered and narrow-hipped, with the faintest suggestion of abs. His skin was warm and rich in the low lamps of the hotel suite, like the darkest shades of amber: gold where he caught the light, and brown in the shadows. He moved like a panther, elegant and self-assured, tiny rivulets of water running down his body over his tattoos as he crossed the room. Kris wet his lips and glanced away.

"You're dripping everywhere."

"I'll leave a big housekeeping tip." Rayne flopped onto his back on the other side of the bed.

Kris headed for the bathroom before he could see how far the towel shifted.

In the shower, he lathered up in complimentary body wash and shampoo. The water was hot, the pressure was perfect, and Kris was not reliving the last kiss they'd shared onstage.

In fact, he wasn't fantasizing about Rayne at all. This preoccupation was just a matter of bad timing. He hadn't gotten laid in over four months since he and his girlfriend had broken up before he left for New York, and they'd been drifting apart for longer before that. They had parted on mutual terms, and there was no bad blood between them, but still—he was getting antsy. And since Rayne's attention onstage was the only action he was getting, it was only natural for him to get a little distracted. It didn't mean he wanted to do anything about it.

Rayne was the kind of tall, dark, and handsome that could make even the most heterosexual man grudgingly admit he was good-looking, and Kris was far from straight. Some might say Rayne was too pretty, but Kris liked that. He liked how Rayne could switch from being a total dork offstage, overenthusiastic, with a braying laugh, to the sultry, slinky predator who stalked around in front of the crowd, and he liked how Rayne was equally sincere in both roles. But they never kissed except during the show. Sex was for the stage, and the stage alone. Passionfruit was equally close, but then, they were odd too. Kris didn't have any kind of baseline for normality anymore. His parents didn't comment on it, his sister jeered and congratulated him, and he hadn't talked to Brad since that phone call in the tattoo parlor.

Would it be easier if he'd been a Chokecherries' fan prior to meeting them? No, it was better this way. Less awkward. He shouldn't overthink things. If he were smart, he'd leave what they did onstage onstage like they'd agreed, and that would be that. He'd compartmentalize.

He sighed, turned the water all the way to the cold side, and stood under the spray until he was shivering. Getting involved with a bandmate was way too risky when his position in the band was so tenuous. Besides which, he still didn't feel ready to come out. It was ridiculous; he was as safe as he would ever be, and the fans and the press all assumed he was some kind of queer anyway. But his heart stuttered when he thought about making that final leap and saying it out loud, so he bit his tongue and kept it under wraps.

Back in the room, Rayne, now dressed in pajama bottoms, was watching something bright and loud on the television.

"I thought hotel nights were for hookers and booze," Kris said. "You're watching a musical."

"If you want hookers, you can get your own room," Rayne said. "There's booze in the minibar, though."

Kris fluffed his pillow and joined him, settling in to get comfortable. "Nah, I'm good. What is this?"

"An Indian movie. I used to watch them with my mom all the time, but I haven't been keeping up the last couple of years."

"Like Bollywood? Aren't those movies all singing and dancing?"

On screen, a man in a chariot slashed through an enemy army.

"A lot of them," Rayne agreed, "but not this one."

"Holy shit, that was epic."

"Big budget." Rayne nodded.

Intrigued, Kris kept his eyes glued to the screen as the battle raged on, men getting torn apart in slow motion. "So movies were a thing for you and your mom?"

"She was an actress in India before she moved to the States with my father. He's Persian. I got more of his looks, but I got her flair for the dramatic."

"That's so cool. They must be proud of you, following in her footsteps, huh?"

"My dad died a few years before I started the band, and my mom moved back to India not long after, to be with her family." Rayne seemed wistful, but not sad. "I hope he'd be proud of me. I know she is."

Kris shuffled sideways to fit himself under Rayne's arm, nestling in against his chest. "I bet they both are. Look at you, man. You're living the dream."

Rayne hummed.

"Do you miss them?"

"Sometimes," Rayne said, after a moment. "I still visit my mom, and I'll always miss my dad a little bit, but I'm okay."

Kris gave him a comforting squeeze. "Is India really like this?" he asked, nodding to the movie.

"Kind of? I mean, this is fantasy, but it's recognizable. You could come see it in person, if you wanted."

"Is the tour going through India?"

"No, but we could go on our own. The rest of the band's already been, but the two of us could visit. I could show you around."

Kris twisted around to look up at him. "Seriously? I've never been outside the States before. I'd love that."

"I'll make it happen," Rayne promised.

Kris smiled and settled in to watch the movie. He'd already missed the beginning and his vision was starting to blur, making the subtitles a challenge, but the cinematography was beautiful. On screen, an elephant reared up, balancing on its hind legs. "You should get an elephant," Kris said sleepily. "Make it part of the show. Or, like, put it in your next video or something. That would be awesome."

Rayne seemed to give that thought way too much consideration. "I don't think we could use it in the live show. A video would be good though. I should ask Brian." He dug out his phone and started texting.

Two minutes later Brian called. "Absolutely not."

Kris giggled into his pillow.

"No wild animals. Never mind the liabilities—do you know how hard it is to wrangle a bus full of musicians? And you want to add an entire elephant to the mix? No. Stop watching TV and go the fuck to sleep, Rayne. And Kris? I know you're listening, and I know this was your idea. Sleep. Now."

He hung up.

"I'll work on him," Rayne decided.

"Maybe we can start with like, a horse, and work our way up."

"Or a snake," Rayne said around a yawn. "A big ball python or something. They're exotic. They'd look great in a video."

"For sure," Kris agreed. The camera panned over an ancient cityscape as the soundtrack wailed. "We can get a snake. A snake must be easier to wrangle than a horse or an elephant." He tried to think of everything he knew about India, which wasn't much. "You want a peacock? They're Indian, right? They've got those at the zoo just roaming around, mingling with the visitors and stuff. I bet we could steal one."

"You want to steal me a peacock? That might be the most romantic thing anyone's ever said to me."

A delightful shiver shot through Kris at the word *romantic*, but he crushed it down. "Fuck yeah, I'll steal you a peacock. Also, you should probably raise your standards, but that's your business. But I will absolutely steal you a giant bird to further your rock star aesthetic if that's what you want."

Rayne tugged him sideways so Kris sprawled the rest of the way across his chest. "You're the best. Don't get arrested though."

"Why not? That's totally rock and roll. How's anybody going to take me seriously if I've never been arrested?"

"Brian would have a heart attack and cancel your contract," Rayne pointed out. "And then I'd have to leave you in jail to stay on his good side."

"That's cold, man."

"That's show business."

A jungle stretched across the TV, calmer now that the battle had passed, and Kris's eyes kept drifting closed of their own accord. Listening to the background music, he could pick out similar themes in The Chokecherries' songs: an undercurrent of Indian influence he'd never noticed before.

"Early night?" Rayne asked.

"So rock and roll." Kris snuggled deeper into the pillow, Rayne's heat a constant burn against his side. "Going to leach your body heat a bit longer, then I'll move back to my side."

"I knew you were just using me."

Rayne ruffled Kris's hair until Kris batted at him. On screen, a chariot horse blinked at the camera like it was judging them. Kris didn't care.

Something nudged him. "Hey. You awake?"

Kris blinked groggily, willing his eyes to focus. The clock on the bedside table read 3:03. He had been awake, more or less, drifting in that heavy in-between place and flirting with consciousness. "Mm?" Rayne was a warm presence against his back, and Kris rolled over to face him. Their knees bumped under the covers as Kris propped himself up on one elbow and yawned. "What's up?"

"Want to talk to you." Rayne looked delicious in the dark, his hair unmanageably mussed from the pillow and his eyes soft from sleep.

"At three in the morning?" Kris asked around another yawn. "Okay, sure. Talk about what?"

"There's this band going to Purple Sage—Dead Generation. They're signed to the same label as us. They're new, but they're good."

Kris woke up properly. This must be about Rayne's secret from the club. "You want to add them to our opening act?"

Rayne shook his head. His hair fell in his eyes, and Kris was momentarily distracted.

"Their front man, Calloway, got outed in a gossip rag the other week, and he and the label have decided to roll with it. They've asked me—the label has, I mean—to step in for a publicity stunt. Something to put the narrative back in their control."

Kris blinked and tried to make any kind of sense out of Rayne's words. He must be more asleep than he'd thought. "Sorry, what? You're going to have to spell it out for me, man. I'm not versed in all this cryptic industry talk yet."

"Me and Calloway," Rayne said. "They want us to go on a few dates, let the paparazzi get a few pictures, spread a few rumors. Just for the length of the festival."

"They want you to . . . pretend to date some guy. Oh my god, they're pimping you out!"

"No, that's— Well, sort of. It's an image thing. Now that he's been outed, the label has to decide how to reinvent his brand. They chose me. Everybody loves me, and I've been out since before I signed. And the papers have been dying to dig into my personal life for ages now. Two birds, one stone."

"This is what Brian was talking to you about in the White Rabbit?" Kris asked incredulously.

"You knew about that?"

"I overheard you talking to Angel about something that night. You had said it was business stuff."

"Right, well, Brian's not impressed with the idea either, but I said I'd consider it."

"Okay," Kris said, slightly dazed. "Fake dating. That makes sense. It's so obvious; why didn't I think of it?"

Rayne rolled his eyes fondly and prodded Kris in the shoulder. "I'm not pretending the music industry is remotely sane."

"So are you going to do it?"

Rayne was still for a moment. Rayne being still meant he was deep in his thoughts, and that was never a good thing. He was the kind of guy who made split-second decisions and never looked back, like lightning in a bottle. He wasn't careless, but he wasn't given to overthinking. Kris leaned in and tapped him on the forehead, right between the eyes.

"I don't know," Rayne said finally. "That's why I'm asking you."

"What? Why? What have I got to do with your fake love life?"

"Right now, you are my fake love life," Rayne pointed out, and Kris's heart gave a thrilling thud. "A good chunk of people—fans, tabloids—think we're a thing, and they'll keep thinking that as long as we keep doing what we do onstage, no matter what we say. If Calloway and I do this stunt, it'll throw all that for a loop, so I thought I'd better ask before deciding."

Not six hours ago Kris had been fantasizing about Rayne in the shower. Now, lying nose to nose in bed together, his thoughts weren't much further ahead, and that wasn't helpful when Rayne was trying to talk about something important. Kris forced himself to concentrate and consider Rayne's proposal. "Would you having a fake boyfriend affect our shows?"

"Brian's advising us to drop the make-outs while I go out with Calloway, but he says that's up to us. People will talk about it either way." Rayne smiled wryly. "The press loves a scandal."

Kris took a deep breath and closed his eyes for a second. His brain was still fuzzy, not used to functioning at this hour, let alone making publicity decisions. Rayne was a solid presence in the dark beside him.

Kris didn't have any right to monopolize Rayne's attention—*or his affection*, his sleepy brain added traitorously. *Or his touches, or his kisses, onstage or off.* Rayne was just being considerate, giving Kris a heads-up like this.

"If the label thinks it's a good idea . . ."

"Brian's skeptical," Rayne said, "but he always is. He stressed it was entirely my choice. They're not going to make me do anything I don't want to."

"They're just going to pointedly encourage you?"

"Right." Rayne sighed.

"Do you know this Calloway?"

"Never met him. Here, take a look."

Rayne fumbled for his phone before handing it to Kris, and the screen lit up with a picture of the singer in question. Calloway was heavily freckled under his sun-kissed glow, with coiffed ginger hair and a blinding smile. He was attractive, but anyone could look like a model with enough airbrushing.

"Irish?" Kris guessed.

"So they tell me. I've listened to his band, and they're good. They're not big yet, but they could be, given the chance."

"Okay. So he's pretty, and he's got talent. That sounds like your type, right?"

"Evidently. So? Are you going to be my voice of reason and tell me it's a terrible plan?"

Kris thought about it. He and Rayne weren't dating. They weren't even friends with benefits. In fact, they weren't anything at all besides bandmates trying to put on a good show, and that was exactly how they were going to stay, because Kris was a goddamn professional and he wasn't going to ruin his shot at making it big with the band. If Rayne were involved with somebody else, even for a single week, even just for the tabloids, that would keep him strictly off-limits from Kris and his increasingly overactive imagination. A week would be more than enough time for Kris to pull himself together and get over whatever this was. It was perfect.

"Actually," Kris said, "I think it's a great idea."

"Really?"

"Yeah. Like you said, two birds, one stone. And you could help jump-start this guy's career, by the sound of it. That's got to be good karma, right?"

"Right," Rayne agreed. Was it Kris, or did he look almost disappointed? No, it was just the way the shadows played over his face.

Kris plastered on a smile and socked Rayne on the shoulder. "It's cool, man. Go sow your fake wild oats."

"We'll have to change our shows a bit," Rayne reminded him.

Just the thought of their shows left Kris burning up from remembered kisses. *Cold water*, he thought. Freezing, ice-cold water. The least-sexy feeling imaginable. "We'll figure something out." He paused, then asked, "Hey, what was that other thing Brian was talking about earlier? Something about not wanting a repeat of what happened last time?"

For a moment it didn't seem Rayne was going to answer, and then he blew out his breath with a rueful smile. "He was worried about you and I getting involved onstage. He knows my history with straight boys, and what happened before—it got messy and ended badly. As these things do."

"Heartbreak and misery?" Kris guessed.

"Something like that." Rayne slumped lower, propped up on one elbow. "It was with Fink," he finally admitted. "Before he got into the hard drugs. We used to fool around—not during the shows, but on tour—and I wasn't great at keeping my feelings in check then. When I told him I'd fallen for him, he just laughed."

"What a dick," Kris said, disbelievingly.

"Yeah." Rayne shrugged. "He said he was still straight, and what we were doing was just for fun. 'A good time,' he called it. I was sitting there pining while he was fucking around the whole time with any groupie who looked his way, acting like nothing had changed between us. I couldn't do the same. After that his drug use got too bad to ignore, and you know how that turned out."

"I'm sorry."

"It was only a matter of time before he left, even if he'd stayed clean. I would have kicked him out myself, I think, heroin or not. Or Brian would have. I could barely be in the same room as him, near the end."

"You can't blame yourself for him getting hooked on heroin, though. Or for bailing on the band like that."

"No, of course not, but I don't think I helped. Brian's right to warn me off you." Rayne smiled and shook his hair back. "It's fine, though. We're good, right? Brian has nothing to worry about."

"We're good," Kris promised, catching Rayne's hand to hold it. "And hey, good riddance, right? You're better off without the guy."

Rayne cracked a genuine smile and squeezed his fingers. "You're a marked improvement over him," he agreed softly.

Kris's insides went warm and melty at that, though his brain was too fuzzy to process everything Rayne had shared. He smiled back and rubbed his thumb reassuringly over Rayne's knuckles. "You got anything else you need to talk about? Any deep, dark secrets you're harboring? Lip-synching onstage? The long lost prince of Genovia?"

Rayne hesitated for a split second before shaking his head, his curls catching the only light in the room. "No, I'm done. No secrets, no royal bloodlines."

"Too bad. Guess you'll have to make do being a millionaire rock star." Kris's head was dropping of its own accord back toward his pillow as sleep rushed in to meet him. "Fancy rock star with a fake boyfriend," he mumbled, reaching over to swat at Rayne one last time. "You're like a walking fantasy, man. All those fics Cassie talks about, they've got nothing on the real you." The last thing he saw before his eyes slipped shut was Rayne's expression, caught somewhere between startled and wondrous.

He was surrounded by warmth. Sunlight filtered through the curtains, covering everything in pools of gold. The bedsheets were rumpled, and the body under him arched as Kris's veins flooded with heat. It was the lazy, unquestionable kind of enjoyment that came from familiarity, when he knew every inch of his partner's body and they knew his. Kris didn't even need to open his eyes; they were connected spirit to spirit, pleasure crashing through them with no regard for where one body ended and the next began. Kris dropped his head to his partner's shoulder and breathed in deep. They smelled like oranges and lemon peel, so fresh his mouth flooded with water. He tasted the salt of their skin as he moved his hips in lazy circles.

"Oh god, fuck," he panted, chasing his climax. It felt like burning coals in the pit of his stomach, spreading out through every limb.

"You feel so good," his partner breathed, nipping at his ear. Kris shuddered. "You feel so good . . . come on, come on—"

"Wait," Kris gasped. "Wait, I want to kiss you." He leaned down to find his partner's lips, and when their mouths met, his eyes flew open for the first time. He knew that kiss. Looking back at him, sun-dappled in the bed, lay Rayne, his hair tousled and his eyes bright and flooded with want.

"Oh, fuck," Kris said, and woke up.

It was morning, and Rayne was spooning him from behind, his face buried in Kris's shoulder. Kris was painfully, achingly hard. So, he noticed, was Rayne. Rayne's breathing was slow and steady, fanning over the back of Kris's neck. It felt damp and too hot. Kris shifted, trying to escape it, but only succeeded in pushing himself farther back into Rayne's embrace.

Kris paused and considered his options. Rayne was asleep, no matter what his libido was thinking. Kris could extricate himself—very carefully—and slip away to the bathroom, have an excruciatingly cold shower, and pretend nothing had happened. Rayne would probably be awake by the time he came back, and neither of them would have to talk about it. Or Kris could pretend to go back to sleep until Rayne woke and left for the bathroom, and again, neither would have to mention anything. Or least advised: he could stay exactly where he was and wake Rayne up to call him on his accidental intimacy. It was a terrible idea, especially considering their last conversation concerning Calloway, but Kris could still see his dream-Rayne glimmering behind his eyelids every time he blinked. That made it hard to remember why, exactly, he should be keeping his distance.

Kris held his breath and waited to see if his erection wanted to subside on its own.

It didn't.

He took the third option, shifted onto his stomach, and elbowed Rayne in the ribs.

"Dude," Kris said.

Rayne whuffled in his sleep and held him tighter.

"You are getting way up in my business here, man." Kris twisted around just enough to see Rayne blink awake, looking baffled and adorably out of place. He stayed pressed against Kris's back from chest to knee.

"Huh," said Rayne, his voice rough and low from sleep. "You don't seem to mind."

"You have to make an honest guy out of me now." Kris kept his tone deliberately light. "Roses and fancy dinners and a big fat ring. No fake boyfriend for you after all."

"You're so high maintenance." Rayne yawned. "Fine, we'll detour through Vegas and get married by some Elvis impersonator, how about that?"

"Perfect."

Kris wriggled onto his side, pretending to search for a way out from under Rayne's arm, but actually pressing his ass back against Rayne's hips, testing how far he could push things. Rayne groaned and buried his face in the pillow.

"You're a menace. Stop moving like that."

"Like what?" Kris asked, all innocence.

"You're doing this on purpose."

"So go jerk off in the shower, rock star."

"Aren't you supposed to be straight? Straight boys don't do this, unless the world's been lying to me this whole time."

Kris bit his lip and hid his face so Rayne couldn't see. "Maybe I'm just getting you back for rubbing up on me all morning."

He couldn't admit he was still chasing that high from his dream, trying to get close to Rayne in any way he could before they reached the festival and whatever complications it was going to bring. It wasn't smart, whatever the excuse. Rayne narrowed his eyes, and Kris had a second to brace himself before Rayne flattened him onto his stomach, swung a leg over Kris's thighs, and pinned his wrists to the pillow. Kris noted Rayne was keeping their hips conspicuously apart.

"What are you going to do?" Kris asked around the pillow.

"You are such a brat."

Kris shrugged as best he could, which was minimal. "You like it." He struggled against Rayne's hold, but only for show. Rayne was taller and heavier than him; he didn't stand a chance if Rayne really wanted to keep him pinned. He was pretty sure Rayne was bluffing, though.

"You going to stare at the back of my head all day, or you going to make good on that threat?" Kris bucked his hips up, and Rayne jolted up to avoid contact. Kris grinned. "Didn't think so."

He could feel Rayne's glare through his skull. Rayne held him there for a moment longer as if considering him, before dropping his full weight on Kris's back. Kris wheezed as he deflated, the air fleeing his lungs.

"Brat," Rayne repeated, more fondly now that Kris had been unilaterally defeated.

Kris pulled one hand free to smack Rayne in the shoulder. "Off," he wheezed. "Dying. You win."

"You sure?" Rayne asked. "You sure this wasn't what you wanted?"

"You're still poking me."

Rayne shifted around and jabbed his elbows into Kris's ribs.

"Okay!" Kris managed. "Okay, I give up. You win. Off."

Rayne didn't move, and Kris wondered if he was really going to be crushed to death under an annoyed, blatantly aroused rock star first thing in the morning. He'd just started drafting his final will and testament when Rayne grinned and pressed a smacking kiss to Kris's shoulder and dismounted, hopping off the bed.

"First shower," Rayne announced.

"Roses and dinner," Kris repeated. "The most expensive shit you can find."

"I can do coffee and a muffin. Maybe weed, if Angel's generous."

"Deal."

Rayne disappeared into the bathroom, and Kris rolled onto his back, flinging one arm over his face as he palmed himself through his shorts with the other. *It was a fluke*, he repeated to himself. It had been a while, and Rayne was the only person he'd touched in months. He wasn't in love—he wasn't even in lust, whatever his subconscious was saying—and he was not going to rub one out over his boss-slash-best-friend, no matter what kind of thrill had shot through him when Rayne had pressed him into the mattress like that. Rayne was going to go meet his publicity-stunt-fake-boyfriend, and Kris wasn't going to get between them, because he and Rayne were just friends. Friends and bandmates. Brian would kill him if he pulled a Fink and fucked up the tour, and Kris would kill himself if he pulled a Fink and fucked up Rayne's heart.

"Fuck me," Kris complained to the empty room.

"Marriage first!" Rayne hollered from the bathroom.

Kris pulled the pillow over his face and groaned into it. He was such a mess.

# CHAPTER NINE
## AN INTERLUDE ON THE
## SUBJECT OF DIVINE BEINGS

Modern spirituality is a strange thing, often made difficult by the unrelenting fast pace of the twenty-first century, but people find ways to make ends meet. Some attend church; some read Buddhist teachings. Some surround themselves in nature and breathe deeply until they feel at peace.

Leif had started a cult.

He hadn't meant to, at the time. But it had gotten away from him, as those things tend to do, and before he knew it people had been coming to him for guidance and spiritual well-being, and he could hardly have turned them away with nothing to believe in. He might have fucked up, but he was damn well going to take some responsibility for once in his life and see it through.

So: cult.

Seven Years Earlier:

The exact moment it began, he was sitting in the rickety foldout chair in front of his rickety little trailer, parked in a lot of other semipermanent ramshackle homes in the Mojave Desert. Leif did his best with what he had, but he'd always felt there was something missing. The outside of his trailer was rough and weather-beaten, and inside wasn't much better. He might as well be living in a cave somewhere, for all the home touches he lacked.

His soul was as neglected as his physical surroundings, and like every other hole in his life, he filled his missing sense of purpose with drugs. When his life changed, he was extraordinarily high on a combination of weed, ecstasy, and LSD, to the point where he was barely tethered to reality. His head swam with shapes and colors; his mind was so far open that the universe was pouring in through his third eye and his soul was pouring out and connecting to every other living being in the cosmos, and he understood everything. It was beautiful, but when he came down, it wouldn't have been marked as truly spiritual.

It was the peacock that tipped the experience into life-altering territory.

Leif had never seen a peacock in real life before, and at first he wasn't convinced the bird was real at all. It was too big, too colorful, too . . . much, to be a real animal existing in three-dimensional space. He flew down to Leif from the sky, surrounded by lights of a billion different colors, colors Leif had never seen before, beyond the spectrum of human visibility. The peacock's wings beat in slow motion as he descended, and Leif's mouth fell open in slack-jawed awe as they fanned his face. The breeze was warm and, it seemed to him, originating from another plane of reality. When the peacock landed on the ground before him, folding his wings back and shaking out his tail in a series of short ruffled waves, Leif was convinced he wasn't looking on any mortal bird, but some divine creature sent from heaven to bring enlightenment to his life.

He was incredibly high, and he knew he was incredibly high, but what really cemented the idea of the peacock being divinity was that he felt the same once the drugs wore off. Hours later, when he was settled back in his own skin and his mind worked slowly and linearly again, the peacock still gave him that same sense of otherworldly reverence. The peacock regarded Leif with bright, shiny eyes that seemed too intelligent to belong to a bird, and his feathers were so glossily iridescent that Leif thought there must be LSD still left in his system.

"You're something else, aren't you?" he whispered, his voice hoarse and his mouth dry.

The peacock screamed, an unearthly wail that sent goose bumps running up and down his arms, and the hairs on the back of his neck raising in alarm.

He called his friend Red.

Red was a uniquely belligerent man whose only source of inner peace came from the drugs he imbibed, and he made sure to carry a wide variety on him at all times, a pill for every occasion. He was the type of man more likely to stare at a wall for six hours when he was high than talk about the wonders of the universe, but he and Leif had been crossing paths for years, and found it easier to call themselves friends than anything else. Red was as logical and down to earth as anyone Leif had ever met, if prone to brawling. If anyone could offer some perspective on the peacock, it was him.

"What do you mean you saw God?" Red grunted over the phone.

"Not God-god, a different god," Leif said. The peacock watched him, seemingly judging his every word. "The god of . . . truth, or beauty or— I don't know. Enlightenment."

"You know you sound nuts, right?"

"Yeah, I know. But listen, get over here and judge for yourself, okay? I'm telling you, there's something about this thing. He's not a normal bird."

Red grunted again and hung up, but he came. He pulled in on his big hulking motorcycle, the machine choking out fumes, and parked beside Leif's trailer. By then the peacock was perched on the edge of the aluminum roof, his tail cascading down over the window, and he looked back over his shoulder to watch Red's approach. Leif rose from his chair to greet him.

"That's a hell of a bird," Red said eventually. "Bigger than I thought. Don't know about it being any god, though. You sure all that shit you smoke hasn't fried your brain?"

"I haven't tried anything you haven't," Leif retorted, but it was the peacock that demanded the last word. He shrieked and launched himself from the roof to assault Red in a flurry of feathers and talons, and Red shrieked in return and fell to the ground, his arms up to protect his face.

"Okay, all right!" he hollered, curling up while trying to fend the bird off. "I believe you! It's a god!"

The peacock hopped back a pace and cocked his head to one side, watching him. Red slowly got to his knees, his arms and face covered in scratches. He and Leif watched the bird, wary in case he launched a second attack. Instead, the peacock took another step back and fanned out his tail, keeping his gaze fixed on them all the while.

Now, Leif wasn't given to superstition. He hadn't been raised in a barn. He'd gone to college and studied poetry and philosophy, looking for anything to give his life a little meaning, though the student loans had piled up too quick and he'd dropped out before finishing his degree. Then he'd gone off grid for a while to avoid the debt collectors, and things had spiraled from there. The point was, he'd had an education, and he wasn't the sort to unquestioningly follow the first thing that showed any promise of spiritual fulfillment. But when the peacock spread his tail, Leif dropped to his knees alongside Red, his hands pressed to the dusty ground as he leaned forward until his forehead touched the dirt. Submitting himself like that brought the strangest sense of serenity, like all his worldly troubles were drifting away, out of reach and suddenly meaningless in the face of this beautiful, radiant creature.

And sure, maybe the drugs had fried his brain. It was possible. But the thing was, once they started showing the peacock to other people, they all agreed that there was something about the bird as well. The peacock made them feel things about life and beauty and the universe that they'd never felt before, and if that wasn't the sign of some kind of godhood, Leif didn't know what was. That, and the fact that as soon as the peacock arrived, his luck had started to change. Things started to go right again for the first time in years. He'd found a twenty-dollar bill on the ground that very day, and that was only the beginning.

From there, the cult seemed like a natural progression of events. He and Red were the only members at first, and they didn't call it a cult then. But the more time they spent communing with the bird, the more attention they attracted from like-minded individuals. Boar came next, a great hulking mountain of a man, like a Viking berserker from centuries past, looking for a community and a purpose. By that time Leif had determined his own purpose in life, which was to devote himself entirely to the peacock in return for his feathery blessing, and he was happy to bring others into the fold. Boar took to worship like it was a lifeline saving him from drowning, and everything escalated quickly after that.

They named their god to better worship it: Incandescent and All-Seeing. They shaved their heads like monks, forsaking all earthly beauty, and tattooed themselves with the images and messages they saw in their visions. Leif sold his trailer and bought a motorcycle, and traveled to hold court in music festivals and hippie camps, preaching the gospel that flowed from the universe straight into his brain. He had a gift for talking; all those years of reading poetry had left him with a deep, lilting intonation and an unusually developed vocabulary that caused his audience to sit up and pay attention, even the skeptics. Leif didn't actively recruit people to the order, but more did join, here and there. Some stayed for a few days, some for a few years. It always hurt when they left, for whatever reason, but the peacock never seemed inclined to smite them for their abandonment, so Leif didn't either.

They rarely strayed out of Nevada. The peacock had come to them in the desert, and in the desert they would stay, haunting the highways on their motorcycles as their god watched over them from above. They took money where they found it, whether from hustling pool at roadside dives, or jacking cars for parts when out-of-state drivers broke down in the desert and had to pull over and call for help. It wasn't always a legal living, but Leif thought it was an honest one. Spiritually honest: that was the important thing. Otherwise, the cops should have caught them by now. Bald and tattooed, they were hardly inconspicuous: dressed all in dusty motorcycle leathers, roaming the desert like great earthbound vultures. They had to be on the right path. Otherwise, the peacock would have abandoned them, and they would have gone to jail.

Now:

"Where to next?" Red asked.

There were four of them now, and they had set up camp off the side of the highway, their bikes parked in the shade of the towering cacti. The desert stretched out vast and orange in all directions as the sun began its descent.

"Purple Sage," Leif said, looking up at the clouds. One of their old members would be there—Calloway, who had turned his back on them, seduced by the call of worldly fame and fortune. Leif didn't have any intention of trying to win him back to the fold, but they had parted on poor terms, and he wanted closure. The new kid who had replaced him just wasn't the same. And the peacock had liked Calloway, before he'd left. Had barely screamed at him at all, and never tried to peck at him the way He did Red and Boar.

Leif sighed. Nothing was the same anymore. He wondered sometimes whether he should have founded the order at all. A selfish part of him wished he'd never called Red that day, all those years ago, that he had kept the peacock a secret between him and the universe. Would that have been such a terrible life?

The peacock screamed and rustled His wings warningly, and Leif abruptly cut off that train of thought. "Purple Sage," he repeated, more firmly this time. He'd made his choice, and he wasn't going to back down now. He couldn't. "We'll find new people there."

# CHAPTER TEN
## THE PURPLE SAGE MUSIC FEST

They were three hours out from the festival grounds, and Kris could already feel the change. It wasn't just that it was drier, the desert soaking up the sun and chasing every last shred of moisture from the air: everything looked sharper in the desert, more vivid, like reality was suddenly realer. The atmosphere crackled with expectation, and Kris couldn't keep still.

"I've never been to a music festival before," he said to Cassie on the phone. He was curled up in his bunk as they trundled down the highway, trying to block out the band's chatter. "I don't know what I'm doing."

"You'd never been to a gig anywhere bigger than a dive bar, either," she said reasonably. "You'll figure it out. We're coming to see you, by the way."

"Wait, what? Who's we?"

"All of us," Cass said. "Me and Brad and Mom and Dad. We're on the road now. We should be there tomorrow. We wanted to see you play live!"

Kris tensed up instinctively. "Why is Brad coming? This isn't his scene."

"He said it had been a while since you two hung out." He imagined her offering a careless shrug. "He said we should have gone to a closer show, but Mom and Dad thought it'd be cool to make a whole trip out of it, so here we are."

"Well, shit. Okay. We'll be here."

"And you'll be awesome. I have to go, but stop freaking out! Go find Rayne and make him give you a hug."

Kris sighed. "Say hi to everybody for me. Love you. Bye."

"Bye!"

He ended the call and climbed out of his bunk. While he hadn't been avoiding Rayne since the hotel, he hadn't been actively seeking him out, either. He found him on the couch chatting with Lenny, and sat down beside him and buried his face in Rayne's shoulder, slinging his arms around Rayne's waist. Rayne put his arm around Kris's back without missing a beat in his conversation.

"Hey," Kris said during a pause, mostly to Rayne's hair. "My family's coming to see us play tomorrow."

"That's great!"

Kris groaned.

"Is it not great?"

"I'm worried my parents are going to give me some kind of talk about life choices because of the makeup and stuff, and the last time I talked to my brother we yelled at each other, and I need you to not kick me out of the band after you meet my sister." He chanced a glance up. Rayne's eyebrows were raised, and Lenny looked amused. Stef and Maki came over to join them, likely drawn by the promise of drama.

"That's a lot," Rayne said eventually. "Is there a reason I should kick you out of the band?"

Kris shrugged and nestled closer. "She's a fan. She has posters of you in her bedroom. It's weird."

"As long as she doesn't have a shrine and an altar, it should be fine. And if your parents or your brother start giving you shit, text me, and I'll say it's an emergency and I need you onstage right this second, no excuses."

"Thanks."

Rayne's hand drifted up to Kris's hair, and Kris purred and leaned into it as Rayne scratched his scalp.

"It's going to be fine though."

"Course it is," Kris agreed. "I'm not even panicking. It's totally cool. What's the festival going to be like?"

"Festivals have a different energy than playing a show in a stadium for a few hours," Rayne said. "More of a marathon than a sprint."

"It's hard to describe," Lenny said thoughtfully. "You have to let it happen and decide for yourself."

"You take a desert, right," Stef chimed in, "and you fill it with drugs and music and kids looking for meaning, or love, or just a week of stories to tell after the fact, and mostly everyone's there for the experience and it's all good, but I've never played a festival where things didn't get weird."

"Weird," Kris repeated.

"Not in a bad way," Maki said, "but Stef's right. Festivals are . . . different."

"None of this is filling me with confidence, guys."

Rayne squeezed him tighter. "It's like if everywhere else is the real world, then festivals are just slightly off-kilter from it. Everything gets turned up to eleven."

Kris glanced out the window in time to see a biker gang pass by in a rumble of tattoos and black leather.

"I don't know if that sounds like a place I want my parents to show up," he said.

"They probably remember Woodstock," Stef said with a shrug. "Bet they know more about the scene than you think."

Kris decided he'd rather not think about that too hard. "There's still my brother."

"What's the worst that could happen?" Rayne asked optimistically.

"He's a Republican."

"Oh."

Kris buried his face in Rayne's shoulder while Rayne patted his arm.

"Maybe it won't be that bad?" Rayne offered. "You'll be pretty busy; you can avoid him if you have to. We'll help run interference."

"We totally will," Stef agreed. "Like secret agent bodyguards."

"At least Cass should have fun," Kris mumbled into Rayne's shirt.

"You will too. We'll get set up and play our show and meet Calloway and Dead Generation later on, and everything will be great."

Kris nodded and clung tighter for a second, savoring the contact, before straightening. Once Rayne and Calloway were involved, there'd be no more of that for a while. Kris and Rayne could technically keep sneaking cuddles in private where the press couldn't catch them, but it seemed safer to stop entirely while Calloway was in the picture, so Kris wanted to store up what he could while he had the chance. "No, you're right. Everything will be fine."

The last of the stages were still being built when they rolled in. The festival sprawled like an oasis in the desert, a tiny city of tents, trailers, and scaffolding all glittering hot as a mirage under the sun. Kris watched it unfold around him, his nose pressed to the window, as the bus made its way through to their campsite. They parked in a clearing, and it dawned on Kris that they were going to be living out of the bus for the next week until the festival wrapped up, outdoor toilets and showers and all.

It was still better than being homeless on the streets of New York.

By the time they started rehearsing, Kris's anxiety had settled into a nervous thrum of excitement. The songs came easily now, and he barely had to improvise at all anymore. He had their set list memorized, and he could anticipate Rayne's vocals as easily as he could his own solos. And he knew Rayne's habits onstage too—how he looked when he was wound too tight, his expression and the set of his shoulders when he was about to prowl over and kiss Kris senseless. Kris kept one eye on him during rehearsal, watching for the signs, but they didn't come. They rarely did, except during the live shows, like Rayne wanted to bottle it all up until the pressure was too much and he couldn't keep it down any longer.

Kris liked it that way. It kept things clear between them, and clarity was what he needed, no matter what his traitorous body suggested to the contrary. A solid line between what they did onstage and how they were off it.

He still thought about that dream when he was trying to fall asleep at night. He tried not to dwell on it, but it crept in through the cracks in his resolve, and before he knew it, he'd be half-hard from a memory that had never even happened.

It was getting ridiculous.

This stunt with Calloway was the best thing for it. And while Rayne and Calloway were busy, Kris would throw himself into the festival and play so hard his mind didn't have time to wander. He and Rayne would cut down on the fan service onstage, and offstage, Rayne and Calloway would be boyfriends, at least while their pictures were being taken. It would all be good. And then later, when his head was clear—after the tour, when Rayne wasn't influencing his decisions anymore—then he would come out as bi.

The first night of the festival—when the shadows grew long in the setting summer sun, the last of the stages had finally been erected, and the lanes were flooding with crowds of thousands at a time—they took to the stage and Kris realized with a heavy drop of horror that his plan was not going to work.

Rayne kissed him like he wanted to eat him alive. He tangled one hand in Kris's hair, wrapped the other around his throat, and reeled him in like a fish on a hook and held him there, helpless, in front of their screaming fans. Kris's knees buckled and he nearly fell, but Rayne held him fast, licking into every inch of his mouth like he had something to prove. Kris moaned, uncaring if Rayne's mike picked it up, and licked back. His hands kept time on his guitar, moving mindlessly over the chords as his whole body lit up with want, his brain blank except for a chorus of *Rayne, Rayne, Rayne.*

After the show, he stumbled backstage, dry-mouthed with a pounding heart and no plan except to douse himself in the coldest water he could find. It was better than nothing, though he doubted it would help. He had made it this far without rubbing one out because of Rayne, and he wasn't about to start now. His guitar stayed on him like armor, even as the rest of the band pulled him into their customary post-show embrace, sweating and panting and bright-eyed all around. He returned it, still riding the high himself, but this time trying to hide his blatant arousal from anyone else.

He didn't know why he bothered. Rayne got worked up onstage all the time; it was a combination of adrenaline and elation and Kris didn't want to flatter himself but he imagined he was no small part of it, either. There were entire websites dedicated to pictures of Rayne getting overly excited onstage, and Rayne never bothered denying them, so why should Kris?

He adjusted the guitar across his lap and skittered back to their dressing room, a separate trailer set up behind the stage, to get changed and clean the makeup from his face. Rayne's kiss had destroyed his lipstick, smudging it and making him look more wanton than usual. Rayne hadn't escaped unscathed either, finishing the show with his own lips darker than usual, but it had only made his smile all the more enticing. The crowd had screamed and wailed, begging them to continue.

"You good?" Rayne asked from the doorway. The lipstick was smeared around his mouth, berry-dark. "You bailed pretty fast."

"Needed water." Kris managed a smile. "I'm good. It's all cool."

Rayne sidled in, ignoring Kris's attempted brush-off. "Still worried about your family coming?"

Kris's family had been the last thing on his mind. "Yeah, that."

"Calloway's arriving with Dead Generation tomorrow morning; we'll tone our shows down once he gets here. Your parents don't have to see you and I doing all that in person. I still haven't committed to anything, though. Not for sure." Rayne's expression was a mixture of tentative hope and nervousness, and Kris didn't like seeing it on his face.

"But you're going to, right?" Kris asked, pushing aside the way his stomach flipped at the thought. "I think you should. If the label wants you to, then it must be a good career move. And who knows, maybe you and Calloway will hit it off for real."

Rayne's face shuttered for a split second before he smiled. "Yeah, maybe we will."

Kris smiled back and adjusted his guitar strap, resolutely ignoring the way he felt faintly sick at the thought of Rayne getting involved, offstage and for real, with a guy who wasn't him. "Cool," he said aloud. Everything was going to be fine.

Kris's family arrived the next morning, hours before The Chokecherries were due to take the stage again. The festival was a hive of constant activity, with additional bands and attendees arriving every hour, the tents and stages bursting with music and partygoers day and night. Dead Generation arrived around ten, but Rayne said they were busy setting up, and he was going to find them later. The energy was unlike anything Kris had ever felt—maybe it was just because the air was hazy with weed and everyone seemed to be high on one thing or another, but it felt brimming with humanity at its best and most expressive, and Kris thought he could get high off that alone.

There was really a lot of weed.

But the combination of performing and connecting with fans he never thought he'd have left him feeling more at home in his skin than ever before, so when his family arrived on site he was dressed half in his stage clothes and half casually, with his hair ruffed up in a faux-hawk and eyeliner smudged around his lids. He wasn't fully done up and wouldn't be until closer to showtime, but he still got a thrill from seeing himself in the mirror with makeup on, so it was creeping further and further into his offstage life. He couldn't apply a convincing smoky eye yet, but if all he needed was a bit of kohl, he was set.

The downside to his increase in comfort was that he forgot he was wearing the stuff when he met his family.

To his parents' credit, they didn't comment. Cassie did, but nonverbally—she pointed at him from behind their parents' backs, exaggeratedly miming at his face while grinning and giving him the thumbs-up. Brad stiffened and said nothing. Kris opened his mouth to apologize preemptively, then changed his mind and smiled instead.

"Thanks for coming all the way out here. You really didn't have to."

"Of course we did," his dad said. "If you're going to go off touring the world, the least we could do was come see you before you left the country."

"I appreciate it. I, uh, I guess Cassie's been keeping you up-to-date on all the shows?"

"You do look like you're having fun up there," his mom commented mildly, and Kris nearly choked on his tongue. "That Rayne knows how to put on a show, doesn't he?"

"He's a natural all right," his dad agreed.

Cass elbowed Kris in the ribs, still grinning.

"Lunch?" Kris blurted. "Let's get lunch. They've got decent food here, unless you want to drive out to an actual restaurant."

"Here's good," his mom said. "We're here for the experience, after all."

Kris led them through the picnic area to the food trucks, where vendors of every possible cuisine had set up shop, from the vegan elites to the place where you went when you were drunk at 3 a.m. and the fridge was empty. They ordered their food and sat at a picnic table. Kris tried not to fidget. He was in his element, and his family was happy for him.

Except Bradley. Brad didn't seem happy.

Kris resolved to ignore him until he couldn't anymore.

"You're going to introduce us to the band, right?" Cass asked, shoveling rice into her mouth. "And Passionfruit too? They look fun. Do you think anyone would let me try their drum kit?"

"You can ask about drumming. And I already warned Rayne you were coming, so sure, you can meet everybody," Kris said. "That won't be weird for me at all."

"We met your last band," his dad pointed out.

"In high school," Kris replied. "This is a bit different."

"Your last one didn't dress you up like a girl and grope you in front of a million people," Brad said.

Everyone stilled and Kris sighed internally. Of course he wouldn't be allowed to ignore Brad.

"It's for the show, Brad," he said, repeating their press line with as much patience as he could muster.

"Hell of a show," Brad replied.

"I think it's great," Cass cut in. "People are loving it. Don't crush his entertainment dreams, Brad."

Brad held up his hands. "I'm not here to crush anything. I just want you to realize how it looks to other people."

"It looks fucking punk," Cass insisted.

"Okay," his dad said, "let's everybody cool down. Kris, why don't you tell us about the rest of the tour? What are your plans after the festival?"

Kris dived in gratefully, talking about the band's plans and where Rayne wanted to go, and where the international tour would take them—not that Kris was officially signed on for that part—but he kept stealing glances at Brad out of the corner of his eye. Brad didn't interrupt again, but he didn't relax, either. Kris finally texted Rayne under the table, demanding that he show up and provide a distraction.

Rayne came over a few minutes later; Kris knew his arrival by the sharp intake of Cassie's breath.

"Sorry to interrupt," Rayne said, and Kris let out a sigh of relief. He loved his family, he really did, but negotiating Bradley's idiot ideals of masculinity was the last thing he wanted to deal with. "I was going to borrow Kris for a minute, but if he's busy . . .?"

Kris stood, grabbed Rayne by the wrist and made a gesture like Vanna White. "So hey, this is Rayne! Rayne Bakshi. Rayne, this is my family."

His parents smiled and Cassie gazed at Kris imploringly, stars in her eyes, pleading for him to stay. He relented, grudgingly abandoning his plan of escape. "You guys want to walk us back to the . . . stage? Bus? Where are we going, Rayne?"

"The bus," Rayne said. "There's been a slight incident." He held out his hand to Frank, smiling widely. "And you're Kris's dad! I've heard about you. All of you," he amended. "Did you have a good drive?"

Kris's dad shook Rayne's hand and smiled back, clearly relieved to find Rayne capable of small talk. "A good drive, yes, thank you. Beautiful landscape, beautiful country. And it looks like you've got decent weather for the festival too."

"Couldn't ask for better," Rayne agreed, offering his hand to Kris's mom next, who seemed charmed. Rayne had that effect on people.

"And my sister, Cassie," Kris said.

Cass squeaked, grinned, and thrust her hand out at lightning speed. "Hi. Rayne. Rayne Bakshi. Hey."

"Hey," Rayne said, his eyes sparkling. "I heard you keep my picture in your room."

"Kris!"

Rayne laughed and patted her shoulder. "No, I'm flattered. He promised there wasn't a shrine or anything, so it's fine. You want to meet the rest of the band?"

"I get why Kris likes you," Cass said, allowing his hand to stay. "You're awful. I love it."

They set out together back to the buses, and if anyone noticed that Brad never got introduced or shook Rayne's hand, no one commented on it.

Kris was surprised to find that there really had been an incident with the bands: Knocks, Passionfruit's drummer, had broken his foot and been whisked away to the nearest hospital, and the remaining band members were huddled outside The Chokecherries' bus, nursing various alcoholic beverages and looking morose.

"What happened?" Kris asked.

"Jay tried to kill our drummer," Billie said.

"It was an accident," Jay said.

"You tackled him into the middle of his drum kit. You're lucky you didn't break his neck."

"I didn't know he was going to get tangled up in the pedals like that."

Billie sighed. "And now we're trying to borrow Lenny for our show tonight instead."

Lenny raised his drink in a salute.

"You're going to play two shows back-to-back every night for the rest of the festival?" Kris asked.

"That's what I said," Rayne cut in, glowering at Passionfruit.

"We need a drummer," Billie returned, "and Lenny knows all the songs. Mostly. Kind of."

Rayne cleared his throat. "Everyone, this is Kris's family. They're here to see the show."

Cassie waved. Kris's parents smiled and fidgeted, keeping a polite distance while Brad stood stony-faced, arms crossed and feet planted firmly on the ground.

"Cass wanted to meet the bands, and the timing kind of sucks, but hey?" Kris tried.

"The timing's fine," Rayne said. "It's a festival. There's always something going on."

Billie sighed again, more heavily this time.

"You know I didn't do it on purpose," Jay muttered, sotto voce.

"We're talking about this later," Billie said.

Kris winced and turned back to his family. "So, this is it. Passionfruit; The Chokecherries. Check out the glamorous life of bands on tour."

"Accidents happen," his mom said diplomatically. "They're rarely the end of the world."

"But obviously you're all very busy, and we should get out of your hair," his dad said.

"No, it's fine!" Billie said. "It'll be fine. Do you want a drink? We've got beer." He glanced at Cassie. "Or water, or Coke?"

"I'll have a Coke," Cassie said, happily undermining her parents' attempt at retreat. "Is your drummer going to be okay?"

"He'll be fine," Jay stressed, pulling a can from the cooler for her. "Grab a seat, hang out with us."

Cassie sat down on top of the cooler and looked at the rest of her family expectantly.

"We really don't want to get in anyone's way," their mom began.

As much as he'd like to avoid Brad, Kris felt bad giving his parents the same treatment. "Stay until we go for makeup in another hour," he said. "It'll be fun."

Rayne nodded. Cassie was already making herself at home as if she were among old friends, smiling and chatting away. Brad scowled—almost imperceptibly; Kris didn't think anyone else would notice—but took a seat with the others. Hatchwork, the mustachioed Passionfruit bassist, drew Kris's parents into a conversation about their hometown, which they were only too glad to have. Lenny was engrossed in a quiet argument between Rayne and Billie.

"You've met Rayne now," Kris said to Cass. "This is Maki and Stef—and that's Lenny, over there."

"Hey," Stef said with a smile.

"Hi." Cassie smiled back. "I've seen your videos. Love your work."

Maki caught Kris's eye and gave him a knowing smile. Kris rubbed his hand over his face, not caring about smudging his makeup anymore.

"I can play drums, you know," Cassie said.

Everyone paused and looked at her.

She shrugged. "I'm pretty good. Kris can vouch for me. Just putting that out there."

"Cassie," Brad said.

"What? I am."

"How fast can you learn a new song?" Billie asked, leaning in.

"I know most of your set already," she said, taking a swig from her drink. "I checked out your albums when Kris said you were opening for Rayne, and I've been watching all your concerts since you started the tour. I bet I could play most of it right now. See?" She offered her phone to show off a recording of her on her kit in the garage. She played as steady as a metronome, and she smashed out her solos with the energy of a hurricane.

"Damn," Billie said. "That's actually amazing." Cassie preened as Billie glanced around at the rest of his band. "What do we think, guys?"

"Hell with it," Jay said. "Let's audition her. What have we got to lose?"

"You can't be serious," Brad said, but though their parents exchanged a few whispered words, they didn't voice any objections.

"Don't worry," Rayne said, ignoring Brad entirely in favor of addressing Kris's parents. "There's a billion people around to keep an eye on her. She won't get into any trouble."

Cassie beamed and finished her drink. "No trouble at all," she promised, and then she was sauntering off with Passionfruit like that had been her plan all along.

Brad turned to their parents. "You're really going to let her go off like that without—"

"Oh, give her a break," Kris cut in. "It's a festival, she's an adult. Let her enjoy herself for a minute. Jesus."

"I'm sure it's fine," their mom said. "Like Mr. Bakshi said, there are plenty of people around to watch out for her."

Kris flashed Brad a spiteful smile. He wasn't sure what to make of Cassie auditioning for Passionfruit, but if it annoyed Brad, he was all for it.

Leif was at home in music festivals, and Purple Sage was one of his personal favorites. He sat with his disciples in a clearing between a ring of tents, their bikes parked nearby and the peacock wandering the grounds, as was His wont. The bird never strayed too far, and it wasn't as if He could get lost, so Leif let Him be. He talked about his spirituality in a low, calm voice as he etched a fresh tattoo on Boar's leg. They had attracted a few onlookers, including a twitchy, strung-out youth named Travis who watched wide-eyed as the needle dug into Boar's skin and the ink set.

"Will you do me next?" he asked, but before Leif could answer, a black girl with a huge halo of curly hair stumbled into their circle as she rounded the corner of the nearest tent.

"Sorry," she said. "Didn't mean to barge in on you like that."

Leif glanced up from his work to see if she was interested in hearing about their god, and she stared back, apparently not expecting to run into such a gathering. Leif knew how they appeared to casual passersby: pale as bone and covered in strange scribbled tattoos, their heads shaved, and dressed head to toe in scuffed-up bike leathers. Anyone who wanted to hear about the universe, their god, and their coming salvation had to see past their rough exteriors to the truth.

"It's no problem," Rikki said to the young woman.

Rikki didn't fit in with the others yet. He was the order's newest recruit: the youngest of them, and the slightest, too, with big pale eyes and a face too earnest to make a living the way they did, though he believed in their god as fervently as Leif could wish. They'd work on him.

The woman gave Rikki a short nod and sidestepped out of their midst. "Enjoy the festival," she said, and left quickly, without looking back.

Leif returned his attention to Boar's tattoo, but he didn't miss the way Rikki watched the woman as she disappeared into the mess of tents.

It was easy for Kris to forget that his family was in the audience by the time The Chokecherries took the stage. Passionfruit killed it, playing even more aggressively than usual, as if to make up for losing a member, but Cassie took to it like breathing. Apparently she had nailed the audition, and while Passionfruit had still wanted to test her in front of a live crowd, they had been vibrating with enthusiasm about her skills, telling everyone who passed that she was a genius and they needed to steal her for the rest of their tour. She broke a stick halfway through the set, and Passionfruit looked pleased as anything about it. When they traipsed offstage, she smacked Kris on the chest as she passed, sweaty and wrung out, grinning from ear to ear.

"This is great!" she yelled. "Way better than our band in high school. I get why you do it!"

"Nice playing, kid," Stef said. "You're a natural."

"Hell yeah, I am. Go get it!"

When their set began, Kris played as he always did, keyed up with tension the second until the opening riff started and Rayne took the stage. By then he wasn't thinking about his parents or Calloway or the future at all. Rayne commanded the crowd's attention with a crook of his finger and shake of his head, and he stole Kris's just as easily. The Chokecherries played with the same passion they always did, and Rayne sang with the same raw energy, but this time, when Kris waited for their midshow kiss, it didn't come.

Kris frowned and tried to catch Rayne's eye, but Rayne wasn't looking.

There was nothing wrong with changing it up. They could always do the kiss later.

Later came and went, and Kris grew increasingly twitchy behind his guitar. He had thought they would keep their shows as they were until Calloway entered the picture, for the fans' sake. Had Rayne already met with Calloway and begun the stunt without telling Kris?

When they only had three tracks left, Kris finally tore a page from Passionfruit's book and launched an attack, barreling into Rayne from the side and jabbing his shoulder into Rayne's chest, all without missing a chord. Rayne took a fistful of Kris's hair, whether to hold him in place or push him away, Kris didn't know. It didn't matter. All he needed was Rayne's hands on him, somewhere, anywhere, especially if it was going to be the last time. He butted into Rayne's space, demanding more, but Rayne still didn't kiss him. He came close, pulling Kris's back in against his chest so Kris could feel their heartbeats thundering in tandem, even above the bass and the kick of the drums, and his lips ghosted over Kris's temple, but they didn't touch.

Kris leaned back, eyes closed as he coaxed the riff from his guitar, and dared Rayne to touch him for real. He let the music swell around him and Rayne's heat soak through his shirt as his mouth parted, throat bared to the sky, waiting.

When Rayne shuddered, Kris felt it in his whole body. They moved into Stef's solo, and Rayne bent forward, his hand splayed against Kris's chest, and he mouthed, "You little brat," against the shell of Kris's ear.

"Why did you skip our thing?" Kris mouthed back. "Is it Calloway?"

"I haven't even met him yet."

"Then stop fucking around."

"Your parents are watching!"

"I'm not asking you to fuck me onstage!"

Rayne dug his nails into Kris's skin, and Kris rocked against him. "Just kiss me before we go backstage again, and give the people their money's worth."

"You're incorrigible."

Kris twisted around in Rayne's grasp, flinging one arm around Rayne's neck, the other holding his guitar between them, to meet Rayne's gaze. They stared at each other for a second, Kris daring him to do something, anything—and Rayne finally smiled in exasperation and leaned down to press their lips together. It was more chaste than usual, but the crowd screamed right on cue all the same, and Kris shut his eyes and basked in it. Rayne's grip in his hair tightened as he laughed into Kris's mouth, smudging lipstick everywhere.

"You're the worst," Rayne said when they parted.

"You started it," Kris said, his heart pounding at the thought that that might have been their last kiss until the festival was over. "Now you have to follow through."

Rayne shook his head, his hair falling into his eyes, and stepped up to the mike stand again. Kris let him go this time as Stef pounded out the last of their solo, and Rayne opened his mouth for the final chorus. Kris returned to his spot, hot all over. He was definitely going to have withdrawal symptoms if he couldn't do that again the next day.

Brad found him backstage after the show. By that point Passionfruit was long gone and the rest of The Chokecherries had dispersed as Kris took an extra minute to pull himself together before rejoining Rayne. Kris glanced up as Brad approached with a guarded expression and leaned against a set of scaffolding, watching Kris for a moment. Kris set his jaw and wiped his face with his sleeve, clearing up the excess sweat near his hairline as he waited for Brad to speak.

"I get that you're doing it for the show," Brad finally said, "and you don't want to let your fans down. I can respect that. But can you seriously not see how he's using you? He's a predator, Kris!"

"Oh, yeah, he's really taking advantage of me up there." Kris rolled his eyes and put his guitar away. "Just let it go, man. I'm having a good time."

"Listen to me. You're my little brother, and I worry about you. And this? What you're doing? I know you think this is the only chance you've got of fulfilling your dream or whatever, but have you stopped to ask yourself if it's actually worth it?"

Kris paused and narrowed his eyes. "Are you worried somebody's forcing me to do all this shit, or are you worried I'm actually into it?"

Brad's mouth twisted.

"No, tell me," Kris said. "What's worse—your little brother being bullied into wearing girly clothes and getting groped onstage, or it being all his idea?"

"Kris—"

"What's worse?" Kris demanded. "That I'm a victim or a pansy?"

"I didn't come here to fight," Brad snapped. "If you don't want my support, fine!" He turned and stalked off the way he'd come, away from the stage and back in the direction of the family car.

"Fuck you too!" Kris yelled after him, before he disappeared into the crowds.

Cass poked her head around the corner. "Bad timing?"

"Fucking Bradley, sanctimonious asshole," Kris muttered.

"Yeah," she agreed. "Just wait till he tries to warn Mom and Dad about the dangers of me running away with a punk band."

"The Passionfruit guys are sweethearts," Kris said automatically. "Wait, are you really joining the band?"

"I passed the audition," she said with a shrug, "and they say I did good on the live show. They need a drummer, at least until Knocks is back on his feet. It's almost as cool as running away to join the circus, and I've wanted to do that since I was a kid."

"Cool," Kris said faintly.

"Cool," Cassie confirmed. "Have you seen Stef? I want to talk to them about something."

"Right, yeah, I'm sure. They were heading back to the buses, last I heard."

Cassie grinned. "Thanks, bro. See you later."

"Cassie? No hooking up on the buses! Tour rule!"

She waved over her shoulder. "Sure, sure. Whatever you say."

Kris flopped onto the baggy couch and pressed a water bottle against his face. Why Brad had even wanted to come to Nevada, he didn't know. The idea that Brad suddenly wanted to spend time with Kris after years of minimal contact was laughable. They hadn't been close since before high school, and by the time they both finished community college, they'd had little in common outside their family tree. If Brad had come along on the Golding road trip out of some misguided attempt to show Kris the error of his ways and guide him back to the conservative, heteronormative light, he was going to have to try harder than that. Even if Kris left the band after they finished the tour and never wore girls' clothes or makeup again, he wasn't going to forget how incredible it had felt to kiss Rayne, or that dream in the hotel, or how he wanted to—

He rubbed his fingers over his eyes and shoved his thoughts back into order. He could barely remember why he had wanted to keep Rayne off-limits in the first place. Closing his eyes, he let a fantasy run wild for a second. He would come out to Rayne; they'd do a press release and kiss onstage. Then maybe they'd kiss offstage too. He'd talk to Brian and assure him that what had happened with Fink would never happen with Kris, and his family would come around quickly enough—apart from Brad. Maybe he should come out just to spite his brother.

"Stop it," he said aloud, sternly. Fantasy aside, there was too much at risk in propositioning Rayne—like his career, and his friendship, and his dignity, if Rayne rejected him. Rayne had never shown any interest in being more than friends, and Kris didn't need to invite awkwardness into their lives, or joblessness into his.

His fantasy ran in full Technicolor, suggesting a few other things he could invite instead.

He groaned. "That's so unhelpful," he muttered to his brain.

The fact that he wanted to sleep with Rayne—not hypothetically, not in a dream, but in a definite, real, messily undeniable way—didn't get the due diligence it deserved. It seemed like the kind of revelation that should come down like a ton of bricks, but mostly Kris was just annoyed.

The timing sucked, but Kris was willing to take the blame for that. He should have figured out his attraction earlier; he should have admitted it the second that dream had come crashing through his subconscious. But just because Rayne had dragged his bisexuality over the threshold from a probability to a mouth-watering surety—right at the moment Calloway was due to enter the picture—that wasn't cause for a crisis. It was cause for a plan.

He had more than a crush, and it was only getting stronger as the days went on; that was fine. His plan could work with that. Rayne would do his stunt with Calloway while Kris worked up the nerve to come out, and if by the time the stunt was over Kris still wanted to sleep with Rayne? Then he'd tell him that too.

# CHAPTER ELEVEN
## THE APPEAL OF DATING
## FOR FAME AND MONEY

Kris was itching to meet Calloway in person and get things underway. Neither Rayne nor Brian had announced anything about the stunt to the rest of The Chokecherries yet, but they clearly knew something was winding Kris up. Kris wasn't about to admit to having feelings for Rayne and to depending on a publicity stunt with a stranger to get him over them, so they all circled around each other pretending everything was normal. It was exhausting, and he was strung so tight he might snap, but when he was a second away from flinging himself from the bus to pace the festival, Rayne beckoned him over. Dead Generation was ready.

Kris headed across the grounds with Rayne and Angel, his nerves twisting around like it was his career on the line and no one else's. Technically, he didn't need to meet Calloway at all. Rayne was perfectly capable of making a decision about the stunt on his own. But Kris wasn't going to turn down any chance to hang out, no matter how stressful, so he accepted Rayne's invitation to tag along. Rayne looked brightly optimistic and Angel seemed amused by the whole thing, and Kris let them walk ahead while he pulled himself together.

"You're not slick, you know," Angel said eventually, her voice pitched softly enough that Kris assumed she was speaking to Rayne alone. "You can't stand publicity stunts. You've always said if somebody's music can't stand on its own, it's not worth listening to."

"I have no idea what you're talking about," Rayne replied loftily.

"You talk to . . .?"

"He told me I should go for it."

Angel glanced back at Kris, who wondered if he should hang farther back to let them talk in peace. He waved, and Angel smiled at him, then turned to Rayne and murmured something too low for Kris to catch.

"If I were secretly pining for him, sure," Rayne said, his voice light, and Angel didn't seem inclined to push the matter further.

The Dead Generation stage was easy to find, their banner a huge black-and-white thing with skulls and crossbones. Beside them, an androgynous creature with pink hair was rigging a banner that read *Neurts and the Synthetic Skunks* between two sets of scaffolding for the opening act. Calloway sat on the edge of the stage, kicking his sneakers against the side as he took a swig from his water bottle. When he saw them approach, he lifted his hand in an easy greeting and hopped down to meet them. He was even more attractive in real life: taller than Rayne, with strong shoulders and a vitality that infused his every movement like he was living entirely in the present, and keen to make the most of it. He was less of a twink than Kris—and Kris suspected twink was basically Rayne's type—but that wasn't a fair comparison. Kris was like, the Platonic Ideal of twinkdom. A few tattoos scrawled around Calloway's arms and peeked out from under the neck of his shirt. Kris tried to imagine him and Rayne in glossy tabloid photos together, arms around each other's necks and knowing smiles on their lips. They would look flashy like rock royalty, and the press would eat it up.

"Hi," Calloway said, offering his hand to whoever wanted to take it first. "I'm Cal. Nice to meet you." He had an easy smile and his words lilted with a rough Irish accent.

Rayne took his hand with an answering smile, turning on the same charm Kris recognized from his press interviews. "Rayne. Nice to meet you too. This is my guitarist Kris, and Angel, my makeup artist and . . . bodyguard?"

"I'm a lot of things," Angel said, taking his hand and flashing a smile. "Moral support and common sense, at the moment."

"Yeah, we could use some of that," Calloway agreed, rubbing the back of his neck with a sheepish air. When Kris shook his hand next, his grip was warm and sturdy. Every inch of exposed skin was covered in freckles, peeking out from in between tattoos, and the hairs that dusted his forearms were gold from the sun. "I've heard about you, of course. You've been making quite a splash in the tabloids with your recent shows."

"I don't read the tabloids," Kris said.

"Neither did I, till quite recently." Cal looked back to Rayne. "So, how do you want to do this? Your manager said you were still thinking it over, and I understand your not wanting to jump straight in. Or at all."

"Well, I thought I'd come and meet you, and we'd have a chat," Rayne said easily, "maybe get to know each other a bit. See if we get along well enough to fake a relationship for a week."

"Right, right, that won't be awkward at all." Calloway smiled again, and Kris could see why the label wanted to keep him around. A pretty face went a long way in the industry, if Rayne's stories were anything to go by.

"Let's head to the picnic tables and grab some food," Rayne suggested. "Talk things out. Angel? Kris? You want to join us?"

"I wouldn't miss it," Angel said, and Kris nodded along agreeably.

They grabbed some food and took a seat in the picnic area, Rayne sitting between Angel and Kris with Calloway across from them, as if they were in an interview. Rayne still had his press face on, the one that made him look perfectly at ease, but which Kris knew to be a carefully constructed mask. He thought about the first time he met Rayne and they'd gone to that burger place—that had been an interview too, of sorts, but he was sure Rayne had been nothing but genuine the entire time. The thought helped melt some of the nerves away.

*Calloway isn't replacing me. It's a stunt to boost album sales, and it'll be over as soon as we leave Purple Sage.*

"A lot of Dead Generation fans love The Chokecherries," Calloway said. "If I have to pull a stunt like this, I'm glad it's with you, at least. Though I'm surprised you're considering it at all—I thought you and Kris had a thing going on."

"I haven't agreed to anything yet," Rayne pointed out before Kris could say anything, "and no. Kris is straight."

"Are you?" Calloway asked him. "My god, that's dedication. I'd never have guessed."

Kris swallowed the panicked lump in his throat—this was his perfect chance to say otherwise—but by the time he opened his mouth, Cal was talking again.

"I assumed the label was pushing you into this to cover up you and Kris, actually, though I couldn't figure out why. But this is cleaner. And hey, if things go well, who knows what could happen?" He winked.

Kris glanced at Rayne and tried to detect any glimmer of interest behind the perfectly professional veneer. Rayne just looked amused.

"We'll see how it goes," Rayne agreed, and Cal grinned wider in response. "So how did you get outed? Not to pry, but if the press comes up asking me about a sex tape or something, I'd like to be prepared."

"Now that you mention it— No, they caught me at a gay club with a friend. The label said if I got a girlfriend and laughed it off, it would blow over fast enough, but I couldn't bear the thought of lying, only to come out on my own years later."

A rush of guilt burned through Kris, and he laced his fingers together on the tabletop until his knuckles went white. Angel glanced at him behind Rayne's back, her brows knitted in concern, but he shook his head. If Rayne or Cal noticed anything amiss, they pretended not to, for which Kris was grateful.

"So they set this up instead," Cal continued. "It really wasn't very scandalous at all, I'm afraid. I'd at least have liked a good story out of it."

Calloway was charming enough; he wasn't obnoxious like some front men could be, and he had an easy air to him, like he wasn't inclined to take things personally. If Rayne turned him down, Kris guessed they could all still be friends. Beside him, Rayne relaxed, likely reading those same signs.

"Tell you what," Rayne said, and Calloway brightened and sat up straighter. "I like what I've heard of your band, and you don't seem like a serial killer. I'll do it. Give me one of your Dead Generation shirts to wear for my next show—that'll be enough to start the rumor mill on its own."

Calloway grinned and leaned over the table to take Rayne's hand again. "This'll be fun," he promised. Up close, his eyes were a dark, sparkling blue, and when he turned his smile on Kris, Kris forced himself to smile back. His inner turmoil wasn't Cal's fault, after all.

"You should come meet the rest of the band," Angel said. "And you three should have a talk about what this means for The Chokecherries' shows, with the kissing and all that."

Rayne elbowed her and she elbowed him back harder, still smiling brightly at Cal.

"Kris and I agreed to tone things down while you and I are together," Rayne said. "No more kissing, but we want to keep a little teasing, if that's cool with you. The crowds are into it, you know?"

"For sure," Calloway agreed, grinning between the two of them. "It's all for the fans. Definitely nothing else going on."

Kris bit his tongue to hide his wince and managed to keep his smile in place.

Rayne sighed. "You're going to be trouble, I can tell. Come on, come meet the others. Let's get this rolling."

Calloway detoured back to his stage to grab a shirt for Rayne, and Angel looped her arm through Rayne's as they waited. Kris stood, leaning his hip against the table as he soaked up the sun.

"So?" Angel asked. "What do you guys think? You like him?"

"I agreed to go out with him, didn't I? Or pretend to, anyway," Rayne said.

"You think he's cute?" she pressed. "Maybe hit that thing for real? He clearly wants to."

"Stop it, you."

"It could do you some good," she said with a shrug, then glanced at Kris, who kept his face carefully neutral. "This is your perfect chance to unwind and have some fun, and you don't even have to hide it from the press. Hell, you get to flaunt it!"

"You're a terrible influence."

"What do you think, Kris?" Angel asked pointedly. "If they're both into each other, can you think of one good reason why they shouldn't give it a shot?"

Kris remembered their inebriated conversation in the White Rabbit—how he'd told her he liked kissing Rayne, and how he'd never declined her offer to find him a label other than "straight" to encompass that. She would never out him without his say, but he wished she would, just to get it over with, since he was clearly having trouble doing it himself. Before he could form a semicoherent reply, Calloway came loping back, waving a black T-shirt with the Dead Generation logo sprawled across the chest. He tossed it to Rayne, who shrugged out of his old shirt in a single smooth movement. As Rayne changed, Kris's and Calloway's gazes met and Calloway grinned knowingly before turning away.

Kris had seen Rayne shirtless a thousand times by now—privacy was a foreign concept on tour—but the sight was affecting him more and more. He'd have to be less obvious about it if Calloway could see through him so easily.

Fully clothed again, Rayne put his arm around Cal's shoulders and pulled him along as the four of them walked back to The Chokecherries' stage. Cal fell in line easily, matching his longer strides to the group's.

"So what did you do before your band?" Angel asked.

"Oh, this and that. Dropped out of university and traveled around. Bit of a vagrant, really. Had a brief fling with a cult; that was exciting, I can tell you."

They all made an inquisitive noise.

"Yeah, not my wisest life choice, but it served as a wake-up call. I cleaned up my act, and now I'm here."

"Wait, you're not joking?" Kris demanded.

"About the cult? Nah. It'll make a good chapter in my memoir, if I ever get big enough to write one."

Angel darted in, her eyes fixed on the arm Calloway had slung around Rayne's waist. "Those tattoos . . ."

"Ah, yeah, I'm covering most of the older ones up. I'm a work in progress."

She frowned and took his hand, bumping Rayne aside with her hip to swap places and walk next to Calloway instead.

"I've seen designs like this before," she said, turning his hand over and examining his arm in full. The tattoos were unintelligible, a million miles from what Jiao Fang and her ilk could do. There were bits of writing in languages and alphabets Kris didn't know, scrawled pictures of flowers or strange animals up and down his arms. There was the outline of an eye on the back of his left hand.

"Yeah," Cal said, "I don't know what most of them are either."

"Where did you get them?" Rayne asked.

"A guy I knew had his own kit. I'm lucky I never got an infection, but I was an idiot kid. He explained what they all were at the time, but it never made a lot of sense. I can barely remember, now. That was years ago. It all feels like a dream, honestly."

Angel dropped his hand and stared at him. "Did you have your head shaved back then?"

He blinked. "Yeah, actually. We all did."

"What?" Rayne asked, glancing between the two of them.

"That's where I saw these tattoos before, on those skinhead guys I ran into earlier," Angel said. "They all had them. You're not joking about the cult. They're here."

"Are they?" Calloway looked around like he expected them to leap out from behind the nearest tent. "I'm not surprised. I met them at a music festival in the first place. They like these sorts of places. They're not so bad," he added. "They're not like some ritual death cult or anything. They just go around on their bikes and talk about the universe, really. Like big leathery hippies."

"I'm . . . a bit lost," Rayne admitted. "Angel? You met a cult?"

"I missed that part too," Kris said.

"Yeah, I ran into them earlier. I didn't know they were a cult, but I got a weird feeling about them." She eyed Calloway. "You sure they're all right?"

Calloway shifted uncomfortably. "They were never dangerous when I was with them," he offered. "I don't think they know I'm here. It's not like we've kept in touch. My manager knows about them, though not the details. I never even mentioned it to the label."

The Chokecherries' stage came into view and they all slowed.

"Okay," Rayne said. "Just . . . try not to mention it to the rest of the band? Definitely don't mention it to Brian. That's the kind of thing that'll give him an aneurysm, and we like Brian. We need to keep him around."

Calloway nodded sheepishly. "Right. Sorry. Pretend I never said anything."

They headed backstage to where the rest of The Chokecherries were waiting, and Kris took a deep breath. They were committed to the stunt. As long as he didn't interfere, it would go off without a hitch. Brian and the label would be happy, Rayne and Cal would be happy, and he would have enough time to settle his nerves before coming out. And hopefully his feelings for Rayne would dissipate too. He had this covered.

"Hey, guys," Rayne said, tugging Calloway forward to make introductions. "This is Cal, from Dead Generation, and we're . . . seeing each other?" The Chokecherries immediately broke into catcalls, and Rayne rolled his eyes at them. "It's not too late to call everything off, you know."

"Nah, you've got this," Kris said. "It'll be great."

"Course it will," Cal agreed. "So, since the paparazzi have been so keen on making up stories about your stage kisses, would you prefer rumors of cheating, or a threesome now that I've butted in?"

The catcalls went up again, led mainly by Stef.

Rayne glanced at Kris with an exasperated smile. Angel scowled at all three of them like she wanted to smack some sense into their heads, a line of aggravation between her brows.

"We don't need either," Kris said firmly. "We'll quit messing around, like Brian suggested, and we'll remind the press that the show stuff was just for the fans, like we've been saying all along. All three of us can tell them at once, if they want. No cheating, and no threesomes."

"A little speculation is unavoidable, but I'm not worried," Rayne said. "The rest of you," he added, addressing Stef, Len, and Maki, "no stirring the pot. It's only while the festival is running; you can give me shit for it later."

"We will," Stef assured him.

"Nothing personal," Maki told Calloway. "He needs to be kept in his place."

"You're all terrible," Rayne said. "Cal? Second thoughts?"

"No, no. If everyone's happy to go along with it, I think it should be fun." Calloway caught Kris's gaze. "Assuming everyone is happy?"

Kris put on a smile. "It's cool." He almost believed it, too. Calloway and Rayne looked good together, and that was the most important thing as far as the paparazzi were concerned. And Calloway seemed amiable: maybe a year or two older than Kris, sure of himself without being arrogant, and quick to smile. "I'm happy for you guys. I hope you have a great fake relationship."

Calloway didn't stay long, citing the need to go back and prep his band for the incoming press. Rayne went with him, flashing one last smile back at The Chokecherries before he and Calloway disappeared into the festival, their arms around each other with the same casual intimacy Rayne showed everyone in his chosen group.

Kris sat on the edge of the stage and watched them go. The rest of the band dispersed, flitting out between the tents to see different attractions, and Kris leaned back as the clouds drifted through the bright-blue sky. Angel joined him a moment later, dropping down at his side and mirroring his position.

"Hey, you," she said. "What do you think?"

"The press will love it."

"Sure, but what do you think?" She punctuated the *you* with a poke to his shoulder.

"I think the same thing I thought when I told Rayne it was a good idea. And Cal seems like a decent guy. They could pull it off."

"Hm."

He turned to face her. "What, hm?"

"Level with me a minute. All the kissing you two do onstage, and all the hand-holding and cuddling up you do off it, you really don't have a thing for him?"

Kris froze, and in that split second of hesitation he knew he'd waited too long. Angel's expression softened. "No," he said weakly. "No, it's not . . . We're not like that."

"Kris, honey. I love you, but lying's not your forte."

"It's just a crush. It doesn't mean anything." He bit his tongue, hoping his lie didn't sound as blatant as it felt. "And now that Calloway's here and they're doing this whole thing, I'll get over it."

"You really don't want to tell him?"

"I don't want to fuck up and make things awkward. Brian's still got me on a trial run, and I don't want to do anything that could get me kicked out of the band." He reached over and squeezed her fingers. "Honestly. It's just a crush because we're around each other all the time, and he's a great kisser. And he's . . . Rayne. But it's fine. I'm not in love with him, and he's definitely not in love with me. I've got this totally under control."

"Why don't you want him to know you're not straight?" she asked bluntly. "You said you weren't ready, and I respect that, but I can see you pining for him. I could see you pining from the moon."

"I'm going to tell him," Kris promised. "But I don't want to complicate things, especially not while he's doing this with Cal. As soon as their stunt's over, we'll talk. And I'm not pining."

She didn't look like she believed him, but he steeled himself and nodded like it was the absolute truth. She finally sighed and patted his knee.

"Okay, hun. Whatever you say."

Kris took a deep breath to calm his pounding heart. Angel would keep his secret. As far as she was concerned, it was just a crush and it was under control.

Nothing could be farther from the truth.

# CHAPTER TWELVE
## THE ROCKY HORROR
## LAP DANCE SHOW

Control was only ever an illusion. Kris knew that, on some deep level, but superficially he still had hope. He lost the last of it—hope and control both—after Angel brought out her costume trunk.

It wasn't her fault— Kris didn't want to blame her for anything that happened. She was simply the catalyst that sent everything else whirring into motion like a terrifyingly unstoppable doomsday device. It started with a pair of gold lamé booty shorts.

"We're doing a *Rocky Horror* tribute," Billie said.

"I have costumes," Angel added.

"Okay," Kris said. "*Rocky Horror*. Why not."

"I'm Frankie, obviously," Rayne said. "Stef dibs'd Riff Raff, as if anyone else would want him. Maki's Columbia, Billie's Meatloaf—Eddie—and everyone else is a Transylvanian. We're throwing everybody in corsets and glitter."

"What about me?" Kris asked, feeling the answer in his gut already.

"You're Rocky, of course," Angel said with a wink. "Not much of a bodybuilder, but I never did like a man with too many muscles."

"I would've thought I was more of a Janet," Kris said, "but hey, whatever floats your boat."

Angel pressed the shorts into his hand, and Kris had to turn them over three times to figure out what he was holding. They seemed a lot smaller in person than he remembered from the movie, and he remembered them being tiny. "Where's the rest of them?"

"Oh hun," Angel said. "The rest of it's all you."

The important thing Kris needed to remember about Purple Sage was that it wasn't part of the real world. It might seem like it was, being in the middle of a desert that could be found on any map, and the tickets were paid for with very real money, but the festival itself—the part where the music happened—that was somewhere else entirely. That part was just left of reality, where the laws of nature and common sense and outside society didn't apply. That was the reason Kris didn't question the *Rocky Horror* getups, or the way Angel carried a veritable cornucopia of recreational drugs, or his own tumultuous, headfirst tumble into heart-throbbing infatuation with Rayne, which he could no longer deny, though he was trying. Questioning was for the real world, as were consequences. He put the shorts on.

"I think I need a bit more to wear," he said, examining his reflection in the mirror in the private dressing-room-trailer he and Rayne had appropriated.

He didn't mind his body. Sure, he was skinny, with no real muscle definition, and maybe his limbs were a little too coltish to belong on a man of twenty-five, but there was nothing offensive about it. It left his gender ambiguous, almost, at the right angle and in the right light. He'd never really appreciated that before the tour. Less ambiguous in nothing but shorts that barely covered the tops of his thighs, but that was probably the point.

"Can I get one of those corsets too?"

"Sure," Rayne said absently. "You have to feel comfortable performing."

Kris turned from the mirror to find Rayne rolling his fishnets up with agonizing care, sitting on one chair with his foot propped up on another. His corset was unlaced, hanging around his middle with no thought for modesty, and he was barely covered by a pair of black shorts under his garter belt.

Kris swallowed.

"I don't recommend wearing stockings, whatever else you're thinking," Rayne said. "This isn't the first time I've worn them, but I hope it's the fucking last. And fishnets aren't even that bad compared to hose." He reached his thigh and clipped the first garter in place, shaking his hair from his face to glance up at Kris. "Don't do it," he repeated, but he was smiling.

"Noted," Kris said, his mouth dry. He coughed. "No stockings. I need something, though. I can't go out there like this."

"It's good, though. You sure you need to cover all that up?"

"When I'm wearing my guitar I'm going to look naked," Kris pointed out. "I'll look like a slapstick sketch. You have to give me more to work with here."

"Fine, fine. Crush all my dreams at once." Rayne rooted through a bag of feather boas, gloves, and costume jewelry to pull a corset from its depths. Like the shorts, it was gold. Unlike the shorts, it covered more than a few square inches of skin.

"Awesome," Kris said, holding it up against his torso as he returned to the mirror. All the gold brought the browns in his eyes to life and made his hair seem even paler. Once Angel did his makeup, he would look like nothing he'd ever seen before. Not even his first time in makeup could compare to this, with so many glittering sequins and so much bare skin.

He'd never worn a corset before. Or, unlike Rayne, any kind of hosiery—or high heels, or—

The list was endless. There were so many things he had never worn or done or thought about before The Chokecherries, and now he wanted to try all of them at once. He glanced at Rayne in the reflection; he was busy fastening a rope of pearls around his throat.

"Hey, rock star, you want to help me into this?" Kris asked.

Rayne looked up, his expression inscrutable in the tarnished mirror.

Kris hefted the corset. "I can't reach the laces by myself, unless you want me to wear it backwards."

"No, I can help you do it the right way around." Rayne stood slowly. His legs were so long out of his usual jeans. He padded quiet as a panther over to Kris and stopped just behind him, not quite touching, but near enough for Kris to feel his heat. "Here, hold it around you like this."

Kris obeyed, offering the edges to Rayne without taking his eyes from their reflections. The mirror was an old one, its surface going silvery and dim, but looking at it, secreted away in the tiny trailer that was all half-lights and dark corners, Kris felt hidden from the rest of the universe, like there was no one in the entire world but him and Rayne. Within this room, no one else existed: not the fans, not the band, not Calloway or the press. It was a dangerous, intoxicating feeling that curled around his ribs as surely as the corset did, and settled in his heart like a bad idea.

It would be so easy to kiss Rayne here, where no one else could see them.

He couldn't do it.

"How tight do you want me to go?" Rayne asked.

"Tight enough to look good."

"Such an exhibitionist."

"Always," Kris said.

He sank his teeth into his lip at the first bite of the laces; Rayne gave no quarter as he worked his way up, but Kris liked the pressure. It was firm in the way the best hugs are firm, and if it left him a little breathless, that only added to the experience. He watched his body reshape in front of him as the corset forced his waist in, giving the illusion of hips—not much of one, as he had always been flat as a plank in all directions, but enough to stop and take notice.

"Okay?" Rayne checked in.

Kris pressed his hand against his belly and felt nothing but firm, unyielding fabric. His stomach fluttered and he smoothed his hand down. "Perfect."

Rayne tied the laces off and then stopped to admire his work. His eyes were dark in the mirror, and Kris held his breath as he awaited Rayne's verdict. The fans would be delighted, but it was only Rayne he wanted to impress. That was easier to admit when it was just the two of them, even if he couldn't say it aloud.

"You look good enough to eat," Rayne said, his voice a pitch too low to be teasing.

"Yeah?" Kris caught Rayne's gaze and held it, his heart beating fast as a hummingbird. "What you going to do about it?"

Rayne's grip tightened on Kris's shoulder for a second, his fingers digging into his bare skin as surely as the corset laces dug into his back, and then he let go and stepped away, shaking his head with a rueful smile.

"Let's get you into Angel's chair and try not to break any hearts on the way."

Kris let Rayne guide him from the trailer, infinitely disappointed in his own lack of courage for not pushing further.

Things only got worse once the makeup was on.

Passionfruit and The Chokecherries crammed into the space backstage, all of them centered around Angel and her makeshift makeup station like she was a queen holding court. Passionfruit did their own makeup, for the most part, though Billie and Angel were collaborating more often as Billie's tastes grew increasingly outlandish. Jay stayed punk and gleefully mocked him, which Billie ignored, and this instance was no exception. Cassie flitted around between the two bands, exploring Angel's makeup collection, unable to hold still, until Angel promised to do her up in turn, if she would just keep her hands to herself for five minutes. Cass compromised by sitting on Stef's lap. Stef, busy applying dark shadows under their eyes, didn't seem to mind.

Rayne's makeup was heavier than usual for his Frank-N-Furter look—Angel dusted him with black and purple from his lashes to his brows, painting his eyes with kohl and his lips with a wine-dark red that made his mouth obscenely shiny and wet. Kris, she coated in the gold Maki favored, so his eyelids glittered and caught the light with every blink. She gave him his usual red lipstick, and then painted his nails black, the same black Rayne most often wore.

"Now sit tight and let that dry," she instructed, moving on to Maki's Columbia makeup next. "If you smear it, I'm putting you in time-out."

"Yes, ma'am." Kris placed his hands palm-down over his knees and tried not to fidget.

Cassie, though making good on her promise to sit still, lacked any incentive to keep quiet. "So, Angel, are you a professional makeup artist? How'd you meet Rayne?"

"It wasn't long after I opened my club, and he was just starting the band," Angel said.

"We didn't have a record deal yet—we didn't even have Brian yet—but I was determined to play every club and dive bar in the country that would have me," Rayne continued. "So I piled everybody into a van and we headed out, usually booking one or two shows ahead as we drove."

"It was insane," Stef said.

"We all nearly quit at one point or another," Maki added. "Our original drummer did. We met Lenny en route."

Lenny tipped an imaginary hat.

"So we rolled into New Orleans with no real plan, but I'd heard rumors of this new club that sounded queer-friendly, and—" Rayne shrugged expansively "—the rest is history."

"Just like that?" Cassie asked.

"Just like that," Angel agreed. "I didn't start touring with Rayne until after he got his record deal, but we kept in touch the whole time. I visited him in LA a few times and nabbed myself a studio space in his house."

"Not New York?" Kris asked.

"New York's my second home," Rayne said. "My LA place is bigger; it came first. As soon as I had enough pull with the label, I got Angel signed as our official fashion director. Now we don't do anything without her."

Angel shrugged. "I can't complain."

"I can't believe I didn't think to steal you first," Billie groused.

"To be fair, honey, Passionfruit was pretty grungy when you started," she said. "I love you, but I wouldn't have had much to work with."

Billie coaxed his hair into a giant bouffant. "How about now?"

"Baby steps," Angel said.

"Why burlesque?" Cassie asked. Stef finished their makeup and slung their arms around Cassie's waist, holding her in place.

"I started with drag shows back in art school," Angel replied, taking over the design of Billie's hair, "but I wanted something more . . . sexual. I liked the camp, but it felt like I was wearing my own skin and pretending it was a costume. Burlesque seemed like the next natural step."

"More sexual," Kris repeated.

She shrugged. "It's fun. And it's safe, playing onstage like that. There's no room for misunderstandings when you're on a stage and everyone else is paying to watch."

"I get that. I'd never have tried this if it weren't for the stage." He drummed his fingers across his knees, waiting for the polish to dry. "I don't think I'd actually strip, though."

"It's not for everyone," Angel agreed. "Billie would never do it. He's body-shy."

Billie rolled his eyes but didn't stop her from fixing his hair.

"I found it really helped with my body image, personally," she continued. "And now that I have the body I want, I like showing it off. I worked too hard on it for it to go unappreciated."

"And unpaid for?" Kris guessed.

"It's worth every penny. You said no to a dance last time; what about now?" She laughed at the expression on his face. "No? What about from your man Rayne? He can dance, you know."

"I can," Rayne assured them, though he threw Angel a look Kris couldn't interpret. "I'm a great dancer."

"Can you strip?" Cassie asked.

"Can't you go back to being all shy and flustered around him?" Kris asked. "He's supposed to be your idol."

"Nah, I'm over it. Can you, though?"

"Not wearing a corset," Rayne said, but when he met Kris's gaze he was positively predatory. Whatever bait Angel had thrown him, he'd taken it. "But I can do other stuff."

Jay whooped and finished drawing on the last of his eyeliner. "Give Kris a dance and I'll give Billie one." Kris couldn't tell whether it was a dare or a threat. Either way, with his nails still wet, he couldn't defend himself.

Rayne stood in a long, languid motion. "How about it, Kris?" He rested one boot on the edge of Kris's chair, in between his thighs. "Say no."

Kris *should* say no for the sake of his sanity, but Rayne looked delicious made up like that, and Kris was only human. He raised his hands in the universal symbol of surrender—ostensibly to keep his nails from smearing, but mostly to keep himself from trying to touch. "Go ahead. See who gets more embarrassed."

Rayne laughed.

"Bad move, honey," Angel said.

"You know me better than that, Kris," Rayne said. "I don't even know what shame is."

Rayne could move: he had the coordination, the rhythm, and the sex appeal to do it. He danced onstage, or in clubs, or on the bus;

something as simple as rocking his hips to the beat had driven Kris to distraction more than once. Kris had just never seen it from so close an angle before.

Rayne returned both feet to the floor and shimmied up, his stance wide, until he stood over Kris's lap, and rested his arms across Kris's shoulders, bending at the waist to reach. He moved slowly, either teasing or giving Kris time to back out, Kris didn't know. He didn't care. His breath hitched in his chest and he blushed, hard. Swallowing, he tried to brush it off and look nonchalant.

It didn't work. His face was burning up; he could feel the fever-bright heat on his cheeks and in his eyes, and the way his lips fell open of their own accord as Rayne leaned in, his hair brushing Kris's face, to whisper in his ear.

"You can still say no," he breathed, for no one but Kris.

"Do it, you giant diva. Show me what you got."

Rayne laughed again, lower this time, and tossed his hair back. "Keep your hands up, baby. No touching."

Jay whistled. "Look at him, all professional. Does it cost extra to touch?"

"Kris isn't touching anything," Angel said. "He tries it, I'll skin him. I'm not redoing his nails before the show."

"No touching," Kris promised, not taking his gaze from Rayne.

Rayne's tattoos showed above the line of the corset, the matching birds dark against his skin. The corset was barely high enough to cover his nipples, and if he shifted in just the right way, they peeked above the border, dusky brown and getting hard from the friction. Rayne either didn't notice or didn't mind as he started to move, striking up a rhythm as serpentine as the tattoo that wound around his arm. Kris still hadn't touched it. The wrapping was off, but after only a week it had to still be tender. Rayne looked like a walking, breathing piece of art, and Kris wanted to fall to his knees in worship, one way or another. He bit his tongue and kept his hands away.

Like when they kissed onstage, Kris was aware of the cacophony of shouts and appreciative jeers around them. Like onstage, he tuned them out and drank Rayne in like it was only the two of them in the whole world. But their stage antics never got close to this kind of concentrated attention. While Kris knew Rayne was playing up the sex appeal for the others, it was still so much closer, so much hotter, so much more of everything that he felt it in every single atom of his being. It had never been like this offstage before, like Rayne was trying to turn Kris on for real—and it was working.

Rayne danced like his body was made for it. He kept his arms wound around Kris's neck, twisting his body down toward Kris's lap but always stopping just shy of contact, his hips working in a mesmerizing pattern that left Kris's mouth dry and his blood flooding south.

Kris wanted to unlace Rayne's corset hole by hole and watch the muscles shift under his skin as Rayne moved; he wanted to put his hands on him and feel them to be sure this was real. He wanted Rayne to sit down in his lap, and he wanted to push his hands through Rayne's hair and drag him down until their lips met, makeup be damned, and kiss him until Rayne was as breathless and shaky as he always left Kris.

Rayne was supposed to be doing this with Calloway, not Kris, but there were no paparazzi backstage. No one else had to know.

Whether it was the dream, the dance, or just the inevitable deepening of friendship to love, something in Kris flipped. Rayne made him want to fling himself into a jungle of unmapped sexuality, and to hell with ever finding his way out again. Kris wanted to taste him and touch him and be touched by him, and with every passing second the thought of announcing his sexuality to the world seemed less intimidating and more exciting. His nerves gave way to curiosity, which gave way to want that squirmed in his belly, taking up residence with his flock of butterflies, which fluttered wildly every time Rayne moved.

Kris didn't touch him. Not even when Rayne pressed his lips to Kris's cheek in a lingering kiss clearly designed to leave a dark-red mark against his skin, nor when Rayne straightened and stepped back as the bands cheered and wolf-whistled. Completely wrecked and so turned on he was light-headed, Kris returned his hands to his knees and tried to pull himself together.

Angel fanned herself with a flyer, affecting a wide-eyed, overwhelmed expression. "Damn, boy. You ever want out of music, come back to the White Rabbit with me."

"I think I got him a little worked up," Rayne said in fake apology.

Kris groaned and covered his face with the crook of his arm, careful not to smudge anything. His heart was beating in triple time and all he could think of was Calloway, fucking Calloway—he wasn't serving as the deterrent Kris needed him to be. If they were dating for real, Kris would never interfere, but it was fake, and his whole body was burning for Rayne.

"You better take care of that before we hit the stage," Rayne said.

"No touching," Angel said, though she couldn't keep a straight face this time. "Sorry, Kris."

"It's okay," Rayne decided. "It's a compliment. I'm flattered."

"Cassie, I know you filmed that whole thing," Kris said, not removing his arm from his face. "For the love of god, don't show our parents. Don't show anyone, ever."

"I'm conflicted," Cassie admitted, still comfortably settled on Stef's lap. "On the one hand, you're my brother, and there's no way anything you're involved with can be hot. On the other hand—oh my god, Rayne. Oh my god."

Rayne nudged at Kris until he dropped his arm to glare at him. Rayne grinned, mercifully not looking at Kris's shorts.

"I don't know what you were trying to prove," Kris said. "I can't remember. But you did it: Congratulations. You proved the thing. I hate you."

"No, you don't," Rayne said fondly. "Come on, Rocky. Up you get. If you play a good show, you might even get a repeat performance sometime."

There seemed to be something wistful in his tone, lingering just below the surface and unnoticeable unless you were specifically listening for it. A second later Kris thought he must have imagined it, because Rayne had him by the wrist and was pulling him to his feet, laughing with the others. Kris accepted his help in getting up, but was privately sure that a repeat performance would actually kill him, especially if he still couldn't touch. He needed to tell Rayne how he felt; it didn't matter if it was unrequited. Not telling was going to be the actual literal death of him if Rayne kept up like this.

Calloway dropped by before the show, talking animatedly about how the press was already paying ten times more attention to Dead Generation on the basis of a few rumors about Rayne wearing their shirt. Rayne got caught up in his high spirits with admirable ease, and rather than watch the two of them play boyfriends, Kris joined Angel on her quest to the food trucks in search of an apple pretzel.

"Not that I don't appreciate the company," she said, "but you seem like you're avoiding something."

"Nope," Kris said determinedly. "I'm just giving them space to do their thing, because I'm a supportive friend."

"Uh-huh."

"And I'm trying to get used to moving around in this thing." It was weird to walk in the corset; it pulled his spine so straight he felt like a toy soldier, though he looked like anything but. The sequins caught the sun and flashed it around with every step, and his limbs seemed much paler and skinnier than he remembered them being. "And I like hanging out with you." He nudged her with his elbow. "If you want me to get lost, you can say so."

"No, you can stay. Honestly, I'm glad you're here. I'm not used to wearing so much glitter in public, and having this many eyes on me outside of the club makes me nervous."

"I'm probably not helping you blend in though, am I?"

"Not especially, no."

Angel's afro always ensured that she would stand out in a crowd, but with the added sequins and sparkles, Kris didn't doubt that every eye in the festival was on her. She might feel self-conscious, but she looked stunning. He grabbed her hand and squeezed it, and she shot him a grateful smile.

As soon as they set foot in the picnic area, a wolf whistle pealed out. Kris cast around for the source, but Angel just squared her shoulders and marched on, making a beeline for the pretzel wagon. Kris hovered by her side as she made her purchase, but the moment they turned to head back to the stage, they collided with a very tall, very wide man dressed in dusty leather, who sent them stumbling back a pace.

"Watch where you're going," the man grunted.

"You the one who cat-called me?" Angel asked. The man's lip curled and Angel rolled her eyes. "Fuck off."

She went to step around him. Kris stayed glued to her side, though he had no idea what he'd do if he had to intervene, but the man blocked their way. An expression of dumb belligerence sat on his face. "You don't talk to me like that."

"Yeah, I do. Now move, or I'll get you thrown out," Angel said. Kris tried to look intimidating, though he barely came up to the man's chest, and was dressed only in a corset, his sneakers, and a pair of uncomfortably formfitting shorts.

Whatever the man was about to say next—and it was doubtlessly going to be asinine—was interrupted by his friends. One of them gave a sharp whistle and the big one's gaze snapped over.

"Boar! Leave that. Come on back," the other man ordered.

"Yeah, go on, dog," Angel said.

Boar glared and stepped forward—Kris and Angel both darted away—when a second one at the table shouted, "She disrespects us!" and vaulted the picnic bench, hurtling toward them like a burly red missile.

Angel smashed her pretzel into Boar's face, its apple filling still hot from the oven, grabbed Kris by the wrist, and booked it. Shouts followed them, from all four of the men now, but Kris didn't dare look back. They lost them after a few turns, the tents too closely packed for a longer chase. Once they were sure the men were gone, Kris and Angel slowed their pace to a halt.

"Fuck," Angel breathed, and finally dropped Kris's arm.

"Fuck," Kris agreed. "And you lost your pretzel too."

"Forget the pretzel—those were the same guys I saw earlier, the ones Calloway said were a cult."

Kris craned his neck to glance back the way they'd come, but there was no sign of the men. "No shit. That was the cult? Cal said they weren't bad guys!"

"Maybe Cal didn't know them so well."

They adjusted their course for The Chokecherries' stage, slower now that they weren't being pursued. Kris took the time to catch his breath as the adrenaline faded, his heart thumping back to a normal pace.

Passionfruit was just starting to set up when they arrived, Billie running through a mike check as festival goers milled around, drawn by the movement onstage. Kris relaxed, confident they weren't going to get jumped by a cult of skinheads in broad daylight with so many witnesses around. Tom the priest-to-be was there too, and waved when he saw them, bright and blond in the sun. Kris waved back and tried on a smile, but stilled as the youngest of the cultists appeared by the far side of the stage, making his way toward them. Onstage, Billie paused to watch, and Tom hesitated in his approach.

"Hey," said the cultist. He was tall and lanky and impossibly pale, no older than Kris, and didn't seem like he'd eaten a decent meal anytime in the past year. Kris looked to Angel for direction, and Angel crossed her arms and leveled a stoic glare at the interloper.

"Sorry about your pretzel," the kid said. "And, um, about Boar. And Red. They get riled easily when they're on the booze, and they forget their manners."

"What do you want?" Angel asked.

"I brought you a replacement?" He held out a little package, butter seeping through the paper. "To make up for it, if you want."

Onstage, Billie cleared his throat conspicuously, and Kris glanced up. The singer appeared ready to jump down and fight the kid if he made one wrong move toward Angel, though Kris doubted that even if he and Billie teamed up they'd be much good in an altercation.

"What's your name?" Angel asked.

The kid broke into a smile that lit up his eyes. They were big and pale and silvery, but they didn't seem malicious. He felt Angel relax fractionally beside him. "I'm Rikki. Do you want it?"

Angel accepted the replacement pretzel carefully, like it might blow up in her hand. "I'm Angel. This is Kris. Your friends are assholes, you know that?"

His smile slipped but he nodded. "Yeah. Sorry. I should get back before they miss me."

"Thanks for the pretzel, Rikki."

His smile bounced back into place before he loped off to find his cult. The pretzel dripped butter over Angel's fingers as she and Kris watched him go.

"You're aware that guy is in a cult, right?" Billie said from the stage.

Tom, perhaps sensing that not all was well, ducked back into the crowd with a little nod of goodbye and a promise to come back later to see the show. Angel tore a chunk off the pretzel with her teeth.

"So, cults, huh?" Kris said. "When everybody was telling me how weird festivals could get, nobody mentioned the bit about cults."

"We should probably tell Rayne and Cal about this," Angel said, heaving a sigh and casting her gaze heavenward.

"And Brian?" Kris asked.

They glanced at each other, wincing in unison. Angel shook her head. Maybe not Brian, at least not yet.

# CHAPTER THIRTEEN
## HOW TO ADOPT
## A STRAY SKINHEAD

K ris didn't get the chance to talk to Rayne or Calloway before the show. While Passionfruit played their set, the two of them were busy flirting with the paparazzi and each other, wrapped up to the extent that Kris was reluctant to interrupt. They really did make a good-looking couple: their arms slung around each other's shoulders, sharing earbuds as they leaned in close to whisper and laugh together, seemingly oblivious to the outside world. Of course it was all an act— Kris saw the way Rayne kept the flashing cameras in his peripherals at all times, making sure he and Cal were angled so the paparazzi saw exactly what he wanted them to see, nothing more or less.

He could always tell them about the cult after the show, though he was no longer sure he had anything to tell. Neither he nor Angel had caught the cult doing anything particularly dangerous; they were just assholes, and that wasn't cause for a group meeting. Lots of people were assholes, especially when you were wearing a corset, a lot of body glitter, and not much else.

Instead, Kris took the time before the *Rocky Horror* show to think things over. Passionfruit had taken the stage almost immediately after Kris and Angel got back, leaving Kris a very small window to gather his thoughts. He pushed the cult aside temporarily and returned to the issue of coming out to Rayne, sexuality and feelings both. It was love, he could finally admit: full-fledged, cavity-inducing, spine-tingling *love*. It was hard to think backstage with Passionfruit playing a few feet away, even more raucous and impulsive than usual, as Billie belted out a Meatloaf tune to the roar of the crowd. Kris's corset didn't help either; he was hyperconscious of it, and the constant pressure made his stomach flip in the most distracting way, like the butterflies in there were planning a revolt. Yet despite the butterflies, the corset, and Passionfruit's aggressive brand of music-making, Kris couldn't stop thinking about the curve of Rayne's mouth, half hidden in the shadows of his mane of messy hair, as he slowly danced over Kris's lap.

Rayne, apparently oblivious to Kris's turmoil, wasn't helping. His flair for the dramatic combined with the energy implicit in a *Rocky Horror* tribute show left Kris feeling delightfully debauched. He was grateful for being able to hide behind his guitar, because his shorts hid nothing, and Rayne knew it. He seemed to take perverse pleasure in winding Kris up—he spent the show draping himself over Kris, rubbing up against him, curling his fingers through Kris's hair or around his throat. Kris didn't fight a second of it—but they didn't kiss. They touched, and teased, and Kris leaned in when Rayne came up behind him and wrapped one arm around his chest, tugging him close to sing in Kris's ear, but their lips never met, and this time, Kris didn't push it. People needed to believe Rayne and Calloway were a thing, and Kris wasn't going to interfere with that, no matter how he felt. But he wasn't the only one getting excited.

The crowd kept yelling for more, hurling themselves against the barricade, singing along until their voices were wrecked, hands in the air, jumping in time. Calloway was up near the front, his ginger hair burnt gold in the stage lights, arms thrown up over his head as he sang along with Rayne. The cult was there too, all pale tattooed skin and black leather off to the side. They could have passed for punks, but there was something separate about them—they didn't throw themselves into the music like the rest of the crowd. Even among the misfits who made up a music festival, they didn't look like they belonged. Tom didn't look like he belonged either, but from what Kris could see from the stage, he seemed to be enjoying himself.

The band played their set and Kris stayed at Rayne's side the whole time. He'd thought the corset would get more comfortable the longer he wore it, but it never loosened and he couldn't stop thinking about how the laces dug into his skin and squeezed him into a new shape. Rayne's wasn't as tight as his—he needed the room to sing.

As they reached the end of their set, their lipstick messed beyond hope, Stef started up the bass line to "Sweet Transvestite." The crowd dropped to silence for a single second and then surged back louder and shriller than before. Rayne caught Kris's eye across the stage and grinned, fluffed up his feather boa, and strutted to the mike.

He'd said he couldn't strip in a corset, but he managed fine. He had laced his backwards, the ties all up the front, to make for easier removal. The boa went first—he leaned over the edge of the stage and wrapped it around Calloway's neck like a gift, dropping a fleeting kiss on Cal's lips before retreating—and then the laces, one hole at a time. Kris didn't pretend to look anywhere else but at him. His heart skipped a beat and lodged in his throat, trembling in anticipation as the corset dropped. The crowd screamed, and Rayne winked and hit the chorus. When he next stalked over to Kris, one hand coming up to trace the lines of Kris's corset, Kris dropped his gaze to his guitar and closed his eyes, dry-mouthed and desperate for the attention. Rayne was more skin than clothes, sleek and fit, his muscles smooth and lithe and barely showing. He seemed to glow under the stage lights, his tattoos coming to life as he moved, and Kris still couldn't touch him. Kris played until his fingers ached, but that hurt less than having all that in front of him, unable to reach out and feel it.

He couldn't even tell if Rayne was doing it on purpose. What Rayne knew, or suspected, or thought he knew about Kris's feelings, Kris had no idea—other than that he was embarrassingly easy to turn on, but everyone knew that, now. That had been very publicly proven. It didn't mean Rayne guessed anything. He was just messing around, high on the adrenaline from the show, and since Calloway wasn't onstage—

Kris wished they'd never agreed to Brian's suggestion of cutting the midshow make-outs. Rayne still lavished him with attention, but it was Cal he was kissing, not Kris, and it was killing him. He'd never been prone to jealousy before, but this was enough to tie him up in knots.

The song ended and Rayne returned to center stage to say their goodbyes, when a scuffle broke out beyond the barricade. Kris couldn't see what happened, but a girl shouted, and Rikki the cultist punched one of his fellows, and then all hell broke loose. Security swarmed over to tear them apart as Rayne turned back to the stage, frowning, and reached for the mike.

"There's no fighting at a Chokecherries' concert," he said sternly, his voice reverberating without the music to back him. "We're here for peace and love, guys. Get your shit together."

"He tried to grab me!" a girl yelled from the front.

Rayne's frown deepened. "Okay, PSA time, kids. Now, I know my fans are better than that. You'd never grab anybody without permission. So listen—you see somebody doing that? Touching, grabbing, trying to throw somebody into the pit who doesn't want to be there? You punch them in the face."

"Peace and love," Kris muttered from the side.

"Peace and love take a back seat when people are getting harassed. We're all here to have a good time, right? So look out for each other."

Security finally succeeded in hauling the cultists off one another. Rikki glowered at his cohorts, who spat at him. They finally separated, security letting them off with a warning, and skulked away into the twilight. Kris saw Calloway disappear into the crowd, away from the site of the brawl.

"Look out for each other, be kind, and take no shit. We'll see you tomorrow afternoon. Go forth with love!"

How he could deliver a halfway rousing speech dressed only in fishnets, boots, shorts, and a garter belt, Kris had no idea, but Rayne managed it. They traipsed backstage, trailing costume parts in a parade of glitter and sequins.

"I heard something going down, but I couldn't see from side stage," Angel said as she helped Kris unlace his corset. Rayne had disappeared to find Calloway right after the show, and Kris tried not to feel abandoned, missing his post-show dog pile of sweaty hugs and bright smiles. The rest of The Chokecherries were still there, but it wasn't the same without Rayne. Angel, probably sensing that, had stepped in to neatly fill the void. "What happened?"

"Cal's cult friends started shit, and Rayne yelled at them. Well, not yelled, but you heard him. Security dragged them out; I didn't see what happened after that."

Angel dropped the corset and turned her back as Kris shimmied out of the shorts and pulled his real clothes on.

"Well, I'll be happy if we don't see them again for the rest of the festival," Angel said. "And I doubt it'll do Cal any good to run into them, either."

"No, well, Rayne's keeping him pretty busy." He bit his tongue, aware that had come out more bitterly than he'd meant. "I'm dressed; you can turn back around," he added as he put his guitar away and avoided meeting Angel's eyes.

"Come on," she finally said. "Let's go get food and distract you from all that pining."

"I'm not pining for anybody," Kris retorted as they headed into the sea of tents again. "I just have to get used to Rayne spending all his time with somebody else. It's no big deal."

Angel mm-hmm'd skeptically, but as they turned the corner of a large but empty tent, they stumbled smack into the middle of a fistfight that stopped whatever Angel had been about to say.

It wasn't a fight so much as a beating: the three older cultists were surrounding Rikki, Boar and Red laying into him with boots and fists as he curled up on the ground, trying to protect his face and underbelly, while a third man stood back a pace, his arms folded as he looked on impassively. It was with him whom they collided when they turned the corner, and they all tripped back as the fight paused.

"Sorry," Kris said automatically, and then frowned. "Hang on, what the fuck."

"Walk away," the man warned.

"Get off him," Angel countered. Rikki curled up tighter, like a hedgehog.

"Mind your business," Red growled, pulling himself up tall to loom toward her.

Kris bristled and tensed his hands into fists, knowing full well that Red could crush him like a bug but willing to throw a punch if he had to. But before he got the chance, Angel swung her handbag and hit Red full in the face. The buckles caught his cheek with just enough force to cut, and he staggered back with his hand pressed to his face in shock, like he'd never seen his own blood before.

"Get lost before I set security on you," she said, and hefted her bag up again when they didn't immediately leave.

They fled.

"Shit," Kris said. "That was amazing. Do you carry a brick in there in case of emergencies?"

She handed him her bag and he peeked inside. It was mostly makeup, and very hefty. Angel toed at Rikki, still on the ground, with her boot. "Hey, pretzel-boy. You alive?"

He uncurled inch by inch, but didn't try to get up. She knelt down and put her hand on his shoulder. Her touch was gentle, but he flinched away all the same. Kris held Angel's bag in both hands and shifted his weight from one foot to the other.

"You want me to call the paramedics?" he asked.

"No," Rikki said, finally lifting his face. "I'm okay. I can't afford the hospital."

"No broken bones?" Angel asked. "Internal bleeding?"

"I don't think so."

Angel kept her hand on him as he righted himself, pushing up on his elbows and checking himself for injuries as he went. His nose was bleeding, his lip split, and at least one eye was going to go black, but he was all in one piece, even if that piece looked the worse for wear.

"You got somewhere safe to stay?" Angel asked. "Somewhere away from them?"

Rikki sat, pulling his knees to his chest. His eyes were shiny with unshed tears and he seemed impossibly young. He shook his head. "We're family," he explained. "We came to the festival together. They said they were going to trash my bike."

"How come they turned on you?" Kris didn't trust the other cultists as far as he could throw them, but it was hard to look at Rikki and see any kind of threat.

"Boar took offense when I called him out for getting handsy with that girl," Rikki said, eyes downcast. "Leif told him off, but he still said I was causing more trouble than I was worth today."

"Listen," Angel said. "I don't want to leave you by yourself out here. You might have a concussion, or those guys might come back for another round. You sure we can't call the paramedics?"

"I'm fine," Rikki repeated. "I've been kicked around enough to know when to worry." He offered a wan smile, ruined by the blood in his teeth. "I've done some kicking of my own before, anyway. Not like I don't deserve it."

Kris glanced at Angel. Her gaze was fixed on Rikki, who hunched his shoulders against her scrutiny.

"Right," she said decisively. "Up you get. Come back to the bus. Let me keep an eye on you through the night to make sure your brain's not going to fall out."

"Can I do anything?" Kris asked her in an undertone. "Should I tell somebody?"

She hesitated. "Hang out with us for a minute, just to make sure there's no trouble."

He nodded and pulled his phone from his pocket, ready to call for help if things went south. Rikki let Angel help him to his feet, and he swayed there a second before steadying himself against her. He was taller than Kris by almost a head, but he was all gangly limbs and coltish proportions, no matter how the leather jacket tried to bulk him up. They set off at a careful pace and he went along meekly, letting Angel keep her hand on his arm. Kris suspected it was the first time in a long time he'd been touched gently by anyone.

When they got to the buses Rikki shuffled obligingly onto the bus couch, and stayed quiet while Angel checked his pupils.

"You're probably right about being fine," she mused as she held his jaw, shining her phone's flashlight into one eye and then the other, "but I ran into a beating or two back in the day, and I know exactly how much it sucks."

Kris fetched Rikki a water bottle from the minifridge and perched in the driver's seat while Angel finished her examination. As soon as she proclaimed him unlikely to keel over and die, Kris tugged her aside to whisper, low enough that Rikki couldn't hear, "You can't just adopt a stray skinhead. Rikki might be okay, but he's still in a cult, and those guys are nuts."

"We couldn't leave him there to get beaten to death," she objected. "And he seems all right. He gave me a pretzel, remember?"

"Cult," Kris stressed.

They both glanced down the bus to Rikki, on the couch. Rikki smiled hopefully.

"You said you guys were a family," Angel said, at a normal volume. "You mean related?"

"Oh, no. I don't have a real family. A blood family, I mean. I don't think any of us do."

"What do you guys do? You said you have bikes."

"Yeah, we've got our motorcycles. We drive around, we do . . . well, I guess most of it's illegal." He rubbed his hand over his head sheepishly. "Leif—he's our leader—he hustles people at poker. Carjacking too, stuff like that. Just to get enough money to stay afloat and keep the Avatar safe."

Kris and Angel exchanged looks before coming to a mutual agreement that they didn't want to dig into the avatar part yet.

"Have you ever been arrested?" Kris asked.

"No." Rikki blinked up at them with earnest eyes. "We're protected. We have the favor of the gods."

"Right," Angel said slowly. "Of course you do."

"Cult," Kris mouthed to her.

"You know a guy called Calloway?" she asked Rikki. "Redhead, Irish? About your height?"

"I know the name," he offered. "The others talk about him sometimes, but I've never met him. I think he used to be in the order before I came."

Kris resolved to press Calloway for details as soon as he saw him again. "What do you guys do besides the hustling and carjacking?"

"We serve the Avatar. We spread His message and we worship Him as He deserves."

Kris could actually hear the capital letters, and he did not like the sound of that one bit.

"Okay," Angel said. "What are we talking about, exactly? Should we be looking out for sacrificial altars? Black magic rituals?"

"Oh, nothing like that," he said earnestly. "No, it's all . . . love. Love, and beauty, and unraveling the secrets of the universe. Leif preaches it much better than I do. And we come to places like this to listen to the music, too. Leif knows almost every band here. You're with The Chokecherries, right?"

"We are."

Rikki nodded. "He's a fan. Anyway, I'm just grateful they took me in."

"Yeah, I can see that. Hang on one sec." She flashed him a smile before turning away to tap out a text to Rayne, which Kris read over her shoulder. *Apparently Cal's old cult has a god. Also, they're violent. Steer clear of them.*

On the couch, Rikki rested his head against the arm, a bruise already forming around his eye. He didn't look dangerous so much as lost, and if Kris knew anything about The Chokecherries, it was that they weren't good at leaving people to fend for themselves.

# CHAPTER FOURTEEN
## LIFE, THE UNIVERSE,
## AND EVERYTHING

R ikki stayed on the bus to rest, promising not to wander off or get in trouble, while Kris and Angel returned to the stage. Evening was setting in, the sunset sweeping over the festival grounds in a great pink and gold wash like the desert was on fire, and people were lighting up their glow sticks like fireflies as the music and the dancing continued.

"You think Rayne and Calloway are meeting the press again tonight?" Kris asked. "They got off to a good start, so I guess they'll want to keep pushing it, right?"

"Yeah, Rayne said he was going out with Cal again this evening," Angel said.

"Cool, cool. Get some pictures, give some interviews . . ." Kris let the sentence hang. He didn't know where he was going with it, and it was too late to reel it back in now. "What should we do about the cult?" he asked instead.

"We'll tell security to keep an eye out, and try not to run into them again," Angel said firmly. "Come on. Let's go find you a distraction."

"From the cult, or from Calloway?"

She grabbed his hand and dragged him backstage with a wink. "Both."

Angel set her purse on the table where she normally did the band's makeup, digging through its many hidden pockets before triumphantly pulling out a packet of semitranslucent, crystalline drugs. Kris had never done anything besides weed or booze, not because he was leaning toward straight edge, but because back home those were the safest options. Everything else was liable to be cut with so much crap that it would as soon kill you as get you high, and Kris had never been curious enough to take the risk.

Angel guaranteed that she had good drugs.

"I get my weed from a friend in LA who runs a dispensary, and I get everything else from another friend in Louisiana," she explained, holding the packet up between her thumb and her forefinger. "I don't fuck with the hard stuff, but as far as recreational drugs? I know them, I've got them, and I only carry the best."

Footsteps sounded from the stage, and she and Kris looked up as Rayne came around the corner.

"I was just introducing Kris to my stash," Angel said by way of greeting. "You joining us?"

"Yes, please." Rayne ambled over to sling his arm around Kris's shoulders, leaning into him in a brief hug before straightening again. "What have we got lined up?"

"I know it's not weed, but that's as far as I can guess," Kris admitted. "It's not cocaine, is it? Because I'm not sure I want that."

"Nope, no coke," Angel said. "That's a hard drug and I'm not about it. This is pure MDMA." The little plastic bag was full of pearly shards of crystal that sparkled in the light. "Or as pure as I've ever found, anyway. You want to try?"

Kris wet his lips. "Should I be worried?"

"If you are, you won't be for long. But no pressure, hun."

She eased the crystals from their bag onto the table, and Rayne took first choice, licking his finger and picking up a single shard on the tip. It glittered there for a second like fairy dust before he wrapped it inside a bit of tissue, put it in its mouth, and let it disappear. Angel followed suit.

"Can you have a bad trip on MDMA?" Kris asked, unable to tear his gaze from the crystals. "Like, if it's my first time, will anything like that happen?"

Rayne and Angel glanced at each other.

"In my experience?" Angel said. "You should be pretty chill. Worst-case, you might get panicky wondering how hard it's going to hit, but if you only take a little, you should be coasting on good vibes all night long."

"If you start feeling weird, find security or one of the paramedics," Rayne advised. "They'll take care of you. Or we will." He ruffled Kris's hair. "Whatever you need, we've got you."

"You want, or should I pack it up?" Angel asked.

"Hell with it," Kris said. "No, I want to try." He dabbed a shard on his fingertip and stared at it for a second. "You guys will watch out for me, right?"

"Course we will," Rayne promised. "Here, wrap it up like this. You don't want to taste that shit."

"Drink lots of water and don't get overheated," Angel said. "It should hit you in about half an hour."

Kris popped his finger in his mouth and swallowed. "Half an hour."

Rayne caught his hand and tugged him toward the door. "Come on, baby. Let's dance."

"Wait. You and Calloway have to—"

"He's meeting us in a bit. I'm not waiting by myself until he shows up. Come dance with me."

They wound up in a tent on the far side of the festival grounds, where electro music blared and neon lights that hung in the air like jellyfish lit the place up as if it were underwater. Kris danced with Rayne at his back, rubbing up against him in teasing brushes, simultaneously reveling in it and shot through with tension, waiting for Calloway to arrive and put a stop to things. Angel danced with anyone who looked at her, her smile flashing white in the darkness.

The drug hit him at the half-hour mark like it had been on a countdown. Between one breath and the next, the entire universe rushed into him. He blinked, and when he opened his eyes, the neon lights were brighter, the music sweeter, his body cleaner from the inside out, like every bad thought had been scrubbed away. His heart leaped in his chest from the sheer wonder of it all, and he turned to Rayne for confirmation that it was real. Rayne put his hands on either side of Kris's face and drew him in, and the touch was electrifying: it ran through Kris's whole body, top to bottom, and he shivered with the pleasure of skin against his skin. He couldn't understand why he'd waited so long before saying anything, or why he'd thought burying his feelings was a good idea. He had love in him, and he needed to let it out, into the world where it belonged.

"This is perfect," Kris said, and it was.

He felt sparkling, like he had never done a bad thing in his life and nothing bad could ever happen again—he was nothing but love, and love surrounded all of them—it was the only thing that mattered in the world. When he looked in Rayne's eyes, he knew Rayne understood it too. He put his hands on Rayne's waist and petted him there, just to feel the fabric under his hands.

"Dance," Rayne told him.

Kris turned and danced. He danced like nothing else mattered, and maybe nothing else did—only his sweat and his heartbeat and the feeling of Rayne pressed against his back, his hands drifting over Kris's body, closer than they got onstage. The lights glowed and made patterns in the air; he could see the shape of the music as it pounded from the speakers in a rhythmic *thump thump thump* that demanded his body move to meet it. He danced until the music filled him up and he breathed in colors and his head flooded with elation, and he had to stagger back from Rayne just to breathe.

"You okay?" Rayne asked, following after him.

"I'm perfect," Kris said. "I'm perfect—I never knew I could feel like this."

"Like what?"

Kris didn't know how to describe how he felt made of love—the same particles that made up the whole universe, but not the universe he had lived in up till now: a different one, a purer one, like it had been at the time of the Big Bang, or even earlier, before anything else got in the way.

"I love you," Kris said instead. It tumbled out of his mouth like he couldn't contain it a second longer, alive and spoken in the same instant it occurred to him. He loved Rayne, completely and absolutely, and now he'd finally said it aloud. He kept talking, too engrossed in cataloging every feeling to panic. "I know you think this is the drugs talking, but I need you to know—I love you, more than I've ever loved anything. You're everything to me. It's not a crush, or a— I love you."

Rayne touched Kris's hair, his cheeks, his mouth. "I love you too. You're beautiful."

Kris felt beautiful, and if Rayne said it, it must be true. Rayne breathed beauty; he bled and sang and exuded it with every minute he spent on Earth. He was beauty incarnate. Kris reached out with one trembling hand to rest it on Rayne's shoulder, where the wild roses twined under his shirt. Though Kris couldn't feel them through the fabric, he imagined them pulsing with a life of their own. He imagined laying Rayne down and stripping him bare and tracing every one of his tattoos line by line, until he had them ingrained in his mind's eye, never to fade. Opening his mouth, his thoughts raced a thousand miles ahead of his body, intending to say these fantasies aloud, safe in the dark glowing crush of the crowd. Rayne looked at him with soft wondrous eyes, his lips parted as if waiting with baited breath for Kris to speak.

"Rayne . . ."

They both moved in at once, as if in slow motion. Kris's heart thudded in his chest like it was underwater, his blood rushing through his veins and tingling in his lips in anticipation of the—

"Sorry, am I interrupting?"

Kris froze as his heart skipped faster and his blood spread through his face in a wave of heat. He turned to find Calloway standing a few feet off, watching them with a smile, even as a faint line furrowed his brow.

"Cal." Rayne smiled and held out his hand. "You made it."

"You sure I shouldn't come back later?"

Kris wished Cal would. He had forgotten, in that rush of love and understanding, that Calloway was coming, that that had been the plan all along. He was so close to telling Rayne everything—they were on the same level, he and Rayne, bonded by the music and the neon lights. He'd been going to tell Rayne with more than words—they had been so close!—but he'd needed to make sure Rayne knew what he was saying first. But now, with Calloway here, his certainty stuttered. He didn't know what to do.

"No, stay," Rayne said, taking Calloway by both hands and drawing him closer. "We were waiting for you."

"You're both very high."

"You're not?"

Calloway shook his head. "I stopped all that when I quit the cult. I don't even drink anymore."

"You can dance, though."

"Yeah, I can dance. Rayne, listen." He glanced at Kris, but when Kris didn't say anything, he continued. "I know where a few guys from the press are hanging out. If we go over there now, by tomorrow everyone will be talking."

"Okay," Rayne said, tracing the lines of one of Calloway's tattoos up his arm until it disappeared under his sleeve. Kris squirmed, longing to do the same to Rayne, somewhere quieter and more private.

"Rayne." Calloway was laughing, his touch gentle as he caught Rayne's hand. "Are you listening?"

"Yeah, I am. We're going to find the press. Kris? Will you be okay staying with Angel?"

Kris had lost Angel somewhere in the crowd. He pictured her dancing with a hundred strangers under those incandescent jelly lights, swimming through the sea of bodies like a minnow dancing under the waves.

"Kris," Rayne repeated.

He and Calloway both looked concerned, clearly waiting for Kris's response. Kris could see their auras, shimmering around their silhouettes like heat waves. Calloway was attracted to Rayne, he realized, even beyond the basic friendly attraction that had prompted him to agree to the publicity stunt in the first place. They were still holding hands, Cal's thumb brushing Rayne's almost unconsciously. Kris watched as tiny sparks of light like fireflies jumped from the point of contact.

He had missed his chance. No—he had given his chance away when he'd told Rayne to agree to the whole scheme. It was supposed to have made things easier, but it had made everything impossibly worse. His thoughts whirled uselessly. He was too high to solve this problem, too high to . . .

He made himself smile and relax and meet their questioning gaze. "I'm good. I'm okay. You guys go . . . go do your thing."

Rayne glanced at Calloway before letting go of his hands and stepping in close to Kris again. Kris leaned in instinctively to meet him, their bodies hot and too complicated for him to consider with his mind like this. He touched Rayne's arm, trailing up to his shoulder and his neck. The wild roses again. He leaned in—

Calloway gave a polite cough from over Rayne's shoulder.

"Kris?" Rayne said, softly, like he didn't understand at all.

"I need water," Kris said abruptly. Rayne and Calloway needed to convince the world they were dating, and Kris had no place in that. Cal's aura shimmered like gossamer, all wound up in Rayne's. Kris pulled his hand back, missing the touch before it was even gone, and retreated a step, forcing distance between them until his head cleared. "I'm going to walk outside," he said. "I want to see . . . everything."

Angel reemerged from the crowd, flushed with sweat from dancing.

"Will you be okay by yourself?" Rayne asked. "It's still your first time on molly."

"I'm good," Kris said firmly. "I'll meet you at the bus later, okay?"

"You sure?"

"I'm sure. Keep dancing. Go find your paparazzi."

Rayne smiled, his hesitation melting away like it had never been, and Angel pressed a bottle of water into Kris's hands. "Remember, if you feel weird, just find festival security," she told him. "They'll get you back to us."

"I'll be okay," he promised. Angel kissed his cheek, and when he touched it after he found that her lipstick had left a little mark on his skin.

Calloway took Rayne by the shoulders, and leaned in close to whisper something in his ear, and Rayne smiled and laughed, low and dark and full of promise. Kris slipped from the tent before he had to see them kiss, leaving behind the jellyfish swimming through the air above the dancers' heads, and into the night air. It was crisp and fresh and it filled his lungs with the sweetest taste he could imagine, the kind he hadn't known since childhood—like bonfires, with pinprick stars in the void, fireflies, and frogs chirping, forever out of sight. It was a relief to replace Rayne, and all the feelings Rayne evoked—love like he couldn't even articulate—with the air and the stars and the insects, if only for a moment.

He walked in no particular direction at all. Half the time he spent staring up at the sky, watching the constellations shimmer in and out of existence, and the other half winding around tents and dancers and makeshift campsites under the open sky. He felt connected to every single person he passed. They were all children, all finding themselves on the same planet, all spinning through space and time and life together. They were all love. He hummed to himself as he walked, skipping between Rayne's lyrics and songs he remembered his mother singing to him when he was a child. He basked in the beauty of the world and the fate that had led him to this particular moment, this moment out of a million, billion possibilities, and then he saw the peacock.

He had wandered to the edge of the festival grounds where tents were scarce and people were scarcer, but it was lit up with pot lights that bathed the desert in a golden glow. Looking around, he cast glances over his shoulder, but there was no one nearby to confirm that the bird was real.

The bird looked at Kris with bright eyes and bobbed his head. He was the most strikingly regal creature Kris had ever seen, but what a peacock was doing in the middle of the Mojave Desert, Kris couldn't guess. The peacock didn't seem lost, in as far as any peacock could seem lost or not, but he obviously didn't belong. Unfortunately, Kris and the peacock were the only living beings in sight.

"Hey there," he said.

The peacock strutted closer, his head cocked as he regarded Kris with frank curiosity.

"I'm Kris. What are you doing out here?"

He didn't answer, for which Kris was grateful. Instead, as if pleased to have found an appreciative audience, the peacock spread his tail feathers in a magnificent fan, and Kris's knees buckled in the face of such overwhelming splendor, and he sank to the ground to stare.

He needed to find Rayne.

The thought came to him unbidden but, once in his head, was undeniable. Kris didn't want to experience this alone, and Rayne was the only person Kris could imagine appreciating it as he did. Rayne and the peacock were kindred spirits, after all, bound by the mandala on the back of Rayne's head. Kris dug his phone from his pocket and texted him, his fingers skittering over the letters.

*You have to see this*, he wrote. *Come find me by the lights.*

The peacock strutted closer, apparently annoyed by Kris's lapse in attention, but preened, appeased, when Kris raised his phone to snap a picture. It came out blurry and unidentifiable, but he sent it anyway.

Rayne texted back a series of question marks.

"Okay," Kris said, staring at his phone screen. "This isn't going to work." He pushed himself to his feet, swaying unsteadily as he found his balance, and held out his hand to the peacock. "I hope you're a cooperative kind of bird, because it's really important that Rayne meets you."

The peacock rustled his fan, blinked, and seemed to shrug. Kris took that as consent and proceeded with his plan. The peacock was amicable enough about letting him approach, and though Kris was nervous about putting his hand in range of the beak, the bird didn't startle or snap or appear remotely concerned about the strange, drug-addled human trying to touch him. In fact, he seemed perfectly at ease with the idea.

"Good boy," Kris said, like the peacock was a strange, colorful dog instead of a misplaced exotic bird. The bird's feathers were soft, and so bright they seemed to glow when he touched them. Kris shuffled nearer, and the peacock obligingly folded his tail down, and allowed Kris to pick him up and tuck him under his arm, his tail trailing to the ground behind him as he settled in against Kris's side.

Warmth unfurled in Kris's chest at his success. Rayne was going to love it.

Kris didn't remember passing out, but the next thing he knew, he was waking up again. It happened slowly. He drifted out of his dreams bit by bit, until his brain was awake but his body wasn't, and another indistinguishable amount of time passed before he could convince his eyes to open. He would have been happy to float in the ether awhile longer, but Rayne approached his bunk—Kris recognized his footsteps even half-asleep—paused, and said, "What the hell is that."

Kris blinked. His mouth was so dry his tongue was glued to his palette, and he had to unstick it an inch at a time before he could talk. It felt like he'd been clenching his jaw in his sleep. The trade-off for a night of life-altering revelations, he supposed.

"What?" he croaked. He rolled over—a wave of dizziness followed him, with nausea on its tail—and found himself face to face with a very large, very glossy blue bird. "Oh."

"Kris, why do you have a peacock in your bunk?"

The bird cocked his head at Rayne and bobbed closer; Kris put his arm around the peacock to keep him from escaping.

"I have an explanation," Kris said, "but it involves a lot of drugs."

"You had one hit of MDMA, the same as the rest of us, and no one else appropriated a wild bird."

"I don't think it's actually wild," Kris said, fishing around his bunk for his water bottle. The bird nestled in under his arm and regarded Rayne with an appraising eye. "It seems pretty friendly." He took a swig, wincing as the water burned its way down his parched throat.

"Should I ask where you got it, or should I keep my plausible deniability?"

"I didn't steal it," Kris protested. He sat up, fighting how his head spun at the movement, and ducked out of the bunk to join Rayne on the bus floor. The bird perched on the edge of the mattress and ruffled his wings. "He was just wandering the grounds, all by himself. I wanted to show you."

"That's what you were texting me about?"

"It was too dark to take a good picture."

"So you brought it back to the bus, but then you fell asleep before you could show me," Rayne guessed. "Did you use it as a pillow all night?"

"He didn't mind," Kris said awkwardly. The peacock screamed pleasantly. "Anyway, it's a present. I said I'd get you a peacock, and I did."

Rayne stared at the bird. The bird stared back.

"I was having some kind of revelation last night about life, the universe, and everything, and the peacock seemed really important at the time. You have to admit it's perfect for your look. Like, it's not an elephant, but it's pretty good."

"It is," Rayne agreed, his reluctance plainly slipping fast as the bird stared him down.

"And I couldn't just leave him wandering the desert. Peacocks aren't supposed to be all the way out here. The coyotes would get him."

"They would."

"So?"

The bird fluttered down to the bus floor, measured how much room he had, and spread his fan, shaking it in Rayne's face until he made the appropriate appreciative noises. Then, despite the extremely tight fit, the peacock began strutting up and down the length of the bus, screaming, until everyone else poked their bleary faces from their bunks to see what the fuck all the commotion was.

"Meet our new mascot," Rayne said helplessly.

The peacock leaped up to land on Rayne's shoulder, where he surveyed his new kingdom with a proud and godly air, his tail feathers trailing down Rayne's back like a cape.

"You do look good," Stef said, before retreating back behind their curtain. "We should bring it onstage next time. Now for fuck's sake, let me go back to sleep."

The bird pecked at a strand of Rayne's hair and seemed perfectly content to stay on his shoulder.

"Okay then," Rayne said. "I guess we're keeping it."

Kris wasn't infused with light and love and an understanding of the universe anymore, but he still got a buzz of satisfaction from knowing his instinct to share the bird with Rayne had been the right one.

Kris found Angel sitting outside with Rikki, both drinking coffee from Styrofoam cups. They sat cross-legged facing each other, Rikki gazing at Angel with unabashed attention, which Angel seemed to accept as her due.

"Morning," Kris said. His dizziness was mostly gone, though his stomach was still churning uneasily. "You two do anything fun last night?"

"We got high; we talked. We slept outside on the ground, for some reason." Angel grimaced. "My back is killing me."

"You said you needed to connect to nature," Rikki provided. "The stars were all sparking in the sky; we watched them for hours. It seemed important to you, so I didn't try to talk you out of it."

"Yeah, no, that was a bad idea." She turned to glance up at Kris. "He told me more about his order's spirituality, their god and all that. That was something."

Kris's eyebrows went up. "Oh yeah? Is he like you guys, that whole shaved-head, biker-gang style?"

"Oh, no. He doesn't look anything like us," Rikki said. "He's the most beautiful being in all creation. He embodies it. We look like this so He won't think we're trying to compete."

"He doesn't sound very compassionate," Kris said. "Maybe you should upgrade."

"Reject the patriarchy," Angel said, raising her fist while bringing her coffee up to her mouth again with her other hand.

Rikki blinked. "I wouldn't know how to find another god. Or a goddess. Or . . . any other kind. I wouldn't know where to start."

"You think they're going to let you back in the cult?" Kris asked. "I mean the gang. Um. The family?"

"I don't know," Rikki confessed. "I don't know what to do if they won't take me back."

Angel nudged him with her boot. "You can stay with us till you figure it out. We'll watch out for you."

"I don't want to be abandoned by my god."

"I'll find you a new one," she promised. "Don't worry, hun. You'll find the family you deserve."

Rikki seemed doubtful, but he asked, "Can I meet yours? It's okay to say no," he added quickly. "Most people would rather not meet me, so I get it." He bit his lip with a hopeful expression, but not much of one.

Angel looked at Kris. Kris looked at Rikki. He didn't have any opposition to introducing the kid to the others, though he wasn't sure what Calloway's reaction would be. Cal seemed confident in having left the cult behind, but Kris didn't want to put that to the test with the publicity stunt at stake. Though Rayne could walk away from the stunt with his career intact, the press would still have a field day trying to connect him to a cult, and Kris couldn't imagine Brian being too pleased about that.

"We'll avoid Cal for now," Angel said, evidently following Kris's line of thought without having to ask. "And try not to mention the whole god thing just yet, okay?"

Rikki nodded, entirely eager to please.

"All right, come on, then." Angel stood up in increments, stretching her back as she rose.

"Do you know where Rayne and Cal ended up last night?" Kris asked, aiming for casual and missing it by a mile.

Angel regarded him knowingly. "I wasn't with them, but I've heard some things."

Kris swallowed. "Is that good or bad?"

"Well, it's good for Calloway." She took Rikki by the arm. "Let's go find breakfast. Kris? I'll see you around?"

"For sure," Kris said faintly. Angel waved goodbye over her shoulder and left him there, wondering what exactly "good for Calloway" meant, and if that meant it was bad for Kris. He needed more information before going to see Rayne again, and if he needed information about paparazzi rumors, he needed to find Cassie.

She was sitting behind the drum kit on their otherwise empty stage, tapping out a beat as she nodded along to the rhythm. Kris watched her for a minute, wondering what might have happened if they'd stuck together in their old high school band after all, before he stepped up to get her attention.

She set her sticks down and grinned from ear to ear, which was a strong indicator that something had indeed happened last night, and she knew exactly what it was.

"Guess what!"

He really didn't want to. "What?"

"Calloway propositioned Rayne last night. It was filthy. If I didn't know better, I'd think they were the real thing."

Kris's throat went dry. "What did Rayne say?"

"Why? You jealous?"

"Cassie."

She rolled her eyes. "They didn't start screwing in the middle of the festival, obviously. Here, check this out. The pics from last night are already online. The label must be ecstatic—look at them! Don't they look good together?"

She handed him her phone, the screen lit up with tiny pictures. They were too small for Kris to see many details, but didn't leave much to the imagination. Either Rayne and Cal were that dedicated to their performance, or there was something more going on between them. Kris bit his lip and scrolled down.

"This is a video. That's, uh. Daring."

"It's not a sex tape, genius, it's an interview."

Succumbing to curiosity against his better judgment, Kris pressed Play. Rayne and Calloway swam into focus, Rayne's arm slung casually over Cal's shoulders, with Cal's hand at his waist. They appeared intimately at ease together, and though Kris knew Rayne had been high, he didn't look it.

"So are you two serious?" the interviewer asked.

"It's too soon to say," Rayne said easily. "Maybe it'll turn into something and maybe it won't; we're just enjoying the chance to hang out at the festival."

Cal nodded along. He obviously wasn't as practiced as Rayne at acting for the press, but Kris was sure he'd get there. Rayne was the best teacher he could hope for, after all.

"So where does your burgeoning romance leave your guitarist, Kris Golding? You're familiar with the rumors that you two were an item on the down-low, of course?"

"He's not into guys," Rayne said immediately, and Kris winced. "We always made it very clear to everyone—press and fans alike—that what we did was just a performance, and I stand by that."

"Kris is a solid guy," Cal added, leaning into Rayne's side and entangling their fingers. "He's a good friend and a great bandmate, but there's really nothing else there. I'm not a home-wrecker."

The interviewer laughed obligingly. "Okay, so Golding isn't interested. What about you, Rayne? You never had any feelings on your end? I hate to push this," she added, "but my viewers would be out for blood if I let it slide."

Kris held his breath as he waited for Rayne's reply.

"No, none of that, I'm afraid," Rayne said, and he winced apologetically at the camera as if in sympathy for his disappointed fans. "I don't get involved with straight boys anymore, no matter how enthusiastic they are. I learned that lesson ages back, and it's not an experience I'm keen to repeat."

"Fair enough. Are your shows going to change, if you and Calloway do get serious?"

Rayne and Cal shared a glance. They were sitting so close they were practically in each other's laps, having apparently decided subtlety was the enemy.

"We'll have to discuss that when it comes up," Rayne finally said. "For now, Kris and I are toning down some of the more risqué performances, just while Cal and I get our bearings."

"The fans are very invested in your perceived relationship with Golding," the interviewer pressed.

Cal intervened before Rayne had to.

"They put on a hell of a show and I'm not trying to mess with that," he said. "I'm sure we can work something out to everyone's satisfaction. The fans don't have to worry about a thing." He smiled broadly and pressed a kiss to Rayne's jaw, lingering there until Rayne laughed and obligingly turned to meet his lips.

The video clip cut out, and Kris stared at the end screen for a second before handing the phone back to Cassie.

"Cool," he croaked. "It looks like it's going well. I'm happy for them."

She narrowed her eyes. "No, you're not. You're being weird."

"No, really. If they want to get together for real, that's . . . awesome. I'm just going to go . . . elsewhere. For a minute. And, uh."

Cassie watched him critically. "You want to tell me what's going on, or am I supposed to guess? You don't want me to guess."

"You don't have to guess anything. There's nothing going on."

Cassie's expression intensified.

"Shut up," Kris said. "It's true."

He nodded definitively, turned on his heel, and left the stage. He heard Cassie pick up her sticks again, a snappy little beat following him as he went. He hadn't lied; he would absolutely congratulate Rayne and Cal if they decided to give it a shot. But he really fucking hoped they didn't, because Kris wasn't just going to tell Rayne he was bi: he was going to tell him he was in love with him too, sober and for real, and he wasn't going to risk waiting till after they left Purple Sage to do it.

# CHAPTER FIFTEEN
## AN INTERLUDE ON CULTISH LOYALTIES

Leif rarely raised his voice or lost his temper, but when neither he nor Red nor Boar could locate the peacock when they got up that morning, he came close. He shut his eyes and forced his temper down, his hands in fists at his sides.

"We'll find Him," he said, his voice admirably calm. "And find Rikki." The boy had been causing trouble the day before; he might have retaliated by stealing the Avatar away. Leif concentrated on his breathing meditation, and gradually his temper cooled to something more controllable. Maybe Leif had been too harsh on the boy—letting Red and Boar give him that beating had been one thing, but threatening to strip his bike down and sell it for scrap metal might have pushed Rikki over the edge. "Fan out; search the grounds. Find them both."

He set off through the heart of the festival toward the picnic area. Eventually, the boy would need to eat. And when he did, Leif would be waiting.

". . . the last time you ate a real meal?" a familiar voice said.

Leif strained his ears, recognizing it but not remembering from where until the speaker stepped into the clearing where the tables were set up. It was the young black woman he had encountered twice already—she'd hit Boar in the face with that pretzel, and hit Red later with her handbag when she interrupted their fight. And at her side was Rikki, the insolent little whelp—Leif was right that the boy had defected. The Avatar, however, was nowhere to be seen.

"You're skin and bones," the woman continued.

"I've always been like that," Rikki replied.

He was all limbs, like a scarecrow that had learned to walk. His cuts were healing up though, even if he was still too pale and the skin around his eyes too dark to look healthy. But he would live; Red and Boar hadn't done him any lasting damage. Leif was sure they would have if he'd let them; their inherent violence was getting increasingly difficult for him to rein in. He couldn't say what would happen when he finally lost control.

"We'll get you some food, then you can meet the bands. Though we should wait before introducing you to Calloway, just in case. Kris is right; that sounds like a mess waiting to happen."

Leif blinked at the mention of Calloway. It was too great a coincidence to be anyone but his former order member, the one who had abandoned them not so long ago. He waited until they were near enough before he stepped out from his hiding place to intercept them.

"You," he glowered, "have stolen the Avatar."

Rikki stopped dead in his tracks, one arm flung in front of his companion like he could protect her. Leif stiffened and puffed himself up, though he kept one eye on the woman in case she decided to launch another offensive.

"Who stole it?" Rikki demanded.

Leif paused. "You didn't?"

"No! I never touched it." Rikki folded his arms over his chest and glared. Leif, broader if not taller, glared back more formidably.

"Rikki was with me all night," the woman cut in. "He hasn't been anywhere near your avatar, whatever it is."

Leif studied her long and hard, and she bore his scrutiny with cool eyes, her chin held high. Finally, he determined she was telling the truth, and turned back to Rikki. "If it wasn't you, then it was someone else, and you're going to help us find it."

Rikki looked at the woman, visibly hesitating. Leif ground his teeth together, his patience fraying. This was the longest the peacock had been away from him since His arrival, and His absence grated at him, worse than road rash. Did his god's protection extend that far? Would his luck finally run dry without the bird? He didn't want to test it.

"Of course I'll help you," Rikki finally said, when the woman did nothing to intervene. "We're family, right?"

"The Avatar is more important than that," Leif replied. Rikki wouldn't be welcomed back into the fold, but he could serve his purpose before they cut him loose. "Come. We should talk."

Rikki nodded and glanced back at the woman one last time.

"You know where to find me," she said.

Leif took Rikki by the arm and dragged him away. The boy kept looking back over his shoulder as they walked, his expression lost, but unafraid. The last thing Leif heard before exiting the picnic grounds was the woman uttering a heartfelt "Fuck."

# CHAPTER SIXTEEN
## SEA SALT AND CINNAMON HEARTS

Kris needed to work up the courage to talk to Rayne. He was sure that once his feelings were out in the open, even if they were unrequited, he would feel better than he did bottling them up and pretending there was nothing there. Once Rayne had all the facts, the ball would be in his court, and he could do what he wanted. He was pretending to date Calloway—so what? Unless they made it real, it didn't have to get in the way. The publicity stunt had always been a weak excuse to keep Kris's feelings from evolving.

But then, Cal and Rayne were getting along well, and Kris couldn't have imagined Cal's attraction to Rayne the night before. The only difference between Kris and Cal was that Calloway was openly gay, and it was his job to make people believe he and Rayne were an item. That gave Cal the upper hand, but Kris wasn't going to give up. Rayne could choose Kris, or Cal, or neither, but the weight would be off Kris's chest. He would reassure Brian that what had happened with Fink would never happen with Kris, because Kris wasn't straight, and more than that, he was in love.

No more secrets. He was going to let it all out.

But first, he got drunk.

And then he got drunker.

It was all Jay's fault. After the first few days of touring, the bands hadn't usually imbibed too heavily. They'd partied hard for a short time, and then the novelty had worn off and the reality of surviving bus life with a hangover sunk in, and they'd stuck to mostly social drinking. But once in a while, someone wanted to turn up, and insisted on dragging everyone else along for the ride.

When their set ended that afternoon, Kris staggered backstage and Jay greeted him by pushing a bottle of whiskey into his hands.

"Tonight we drink!" Jay crowed. A ragtag cheer, more confused than enthusiastic, went up around him. The peacock, which Rayne had christened Freddie Mercury, shrieked. Brian had read them the riot act about what would happen if the bird got hurt onstage, or hurt one of them, or turned on the audience, as if he were a stampeding elephant after all, and not just an overgrown and unusually vain bird. However, it turned out to be too much work trying to keep him offstage and safe. Like his namesake, Freddie had a thirst for fame, and escaped his handlers to insinuate himself in the center of attention at every opportunity, to Brian's despair. Of course Rayne also enjoyed the extra attention, and Kris was pleased that his gift—however drug-induced—had gone over so well.

Freddie seemed equally pleased with his newfound stardom.

Only Calloway was uneasy about it, asking repeatedly where Freddie had come from and appearing worried when Kris told him that the bird had been wandering the festival grounds, then downright shaken when Kris offered up his drug-addled spiritual experience on finding him.

"Maybe you shouldn't share that story too widely," Calloway suggested. "People might come looking for him."

"What, like animal-control guys? Do you need a license to tour with a bird like this?"

"Just be careful, that's all I'm saying. Maybe he escaped from a zoo or somebody's private collection or something. It might cause trouble for you."

"I'm sure Brian's taking care of any legal stuff." But Calloway's concern was palpable. They might be in competition for Rayne's attention, but it was hard to dislike the guy, especially when he was so clearly distressed. Cruelty didn't come naturally to Kris in any case, so he smiled and gave Calloway a reassuring thump on the arm. "Don't worry about it. It's not like we adopted a stray tiger to take onstage."

Kris got drunker than he had since their going-away party, maybe more so. He wound up on the bus couch with his head in Angel's lap and his feet in Jay's, watching Rayne tell a story about his first show with Passionfruit, and trying not to look at Cass and Stef sitting on top of each other in a near acrobatic feat of intimacy that he really didn't need to see, like, ever. Calloway stood near the bunks, leaning against them as Rayne talked. Kris's attention kept drifting from Rayne to Cal and back again, the alcohol pushing him to search for clues. Were they together for real? Should he ask? No, Rayne would have told him.

"And then the drum kit caught fire," Rayne said with a flourish, nearly spilling his drink.

"Knocks, you have the worst luck," Cassie said.

"My luck's just fine," Knocks said, tapping his rocker boot and pointing to Jay. "It's this little asshole who keeps fucking me over." Knocks was more or less ambulatory since getting back from the hospital, but unable to play drums in the cast. So while Cass stayed behind the kit, he'd taken up rhythm guitar rather than sit out entirely.

"How was I supposed to know it was flammable?" Jay asked. "It was a total accident, and I already apologized about your foot today. Anyway, you're having a great time on guitar."

Knocks glared in a way that said he knew Jay was right, but he refused to give him the satisfaction of agreeing.

"Anyway," Cass said loudly. "We're cool. Right?"

"We're fine," Billie said. "Jay's a live wire; we all know to give him a wide berth onstage."

"As if," Cassie snorted. "You guys can't keep your hands off each other for five seconds."

"Stealing all our ideas," Rayne said mournfully. "You used to be so much more innovative, Billie. What happened?"

"We're not— Jay, stop it," Billie said, as Jay dropped Kris's feet to the cushions and rose, advancing on Billie. "It's just for the show!"

"Giving me a wide berth," Jay said. "I'll show you a wide berth—"

"That doesn't even make sense!" Billie howled, before Jay pounced and took him from his chair to the floor.

Cassie whipped out her phone without moving from Stef's lap. "Sending this to both your girlfriends," she sang. Jay flipped her the finger without getting off Billie, who thrashed weakly, making strangled cries of exaggerated anguish as he tried to shove Jay off. Kris made himself comfortable, stretching out along the couch.

"I feel like I should intervene," Rayne said, "but the view's too good. I can't bring myself to do it."

"Fuck you," Billie said from the floor. "I would've helped you, you traitor."

"I don't know if I'd be complaining," Calloway said.

"Well, I might if it was Jay," Rayne mused.

"Fuck you!" Jay laughed. "I'm a fucking catch and you know it."

"I don't know, you're not quite my type . . . I mean, if it were Kris or Cal, that's a different story."

"If I were what?" Kris asked.

"Engaging Rayne in an impromptu wrestling match," Angel said.

"Oh. Do you want me to?" Kris asked Rayne, looking for somewhere to put his drink. "I can totally do that, hang on." He handed his drink to Angel and got to his feet. The change in elevation brought the drunkenness on suddenly, and he had to take a moment to collect himself.

"Don't think you're going to be wrestling anybody, sweetie," Angel said, her hand on his hip to steady him.

"Nope, I got this. Bit drunker than I thought, but I got this." He leveled one finger at Rayne. "You stand there and hold still, okay?"

"I'm not sure this is a great idea," Rayne said, but he didn't move. Calloway backed up a pace, out of the line of fire.

"Get him!" Jay yelled from the floor.

Kris made a valiant attempt, but the floor tipped sideways under him and Rayne met him halfway, sweeping him up in an embrace that took Kris off his feet, laughing helplessly as Rayne swung him around before setting him down again.

"That's not wrestling," Kris said. "This is just, like, a hug."

"I like hugging better."

"Get a room," Cassie called.

It was the best idea Kris had ever heard, but he swallowed it with the rest of his whiskey and smiled and tried not to let his heart show too obviously. He had no idea whether it worked, but Rayne laughed and poured him another drink. Calloway watched them without saying a word.

They carried on until well after midnight. The stars peeked out one by one until the sky was a dazzling array of rhinestones against the black, and the desert air grew cool and sharp. Somewhere beyond the festival perimeter, a coyote howled intermittently. Gradually the bus quieted until everyone had retired save for Kris, Rayne, and Calloway. Cal didn't drink, and outstripped them in terms of sobriety by miles, but seemed happy to keep them company. Finally, when Passionfruit had returned to their bus and the rest of The Chokecherries had lost the battle with consciousness, he stretched and got to his feet, gesturing to the door. Rayne nodded and drew them both outside, leaving the others to sleep.

"I should head back to my bus," Cal said, his voice soft in the night.

"We'll walk you." Rayne put his arm around Cal's waist and leaned into him, looking back expectantly at Kris. "Coming?"

"Don't want to get in your way," Kris said.

"I don't think there's anyone around worth putting on a show for," Calloway said. "Come on, walk with us."

Kris walked a pace behind them, cataloging how their arms looped around each other's bodies and how Rayne leaned against Cal, his boots scuffing through the dust as he walked, remarkably sure-footed, through the maze of tents and stages. Kris was pleasantly drunk and getting sleepy, though the sharpness of the air canceled out some of the haze. *Rayne and Cal complement each other nicely*, he thought blurrily. Rayne's slender, darker figure bent flower-like toward Cal's broader, sun-kissed frame. When they reached the Dead Generation bus, they paused, three points under the vast night sky.

"I'll see you tomorrow," Calloway said. "Take care of yourselves, all right?"

Rayne darted in to press a kiss to his jaw, his curls brushing Cal's face for a second before he pulled back. "We'll be fine. It's just us and the stars out tonight."

They let go of each other and Calloway nodded to Kris. "Good night."

"Good night," Kris echoed as Cal disappeared into his bus.

Rayne swayed back to him and dropped an arm over his shoulders. "Okay?"

"Do you like him?" Kris asked, his heart in his mouth as he waited for Rayne's reply.

"Sure I like him. Don't you?"

"No, I mean—Cassie said he propositioned you last night."

Rayne broke into a smile. "Yeah, he did. I have to say, he made a very tempting offer." The night cast his face in shadows of blue and violet and his expression turned thoughtful. "The possibility's there. He asked if I wanted to do more, since we were already—for the press, you know? I didn't say yes, but I didn't turn him down, either."

"Do you want to?" Kris asked, biting the tip of his tongue. If Rayne said yes, Kris was done. If he said no—

"A lot of things seem like a good idea on MDMA," Rayne said vaguely. "I might . . . I could like him. Or more than like. But I don't, not yet."

"Is he a good kisser?"

Rayne grinned and pulled Kris tighter, so Kris tripped over his own sneakers and stumbled against Rayne's side. They both laughed in hushed voices as they righted themselves.

"Yeah, he is. We had fun."

"A better kisser than me?" Kris pushed, not entirely joking.

"Course not. You're my favorite, baby. Always will be."

Rayne pressed a kiss to Kris's temple, sloppy and a bit off the mark as he laughed, but Kris closed his eyes and hummed, warm all the way through. He knew Rayne was only teasing, but that didn't mean he was lying. Kris tilted his head back to take in the stars. The sky looked infinite, and he found a weird comfort in his own insignificance. Gazing up at the stars like that, it didn't matter what he did or didn't do; the universe didn't care.

"Hey, Rayne. Remember what I told you last night? When I was high?"

"About the peacock?"

"No, dumbass, about you."

Rayne bit his lip. Kris looked away. He had the whiskey bottle by the neck, dangling loose from his fingers, its glass catching the scarce light left to them.

"You want a nightcap?" Kris asked. "Come on, come back to the stage."

The festival never slept, even if individuals had to. Kris and Rayne wound through music tents and raves and drum circles until they reached their stage, which was dark and empty for the night, and crept through the back to their tiny makeshift dressing room, where Kris set the whiskey bottle down on the table and took a minute to consider how drunk he was. Drunker than Rayne; they were evenly matched for consumption, but Kris's size had always made him a lightweight. Drunk enough to do something reckless, like tell Rayne how he felt for real. Maybe not drunk enough to regret it in the morning.

He'd have to wait and find out.

"When I told you I loved you," he said, "and you said you loved me too. You said I was beautiful."

"Yeah?"

"I meant it."

"You were so high," Rayne giggled.

"And now I'm so drunk," Kris agreed. "Tell me I'm pretty?"

"God, you're the prettiest." Rayne reached out to pet Kris's hair and Kris leaned into it, his eyes fluttering closed for a second at the feeling. "Even without the makeup, your face— I love that you wear it, though. I love that you don't care what anybody thinks."

"I care."

"Not enough to stop." Rayne carded his fingers through the tufts and down the back of Kris's neck to hold him there, warm and steady. Kris blinked up at him.

"Fuck, Kris," Rayne breathed. "You don't know what you do to me."

"You and Calloway—"

"We're just friends, I don't know if we'll ever be anything but friends, I don't even know if I want to be more—fuck, it's not like you and me, you know that—"

With more coordination than the drink should allow, Kris pulled Rayne in for a kiss. He closed his eyes, expecting the roar of the crowd; his heart skipped a beat when it never came. The only sounds were their own hurried breathing, the wet sound of their mouths meeting, and the rustle of their clothes as they pressed together. Kris threw himself into the kiss like he was dying for it, and Rayne returned with equal fervor. They only broke apart when they had to pant for breath, their foreheads touching as they held each other's faces, eyes wild and chests heaving.

"I want—" Kris began, but he didn't know how to finish. The booze swam in his head, dizzying and pushing him off-balance. Rayne hadn't let go: he stood with his eyes closed, his hair falling in his face. His lips were dark and swollen from the kiss, and Kris darted in to nip at them, pulling a desperate moan from Rayne's throat.

"Kiss me," Kris said against Rayne's skin. "Just kiss me—"

Rayne kissed him. He started at Kris's jaw and bit and sucked his way down Kris's throat until Kris was panting breathless syllables into the dark, one hand knotted in Rayne's hair. By the time Rayne reached his collarbone, mouthing at the bend where his neck met his shoulder, Kris was aching for it. He wound his arms around Rayne's neck and buried his face in Rayne's hair, breathing in the smell of his shampoo, needing to feel and touch and taste nothing in the world but him.

He didn't know which of them moved first; maybe they moved at the same time, an inevitable collision of bodies and wants. The first touch brought the best kind of friction, relieving and desperate both at once, and Kris bucked his hips forward, instinctively seeking more.

When their hips met, they both froze.

"Okay?" Kris asked, not raising his face from Rayne's hair.

Rayne stroked his hands up and down Kris's sides. "Fuck," he whispered. His voice was rough. Kris shuddered and twitched forward again, a fraction of an inch.

"We're really drunk," Rayne said.

"Is that a no?"

"No, god, no. Please don't stop."

As far as sex went, it was the least sophisticated Kris had had since his adolescence, but he didn't care. Burning up in the wake of Rayne's touches, he was too drunk for anything more complex. He finally had Rayne and Rayne wanted him back. He couldn't believe he'd wasted so much time.

They made out like teenagers, rubbing up against each other fully clothed, stealing kisses with every breath. Kris went into it harder and faster than he'd meant, crashing up against the edge of orgasm without any finesse, wanting to draw it out longer but too desperate for Rayne's touch to manage. He came without even undoing his jeans, gasping out a curse in the dark and clinging to Rayne like a lifeline. Rayne pressed his open mouth to Kris's neck, muttering a steady litany of *fuck, fuck, fuck* against his skin, and followed a second after.

Afterward, neither of them spoke at first. On the other side of the room, the mirror stood like a silent witness. Rayne's pupils were huge, blown out with lingering lust and a look so fond that Kris's heart leaped giddily in his chest. He was less drunk than he'd been a minute before, but drunk enough to dare to run his finger over Rayne's face, from his brow down his nose to trace the curve of his lips. Rayne smiled against his fingertip and Kris smiled back, helpless and glowing.

"Good?" Kris asked, before he could stop himself.

"You're perfect," Rayne said, catching Kris's hand. "How are you even real?"

"Magic."

Rayne kissed his knuckles, a wet press of his lips, and led him down the steps and past the stage, back into the night. The air caressed Kris's skin like a lover. He felt on top of the world, and when they returned to the bus and he crawled into his bunk, his eyes drifting closed as the last of the whiskey chased itself through his blood, he could still taste Rayne on his tongue, like cinnamon hearts and sea salt. He fell asleep promising himself that it wouldn't be the last time.

Kris woke with a hangover so bad he thought he might die. He hadn't drunk enough to black out so there was no reason he should feel so close to death, but maybe there was something in the whiskey that did it; he didn't know. He got up as slowly as he could, his head throbbing, and resolved to never accept a drink from Jay ever again. Playing that afternoon was going to be a nightmare. He'd be lucky not to puke halfway through the set. He settled one hand protectively over his stomach while the other groped blindly along the bus as he staggered outside into the sun.

He instantly wished he'd stayed in bed. The sun was blinding and his head protested with a scream so shrill he actually flinched; he forced his eyes open and found Freddie staring at him judgmentally. He flipped the bird off and stumbled his way to the picnic area, dreading solid food but hoping a Gatorade might fix him. He hadn't had enough water the night before, and felt like he'd been keelhauled fifty miles down the desert highway.

Despite feeling like death, there was an undeniable spring in his step, and he gave a bright wave to Cassie and Stef breakfasting together as he passed. He'd finally gotten with Rayne and it had been amazing, and no amount of alcohol-induced misery could take that away from him.

Rayne was sitting at a picnic table beside Calloway, nursing a coffee and a quiet conversation. He looked bleary and barely able to keep himself upright, while Cal appeared healthier, but vaguely apologetic about something. Kris couldn't hear their words, but they seemed intimate. Cal straightened and nudged Rayne in the side at Kris's approach, and Rayne let whatever he'd been saying trail off.

"Morning," Calloway greeted. "Coffee?"

"Morning," Kris said, "and yeah, I need it."

"I'll get you one," Cal offered, his hand on Rayne's shoulder. "Anything in it?"

"Just black, thanks. Extra-large. Extra-triple-large. Or bigger."

Cal nodded and headed off to the vendor, glancing over his shoulder as Kris leaned one hip against the table.

"Morning, sunshine," Kris said to Rayne. "How's your head?"

Rayne grunted and tipped nose-first into his drink. "Probably not as bad as yours. About last night . . ."

Kris broke into a stupid grin. "Yeah?"

Rayne patted the table. "Sit."

Kris slid onto the bench on the opposite side. Calloway returned a second later with the coffee, and reclaimed his place beside Rayne. That was where Kris wanted to sit, pressed up close beside him to leach his warmth in the morning sun, but they were in public and Cal and Rayne had appearances to keep up.

"You look miserable," Cal said to Rayne. "There's a guy with a camera just over there—give us a smile?"

"I am miserable," Rayne complained. "I'm hungover, among other things." He smiled anyway, and Kris doubted anyone else would notice how it seemed strained around the edges. He wondered what the "other things" were.

"Listen," Cal said. "Why don't you two go someplace private for a chat? I'll come find you later and we'll do lunch."

Rayne nodded and beckoned for Kris to stand.

"Okay, sure," Kris said, glancing between the two of them in confusion. They had obviously been talking before his arrival—about the night before? Rayne wasn't meeting his gaze, but Calloway carried an air of sympathy. "Thanks for the coffee," Kris said, at a loss for any other words.

Rayne led him back to the dressing room, closing the door behind them and leaning against it. He did look miserable, the tension etching lines between his shoulders like he was expecting a blow. Kris couldn't imagine from whom.

"About last night?" Kris prompted.

"We were really drunk."

"Yeah." Kris frowned. "You don't think it was a mistake, do you?"

"No," Rayne said quickly.

"Because I don't regret it. I regret the timing, and I regret drinking that much, but I needed some liquid courage to—you know. It might get messy with us both being in the band, and I never want to compromise that, or your stunt with Calloway, but I meant what I said, Rayne."

"What you said when you were high on molly." Rayne raised his hands before Kris could protest. "I believe you. I just— We had a good thing going on, onstage, didn't we? It was all for the show. And now I don't know what you want from me."

Kris floundered. It had never occurred to him last night that they weren't communicating on the same level. "I want . . . more. Of what we did. I liked it. I thought you did too?"

Rayne raked his fingers through his hair, tousling it up as he looked away. "Kris, when you joined the band, you told me you liked girls. You said you were straight."

"I do like girls. Back home, I always said I was straight, but that was different."

"And when we were messing around, we said that was for the fans. No strings, no complications."

"Last night wasn't for the fans," Kris pointed out.

"Last night's why we're having this conversation. Kris . . ."

"I said that I'd only ever been with girls, which was true. I never got a chance to explore anything in Kansas, and I didn't want to accidentally lead you on, or let you lead me on, because we're in a band together and I didn't want to fuck that up. And I still don't, but I do want . . . more. Of everything. From you."

"You've never even been with a man."

"I'm trying to be with one right now," Kris said.

Rayne sighed.

Kris's heart dropped like a rock. He folded his arms like he could keep it from dropping any farther, and gnawed on the inside of his lip. "This isn't how I imagined this going," he admitted. "I know you're into me. I know you were into me last night."

"I've tried it on with straight guys before," Rayne reminded him, "and it's not something I want to do again. If you're bi, or pan, or . . . whatever else, that's great, and I'm happy for you. But I don't want to be the person you experiment with to figure it out." He raked his hair back from his forehead and finally met Kris's eyes. Kris couldn't make out his expression in the shadows, but it seemed like it might be one of regret.

Kris cast around for any way to drag the conversation back on track. "We had fun though, didn't we?" he tried. "It was good—"

Rayne's expression shuttered and Kris knew he'd fucked up.

"Wait, that's not—"

"I'm sorry, Kris. I can't go through another scenario like Fink where I get dragged through the mud for someone else's entertainment, especially if they don't even feel—" Rayne took a deep breath. "It's not fair to me—it's demeaning, and I can't—I won't do it."

"That's not what I meant," Kris finished in a small voice.

"We were drunk," Rayne said. "And I've got a chance with Cal. I like him and he likes me, and he's openly gay, Kris. He knows what he's about, and he told me so right from the start."

"You and Cal are just a publicity stunt."

"So are you and me," Rayne said gently.

Kris swallowed. "Fine. I'll see you onstage."

Rayne nodded and slipped from the room. As soon as he was gone, Kris leaned back against the wall, his head throbbing from a hangover and from grief. He couldn't figure out where he'd gone so wrong.

# CHAPTER SEVENTEEN
## THE HIGHWAY TO, FROM, AND THROUGH HELL

"What did you do?" Cassie asked bluntly.

They were waiting for their parents to come by and take them for brunch; the sun was sweltering and the highway asphalt was hot enough to melt rubber.

Kris shuffled around and didn't answer. Cassie rolled her eyes.

"I know something happened," she said. "You got up this morning like you were on top of the world, and now you're all mopey. What's up?"

"Me and Rayne," Kris finally said.

Cass whooped.

"No, no whooping. I fucked up and now it's all weird."

She quieted, but it took visible effort. "But you two did get it on," she confirmed. "Like, offstage, in private, just the two of you? How far did you get? Third base? Homerun?"

"I hate sports metaphors. We, uh." He made a gesture. Cassie screeched. He sighed and covered his face with his hands. "We were so drunk, Cass. It was such a mistake."

"Is that what he said, or are you having an identity crisis because you got off with a dude?"

"Why does everyone keep assuming I don't know what I want?" Kris demanded. "I didn't wake up one morning and think, 'Oh, I wonder what it's like batting for the other team.' Like, I'm into guys. I always have been. Just because I haven't had a ton of—any—experience, that doesn't mean I don't know what I like."

"You've never talked about it before," Cassie pointed out.

"Neither have you," he countered.

"Point. So you're—what? Bi?"

"Bi," he said. "I'm bisexual." It was the first time he'd said it aloud, and it felt scary and thrilling and relieving all at once, like going out in makeup for the first time, or lacing up a corset.

"Okay, well, does Rayne know that?" Cassie asked. "Or does he still think you're straight? And why would you even let him think that if it's not true? These guys shit rainbows, dude. You're not going to get a better opportunity than this to come out."

"He thinks I want to use him to experiment." Kris's insides went leaden at the reminder, and he curled in on himself, wishing he could disappear.

"Oh my god, are you in love with him?"

"I—" He couldn't be, not now that Rayne had so thoroughly rejected him, no matter what Kris had thought he'd seen in Rayne's face in that dressing room the night before—

"You are," Cassie breathed. "Oh, shit. That sucks, man."

"Well, he doesn't want that," Kris said, with heavy resignation. "He was talking about maybe trying to get somewhere with Cal. So it doesn't matter."

"You should really talk to him." She poked him in the arm. "You guys could still work it out."

"Maybe?"

"Talk to him, Kris. You're both adults—physically, if not mentally some days—and this might just be a huge misunderstanding."

Kris wanted to hole up somewhere dark and lick his wounds, but not talking was what had led to this mess in the first place. And regardless of whether he and Rayne could work things out, Cassie would be after him like a dog with a bone until he made an attempt. He sighed. "Fine. We'll talk."

She settled back. "You better. See me missing my chance to have Rayne Bakshi for a brother-in-law—I don't think so."

Their parents' car pulled up and they got to their feet.

"As soon as we get back," Kris promised. "I'll find him and we'll talk it out."

Their parents took them outside the festival to a little diner on the side of the highway, a quaint, family-owned place that proudly advertised its famous pies. Cassie hijacked the conversation, steering it clear of Kris with an ease born of years of jostling for attention.

Kris didn't object; he only pitched in occasionally to corroborate some of her less believable Passionfruit anecdotes, all while Brad sat quietly, humming here and there to contribute, but mostly leaving well enough alone. Kris was glad for the respite—he didn't want to pick a fight in the middle of the restaurant, not with his parents trying to treat him, but he didn't think he could resist if Brad started in on him.

"The festival's nearly over," his dad said. "Are you looking forward to a change of scenery?"

"It'll be good to be back on the road," Kris agreed. Purple Sage had left a sour taste in his mouth now, and he didn't want to set foot in that dressing room ever again. The fact that he and Rayne would still be sharing a bus—he didn't know what to do about that, but quitting the band was out of the question.

*I'm going to talk to Rayne as soon as I get back*, he told himself firmly. Cassie was right: he had probably blown this whole thing out of proportion. He should have taken Rayne's history with Fink into account and been more sensitive; he would apologize for that, and they could salvage things. Even if Rayne didn't want anything more than friendship, surely they could still have that.

"I think I'm still a bit hungover," he apologized.

Cassie slid his plate into her spot without a word and tucked in to the remains of his meal. "Lightweight," she said cheerfully, around a mouthful of pancake. "I think it'll be great to hit the road! I've never been on a road trip before, unless you count driving out here."

"With your Passionfruit band?" their mom asked.

"And The Chokecherries," Cassie said, moving onto the hash browns. "At least until Knocks can play again, but I'm having a great time, and the guys all like me, so." She shrugged. "We'll see how it plays out. I'm happy to stay as long as I can."

"You'll be careful though," their dad said. "They seem like a rowdy lot."

"I'll be careful, Dad. Jay's and Billie's girlfriends are joining us like two stops over anyway."

Their parents looked mollified at the thought of chaperones.

"And what about Rayne?" their mom asked Kris. "I've heard rumors flying about some young man he's been spotted with a few times now."

Brad clenched his fingers around his fork.

"I don't know that it's anything serious," Kris said, keeping his voice even. "I think it's hard to date on tour. I wouldn't want to try it."

"Well, there'll be plenty of time for that after," she said, "what with you being so successful now. I've seen how the girls scream in the audience, you know, throwing all sorts of things at the stage. Young women will always love a man in a rock band."

"Seen some of the boys screaming too," their dad added.

Kris coughed and quickly took a drink of water. "I'm just happy they like the music," he choked out.

Cassie thumped him on the back without looking up from her plate. "I'm dating Stef, by the way," she said. "The bassist? You guys met the first day we got here."

Kris sank deeper into his seat, grateful the attention was off him again. What he needed was to collect himself before his parents asked for any more details about Rayne, or Cal, or anything else.

Their parents glanced at each other.

"We'll have to talk to—er," their dad began.

"Them," Cassie supplied.

"It would be nice to get to know them better," their mom finished. "We'll take you both out to dinner before we leave."

Cassie brightened before glancing at Brad, who thinned his lips but only said, "Congratulations."

"That would be nice, Mom. I'm sure Stef will like that."

"They definitely won't turn down a free dinner," Kris said. "I didn't know you were actually dating."

"This is a family restaurant, Kris," Cassie said. "We're calling it dating."

Their dad cleared his throat as the waitress returned with fresh coffee. "Anyone want pie? I'm getting pie."

He and their mom both ordered; Cassie, having already eaten her waffles and most of Kris's pancakes, begged off.

Kris jumped at the chance for a minute alone. "I'm going to go for a walk, see if that'll help my head. I'll meet you back here when you're ready to go, okay? Enjoy the pie."

He headed out to do a few laps around the parking lot, hoping the sun would bake the angst from his brain.

Brad joined him a minute later.

"Hey," he said. "We got off on the wrong foot the other day. Can we talk?"

Kris squinted at him, then shrugged. It couldn't go worse than their last talk; it definitely couldn't go worse than his talk with Rayne.

"Jump in the car," Brad offered. "Let's go for a drive."

Brad slid into the driver's seat and waited for Kris to buckle up next to him before pulling out onto the highway. It stretched endlessly in either direction, cutting through the rust-colored desert rocks. Brad steered away from the festival, drumming his thumbs against the wheel. Neither of them spoke for the first few minutes. Something with a banjo twanged on the radio.

"Are you really happy?" Brad finally asked.

Kris didn't know where to begin, but he wasn't going to prove Brad right by saying so. "Sure I am. You still hung up on how I look onstage?"

"You're wearing makeup right now."

Kris stole a glance in the side mirror. Whatever he'd been wearing last night had smudged around his eyes, making him look more goth than glam.

"It's hardly drag. So?"

The highway lines passed under them in streaks.

"You and Rayne. Tell me he's never tried anything with you offstage."

Kris laughed. It sounded unpleasant, even to his ears. "You trying to protect my virtue, Brad? That's a losing fucking battle, man. I've done more in the past week than I've done in my entire life, and if me and Rayne did do something, what's it to you? We're both adults."

Brad's mouth twisted. "You're still my little brother. I don't like seeing you like this."

"Successful?" Kris offered. "Getting paid to make music and hang out with some really cool people I respect and admire?"

"It's degrading."

"Sorry, what?"

"I'm not saying anyone's forcing you to do anything," Brad said, "but someone's clearly influencing you. Makeup, girls' clothes, letting some gay rub up on you like that—you would never have agreed to any of that before you moved away."

"No shit. You giving Cassie this talk too, or am I just special?"

"She's twenty. Every college girl goes through a phase like this; it'll pass. You—you're old enough to know better."

"Wow. Say that to her face—she'll have your balls, man. I wish I'd had half her guts at twenty to be myself."

"Mom and Dad think you can take care of yourself," Brad continued, as if Kris hadn't spoken. "Cassie will always side with you to spite me. But I didn't come all the way out here just to fight with you, Kris."

"No? Why did you come, Brad? Because I don't believe for a second that you missed me. We've barely talked since you went all right wing, and honestly, I was good with that. That was working for me. So what changed? Why are you suddenly pulling this concerned-older-brother crap that we both know is bullshit?"

Brad's mouth was set in a thin, hard line. "Did you ever think how your little stage antics would reflect on the rest of us? Dressing up like this, the makeup, the kissing, like you're some kind of sex toy for him to play with up there, while he's fucking some other guy the rest of the time—did you stop and think how that would make the rest of us look?"

"Mom and Dad don't care—" Kris began, and then he stopped. "I'm embarrassing you."

Brad's knuckles whited out around the steering wheel.

"All your straitlaced conservative friends found out about me, and you freaked." Kris barked out a laugh. "This is pathetic, man! You came all the way out to Nevada to bully me into quitting the band so you could save face with those assholes? Like that was ever going to work. Just get better friends."

"You don't understand anything," Brad said coldly, in a tone that meant Kris was exactly right. "But I want you to know, I'm doing this for your own good."

A thread of fear slipped through Kris. They were fifteen minutes out from the diner, and another fifteen after that from the festival. They hadn't passed a single car on the entire drive. "What are you talking about?" he asked, fighting to keep his voice level.

Brad pulled onto the shoulder and let the car roll to a halt. "Consider this an intervention. Give me your phone."

"Like hell!"

"Now!" Brad snapped.

"Fuck you. I'm calling Mom."

Kris made it to the second ring before Brad grabbed his wrist and smacked the phone away, sending it clattering to the car floor.

"Get out of the car," Brad said, his hand still wrapped bruisingly hard around Kris's wrist.

Kris tried to yank his arm free to no avail. "You're kidding. You're fucking nuts, Brad. Do you really think this is going to get you anywhere?"

"Everything's going to be fine," Brad said through gritted teeth. "Now get out of the goddamn car before I drag you out."

"Fuck you."

"You think you can play guitar with a broken wrist?" Brad twisted his hand, and Kris's bones ground up against one another until he swore and hit the car door with his free hand.

"Fine! Fucking—fine. Let go of me."

Brad let him go incrementally. His fingers left white marks like bands, which throbbed hotly around Kris's otherwise red wrist. Kris rubbed it as he braced himself against the door and squared his shoulders. "Asshole."

Brad growled and before Kris could defend himself, lunged over like a juggernaut to force the passenger side door open, undo the seat belt, and shove Kris out to land on his ass on the road.

"What the fuck!" Kris scrambled to his feet, but Brad had already pulled the door closed again and locked it.

"I'm telling Rayne you want out," Brad said through the window, retrieving Kris's phone from under the seat.

"He'll never believe you."

"I'm texting it from your phone. I'm not an idiot; I know you two fought earlier. He'll believe it if you're the one who says so. And then you can move on with your life, and forget this whole dumb stunt ever happened. Go back to acting like a man again." He rolled the window down far enough to toss a water bottle into the dust at Kris's feet. "Somebody will pick you up before you starve to death. You'll thank me for this, one day."

"Fuck you," Kris said. "Fuck you with a giant fucking chainsaw, Brad, I swear to god, if you drive away—"

Brad drove off before Kris could finish the threat, a spurt of dust exploding from the back tires and, to add insult to injury, sending Kris into a coughing fit that only made his lingering headache worse.

The car disappeared from sight, heading toward the diner where the rest of his family waited. He wondered what Brad would tell them.

"Lying bastard asshole."

No one replied.

Once Leif put his plan to recover the Avatar in motion, it was easy. According to the grapevine, it was The Chokecherries who had stolen it, so all he had to do was go to them to get it back. He knew the band; he had been to enough festivals to have encountered them prior to Purple Sage, and Rayne Bakshi stood out even among the throngs of music artists and crowds of partiers. Finding the band wouldn't be an issue. Convincing them to return the Avatar without getting security involved would be a greater challenge, but Leif had a plan for that as well.

"Travis, would you like to do a favor for the All-Seeing God?"

Travis nodded fervently. He wasn't ideal as far as new order members went—he was too skittish, too twitchy, and too strung out for Leif's liking, but Leif had worked with worse before. Travis seemed curious about the order, and most importantly, eager to please.

"I want you to go to the north edge of the grounds and create a diversion. As loud and as riotous as you can manage."

Travis's eyes lit up and he nodded again, even more frantically this time. "I can do that. What kind of diversion do you need?"

"Something big enough to distract the festival security. All of them. Can you do that?"

"Hell yeah. I know a guy with fireworks—give me ten minutes and it's done." He hesitated, seemingly on the brink of running off to find the guy in question. "And after, you'll introduce me to your god, right? You'll let me talk to Him?"

"If you do this well, you'll be one of us," Leif promised.

Travis's face split in a grin, and he bounded away to wreak havoc on the north side, leaving Leif and the rest of the order to find Calloway.

It wasn't difficult. All Leif had to do was walk and let the All-Seeing God guide his steps. Fifteen minutes later he found Calloway at his stage, his hair shining like a golden beacon in the sun where he sat under the great sweeping banner that called people to worship him and his band. Leif had been a little disappointed when he'd learned of Dead Generation; Cal had always been a good disciple, and to find he'd thrown the order aside for a taste of fame still sat uncomfortably.

Red, Boar, and Rikki followed Leif like great loping shadows, awaiting instruction. Rikki had been reluctant to rejoin them, and he'd soon leave the order one way or another. Leif was willing enough to let him go peacefully, especially now that Travis was primed to take his place, but Red's temper was shortening by the day, and Boar had never liked the boy. It was doubtful he'd be allowed to go without some bloodshed.

He put it from his mind and stepped into Calloway's line of sight. The man froze like a rabbit, and they stared at each other for a long moment. A cluster of security personnel at the far edge of the stage kept an eye on them but didn't move to intervene.

"Leif," Cal finally croaked. "What are you—"

"Don't bother calling for help," Leif warned. "Security will be busy elsewhere in a minute. This will be easier if you cooperate."

On cue, the nearest security officer's radio screeched to life, and he frowned, raising it to his ear as the person on the other end said something about "a disruption" between sharp bursts of static. The officer nodded to his fellows and they took off at a run, heading north.

Calloway glanced around furtively before edging closer and dropping his voice. "Why are you here?"

"The Avatar is missing and you know where it is."

Cal looked panicked. "No, I don't."

"The Chokecherries have been bringing a peacock to their shows. You know Rayne Bakshi. You're going to take me to him to help negotiate its return."

"I don't know what you're talking about," Cal insisted, but his eyes gave him away.

Leif stepped forward and Cal scrambled back, but not quickly enough—catching him by the forearm, Leif dragged him in close.

"You're coming with me," he growled, "and you're going to ensure this negotiation goes smoothly for everyone involved. Do you understand?"

"Why can't you talk to him yourself?"

"Because I don't want to escalate things if I don't have to." They both briefly eyed Red and Boar. "He trusts you. He's more likely to return the Avatar if you ask than if I do, and then no one has to get hurt."

Cal hesitated before finally nodding, dropping off the stage to take his place at Leif's side. Leif kept his grip firm around Cal's arm and set off through the festival without looking back.

"Slow down," Cal hissed, stumbling in his efforts to keep up. "If you're trying not to look suspicious—"

"I don't care why they've stolen it," Leif said as he walked, ignoring Calloway's protests entirely. "I don't care what they were thinking. We need the Avatar back; I don't have to tell you its importance. Once we have it, we'll let His Serene Majesty decide their fate."

"I'm sure this is all a huge misunderstanding," Cal said, trying in vain to pull his arm from Leif's grasp. Leif tightened his grip until Calloway's bones shifted under his fingers, and Cal stopped struggling. "Maybe the bird just wandered off on its own."

Red and Boar scoffed from behind them, and Leif paused long enough to level a truly fearsome glower in Cal's direction. Cal shrank back and shut his mouth.

"We're going to The Chokecherries. If you try any tricks, I'll make you regret them."

Cal nodded, eyes downcast, and pointed in the direction to go. Leif nodded stonily. They walked in silence, and whenever Calloway looked like he might try to lead Leif astray, Leif tightened his grip until Cal got back in line. Calloway might have left the order, but he wasn't stupid; he knew the All-Seeing God's power, and he knew Leif wasn't so easily fooled.

"What are you going to do to them?" Calloway asked in muted tones.

"Whatever His Serene Majesty dictates, as always."

Truth be told, Leif had no interest in punishing those who had stolen the Avatar any more than would mollify Boar and Red. He was growing tired—not of his god, nor of caring for the Avatar, but of the never-ending parade of festivals and acolytes, spreading the word day after day to countless unbelievers. It was exhausting, and after so many years, it was beginning to take its toll. He wanted to retire, and care for the Avatar in peace. Maybe he would rent another little trailer, somewhere he could sleep every night and call home, eating ramen and drinking beer and letting someone else preach about the wonders of the universe.

But Boar and Red were still fervent in their faith, and they would demand retribution for this slight. All Leif wanted was to keep them content so they would leave him be.

Unfortunately for The Chokecherries, what kept them most content was violence.

Calloway led Leif and his ragtag order to The Chokecherries' bus, and there he stopped, digging his heels into the earth. "I don't want any part of this. I never wished you any ill will when I left, Leif."

Leif inclined his head. That was true, despite the hurt he'd felt at the time.

"I have a career now," Cal continued, his voice pleading. "I have the chance to really make something of myself. I can't— I'll do anything to keep that alive. Please, just—"

"You'll be fine," Leif interrupted, "as long as you do as I say. You'll find a lot has changed since you left; I have far less patience than I did. But you were a good one; I'd hate for anything to happen to you as a result of this . . . unfortunate incident." He gestured to the bus. "Get your friends."

Calloway tugged his arm free, and this time Leif allowed it. Cal crept to the bus door, standing open in the desert heat, and paused to peer up the steps while keeping out of sight from the bus's occupants.

"I don't see the peacock," he whispered.

"Find out where He is," Leif returned. "Maybe they've hidden Him in one of the bunks."

Calloway put one finger to his lips and turned all his attention to the conversation within the bus. Leif followed suit with his arms crossed, waiting one pace back.

Rayne Bakshi sat on the bus couch like he'd been shot, staring at his phone with an expression somewhere between shock and heartbroken bafflement. The last time Leif had felt either of those emotions was when he'd woken to find the peacock gone, and it was doubtful the rock star had ever lost anything half as important. He watched as Angel scooted in beside the man and leaned into his shoulder to look at the phone.

"It's fucking Fink all over again," Rayne said.

Angel frowned and took the phone. She read: "'I've finally had the chance to think things over, and I don't want to do this anymore. I'm sorry I have to do it this way, but I feel it's my only chance to get out. I never should have let you do the things you did, or let things get as far as you took them. Sorry I couldn't give you more notice, but this is best for everyone. Please don't try to get in touch.'"

"He's gone," Rayne said.

"You have a show in four hours. He wouldn't bail on that, no matter what happened." Angel twisted around to sit cross-legged on the couch and face him. "But something did happen between you two. You finally hooked up in private, didn't you? He was practically glowing when I saw him this morning."

"We hooked up," Rayne admitted. "We were both so, so drunk. It should never have happened. God, why didn't I listen to Brian? He's going to have a fit when he finds out."

Calloway winced in apparent sympathy, and Leif dropped his hand on Cal's shoulder, wordlessly ordering him to focus.

"Kris didn't look like he regretted it. He looked pretty damn happy about it, from what I could see," Angel said.

"That was before we talked."

She fixed Rayne with a stare so unimpressed that he flinched.

"I told him I didn't want to be his experimentation project," he said. "Which, if I'd been halfway sober the night before, I would have said in the first place and we could have avoided all this."

"But you didn't."

"Because I got distracted by him kissing me when he didn't have to just for the show," Rayne said miserably. "I was so fucking happy he wanted to, I didn't stop to think it through."

"I've seen the way that boy looks at you," Angel said. "If you think he's using you to experiment, you're fucking blind, honey."

Rayne seemed unconvinced.

"Call him if you don't believe me," she said.

"His phone's turned off." He pushed his hands through his hair, bleeding distress.

"Then talk to Cassie. She must know where he went."

"I don't have time for this," Leif told Cal in an undertone. "They haven't mentioned the Avatar once. If you're just stalling—"

"I'm not!" Cal insisted, his voice pitching up.

Rayne and Angel froze, looking first at each other and then to the door.

"I've had enough," Red growled, shoving forward to take his place at Leif's side behind Calloway. "This is a waste of time. We can make them tell us where the Avatar is."

"Don't—" Cal started, but before Leif could intervene, Red drew his hunting knife from the sheath at his hip.

"Red—" Leif began warningly, but it was too late: Cal broke away from the others and bounded up the bus steps to slam into the driver's seat.

"I'm so sorry," he gasped. "I didn't want to bring them here. You have to get away—"

Red's shadow stretched up the steps and into the bus ahead of him, the knife's blade long and glinting dully in his fist. "Rayne Bakshi," he said, the sun reflecting off the knife and his shaved skull like a twin spotlight. "You've stolen something important from us, and we're going to take it back."

Leif rubbed his hand over his face and took a fortifying breath. Things were escalating very quickly.

# CHAPTER EIGHTEEN
## THE CULT OF HIS SERENE MAJESTY, INCANDESCENT AND ALL-SEEING GOD

"I'm so sorry," Calloway repeated. He had Rayne by the arm, guiding him quickly through the grounds as Leif and the rest of the order followed behind. Rikki held Angel in a similar way, and Leif watched her in case she chose to launch another handbag-based assault, and Rikki in case his fraying loyalty finally broke and he abandoned the order once and for all. Leif saw the way he looked at the woman, like she had hung the stars and the sun. It was how he should be looking at the Avatar.

But Angel didn't seem to like her chances against the entire order at once, not now that they had their knives out, and let Rikki guide her, however begrudgingly.

"They found me," Cal was saying in a strained whisper Leif chose to ignore. "They knew you had the bird, and they said— I couldn't risk it. I'm not with them anymore, I swear I'm not, and I never told them anything, but they knew."

"What are you even talking about?" Rayne asked.

"We're getting the rest of your band," Red cut in. "We tried this your way," he added, turning to Leif, "using Calloway as a negotiator, and he betrayed us. So now we do it like this."

"I didn't betray anyone!" Cal snapped. "You pulled a knife! Everything would have been fine—"

"Am I being held hostage?" Rayne demanded.

"No!" Cal said. "Well, technically, yes, a bit. Please cooperate. I don't like this any more than you do."

"This is insane," Rayne said, but no one paid him any attention.

Festival security had all but disappeared, presumably converging on the north side of the grounds where Travis was providing his distraction, leaving Leif, the order, and their hostages to move through the festival unimpeded. When they encountered Rayne's personal security guard, Rayne asked him through gritted teeth to fetch something from the far side of the festival grounds. Though Rayne was clearly banking on him to see it for the wild-goose chase that it was, the guard ambled off agreeably. Leif took it as a sign that luck was still on his side, despite Red's mutiny, and smiled grimly to himself. It was the kind of smile that made other people back away nervously and avoid eye contact.

After that it was a simple matter of rounding up the remaining Chokecherries and their opening act. The order steered them at knifepoint with unerring finality into an empty tent at the southernmost border of the festival, as far from Travis and the security personnel as possible. Red had Cal by the scruff of his shirt, his knife held up warningly the entire time, while Boar took up the rear, looming mountainously as he shepherded the captives along. Rikki kept his hand on Angel's arm, and no matter how she glared at him, he ducked his head and refused to meet her eye.

The order deposited them in the tent and herded them into the center, where a large pole was erected like something out of an old Western, and tied their hands behind their backs, tethering them to the pole in prisoners-of-war style. Calloway was tied up alongside them; he would never rejoin the order, especially not after this debacle, and Leif had no further use for him. By the time the order was done securing everyone, both bands were accounted for, with the exception of Kris Golding, Stef Morganstern, and the new girl with Passionfruit.

"I feel like we're missing some really important context here," Billie said, his voice slightly strangled despite his calm words.

"We are the Worshippers of His Serene Majesty, the Incandescent and All-Seeing God," Leif said, drawing on every ounce of his poetic theatricality as he wrestled control of the situation back from Red, "and you have stolen His Avatar."

"Um," said Billie.

"What the fuck," said Jay.

"Rayne," said one of the captives, in a deliberately calm voice, like the sea before the storm, "can you explain?" He was the only one

Leif didn't recognize: middle-aged, beleaguered, and obviously not a performer. He must be Bakshi's manager, Brian.

"Oh my god," said Rayne. "It's the fucking peacock."

Red and Boar visibly bristled, and Leif raised his hand to hush them.

"You don't speak of His Serene Majesty in those tones," Red hissed, ignoring him.

"The bird," Brian repeated. "The one Kris found the other night."

"That's the one," Rayne confirmed.

"Well, give it back so I can return to civilization and press kidnapping and unlawful confinement charges."

"I don't have it! Do I look like I have a peacock on me right now? He's probably wandering around outside somewhere, like he was when Kris found him."

"You should try keeping your Serene God on a leash next time," Jay suggested to the order. "Since this seems to be an ongoing problem."

Boar glowered and Red stepped forward, brandishing his knife as if he intended to gut his captive then and there. Jay flinched back even as he curled his lip in a snarl, and the rest of the hostages went rigid.

"You shut your mouth, boy," Red warned, the blade dangerously close to Jay's throat. "Or I'll shut it for you."

"Jay, shut the fuck up," Billie whispered frantically.

Leif wondered, not for the first time, whether he could actually hold Red and Boar back if they decided to kill their hostages. They had never killed anyone before—not in the time Leif had known them, at least—but then, no one had ever stolen their Avatar before, either. The Avatar gave their lives meaning, and Leif realized, watching them loom over the hostages, just how far they were willing to go to protect that meaning. He sighed and wished again that he had never told anyone about the peacock at all.

"Rayne, I swear to god, if I die in here, I am holding you personally responsible," Angel hissed to her companion.

"Nobody's dying!" Brian said loudly.

"How is any of this my fault?" Rayne demanded.

"Kris brings you a peacock and you don't question where he got it?"

"Are you saying I should have assumed it was attached to a cult? And you," he added, twisting in his ropes to face Calloway. "You knew! Why didn't you warn us?"

"There are lots of peacocks in the world," Calloway said under his breath. "I couldn't be sure it was the same one. I told Kris to be careful—"

"Where is Kris, anyway?" Brian interrupted.

Leif and the order frowned.

"He left," said Rayne.

"For brunch," Brian said slowly.

"The band."

Brian's face went white, then red, and a vein in his forehead throbbed like it was going to burst. For an instant Leif was less worried about the hostages meeting their end by Red and Boar's hands, and more worried about the health of the band's manager.

"He has a contract," Brian said, still speaking with deliberate slowness, as if he could put the universe back in order through sheer force of will alone.

"I'm sorry," Rayne said, his misery evident in his voice. "I know you warned me—"

"We'll talk later," Brian said.

"This Kris is the one who stole the Avatar," Leif said, hauling the conversation back under control.

"He didn't know it was the avatar," Calloway said quickly. "He just thought it was a fancy bird. He didn't mean anything by it."

Leif silenced him with a look. "Then why did he steal it?"

"He wanted to show me," Rayne said. "He thought I'd like it. And he was high as balls, but, uh." He glanced at Brian. "I don't think that's a legal defense."

Brian shook his head.

"This is insulting," Boar said. "His Serene Majesty the All-Seeing God should smite you for this."

"Let him fucking try it," Jay said. "You'd think he would've done it already, though. Since we stole his avatar and everything."

"Please stop antagonizing the cult," Billie said.

"They ain't shit."

Red stepped in and dealt Jay a vicious backhanded blow across the face, snapping his head to the side as the rest of the hostages burst out in yells, struggling against their ropes. Jay glared and jutted his chin out like he was actually going to fight the order from the floor with no hands.

Leif rubbed his temples and wished he were high enough to deal with this calmly. When they got out of this, he was going to try switching Red and Boar from psychedelics to sedatives for a while.

As Jay and the others continued to bait Red and Boar, shouting increasingly derogatory things about their god, Brian cleared his throat and Leif circled around to him to begin negotiations. After a few minutes it became apparent that the man had no concept of the peacock's importance to either the order or the All-Seeing God, so Leif dismissed him to turn his attention back to Rayne.

"Ah," said the rock star. "Yeah, you missed a bit."

Leif stared. There was an empty space beside him where Angel had previously been sitting, and she and Rikki were nowhere to be seen. The ropes had been hacked away—Rikki's switchblade, Leif realized belatedly. No one had thought to disarm him, despite his obviously wavering allegiance. A long slice in the side of the tent's canvas confirmed their escape.

"Yeah, you dumb fucks," Jay crowed from the other side of the pole. "That was worth a black eye, right?"

Red aimed a kick at him but Jay just laughed. He sounded slightly manic.

"Oh, for fuck's sake," said Leif.

Kris kept up a steady litany of curses under his breath as he trudged back toward the festival, his shoulders set and his jaw squared. The sun was deathly hot and the highway stretched bare, disappearing over the horizon into the eternity of rocky orange desert on either side. It would be pretty if he weren't so fucking furious. He tried to calculate the distance in his head—over half an hour by car, on the highway—and when he might reach the festival grounds.

Whatever fuckery Brad was causing, The Chokecherries had a show at four, and it was already half past one.

Kris didn't like his chances.

Also, his math was telling him it was going to take eight hours to walk back, and that didn't sound right, but he couldn't check the numbers because Brad had stolen his fucking phone.

He was going to throttle Brad with his bare hands when he finally caught up to him.

A car engine rumbled in the distance, and he flung himself into the road in his haste to flag it down. It slowed to a crawl as it drew up alongside him, pulling over to the shoulder and rolling the window down.

"Hey, Kris. You need a ride?"

Kris squinted and pushed his hair back to make sure he wasn't looking at a mirage. Tom smiled at him from inside the car, leaning over to wave as Kris panted in the sun.

"Fuck, please. It's an emergency."

Kris stumbled into the car and slammed the door shut behind him, gulping down his now-lukewarm water while Tom watched in consternation.

"You okay?"

Kris wiped his mouth, shook his head, then nodded. "I need to get back to the festival. My brother's sabotaging my career and Rayne thinks I hate him, which I don't, but he might hate me. I don't know. I need to fix everything. Can you drive me back?"

Tom looked taken aback, but he adjusted the rearview mirror and set his hands back on the wheel. "Sure, of course." He pulled onto the road and Kris sank into his seat. Tom glanced at him before cranking the air-conditioning. "Tough day, huh?"

"Understatement. But I'll make it work. I'll talk to Rayne—everything will be fine. Or, at least—almost fine. Manageable, anyway."

"That's a good start," Tom said encouragingly. "Is there anything I can do?"

"Honestly, just being in the right place at the right time like that was the most I could ask for. If you hadn't picked me up, I don't know where I'd be."

"It's dangerous to hitchhike. I always want to believe in the best in everyone, but you hear stories about girls— Well. I'm sure you've heard them."

"Lucky me it was you, then."

They drove in silence for another mile.

"So is Rayne your boyfriend?" Tom asked eventually. "I only ask because what you said earlier— Well, it sounds like relationship troubles. I don't mean to pry."

"Seems Rayne's love life is all anybody wants to talk about."

"Sorry. Forget I asked."

"No, it's okay." Kris took a deep breath, scrubbed his hand over his face, and confessed everything in a single exhalation. "You've seen our shows. You know what we do onstage. Up until last night, that was all we did—and then I pushed for more because I got tangled up in feelings for him, but I didn't have the balls to say it without a drink first, so he didn't take me seriously. He's fake-dating somebody else for the publicity but now he's talking about doing it for real, and if he does, I've lost my chance to convince him I'm not just messing around. Everything's fallen apart, and I don't know how to fix it. I wouldn't know how to fix it even without my brother interfering. God knows what he said to Rayne." He sucked his next breath in with a gasp of relief. It was easier to talk to a stranger than a friend, and anyway, wasn't that the whole point of a priest? "And now he thinks I've pulled the same shit on him that his heroin-addict ex-guitarist did earlier—fucking around and then quitting the band—which is the furthest thing from the truth!—but I need to tell him that so he believes me."

"I'm sure it's not as bad as you imagine," Tom offered. "Things rarely are."

"I'm in love with him, you know."

"I guessed," Tom said. "I'm not blind. I hoped you might— But I guessed."

"I should have told him I was bi right from the start, but it's so stupid—I was scared, you know? For no reason. It's not like anything would have happened to me. Even my parents . . ." His parents would be fine with it. They'd always been decent about that stuff, if not necessarily vocal in their support. "When you get ordained and you start preaching and stuff, promise you'll never say anything to make people scared of coming out? Not even accidentally. Because it gets right inside your head, man, so that even when you know nothing bad's going to happen, you're still nervous to do it, years later on the other side of the country. And it sucks."

"I promise," Tom said, and crossed himself with a painfully earnest expression. "No, I would never. No one deserves that."

Kris stared out the window. The desert stretched on and on, like a green screen on a loop in a cheap movie. "I don't know about God, but somebody's been playing a hell of a joke on me since I touched down in New York."

"The Lord works in mysterious ways. What else can I say? I feel like I should have more answers if I'm going to be a priest and offer guidance, but I don't. I'm not sure what that says about my calling." Tom shrugged helplessly. "All we can do is our best."

Kris tapped his fingers against the door. His nail polish was chipping; he should fix that when he got back to the bus. There was something soothing about dragging the brush over each nail, one by one. Angel had been right about the calm a makeup ritual could bring.

"I'm not a girl," Kris said.

Tom blinked.

"Since we're confessing shit," Kris added. "I thought you should know."

"Okay," Tom said, after a minute. "You just said you were bi, and I didn't realize—now I feel a bit silly, but okay."

"You seriously thought—"

"I met you in the White Rabbit. I assumed you were one of those, you know, punky androgynous girls. I was tipsy. You never corrected me."

"Sorry. I found it kind of flattering at the time. I was figuring some stuff out. Are you mad?"

"I wish you'd said something sooner, but no. Getting mad never makes anyone feel better about anything."

"I like that," Kris said thoughtfully. "That's a good philosophy. Sorry if I, like, embarrassed you."

"Oh, I've had worse. I can absolve you though, if you like," Tom offered. "Not officially. I'm not sworn in yet. But I think, as far as misdeeds go, your brother's outstrips yours by a long shot. There's no sin in wanting to feel loved."

"I hope not," Kris said. The highway in front of them shimmered in the heat, and he held his breath, waiting for the festival grounds to roll into sight.

Kris threw himself from the car before Tom had it in park, and made a beeline for the buses. He'd make it up to Tom later—a bottle of wine, the really nice stuff, or expensive chocolates or—something. A house, maybe. He'd figure it out later.

The buses were empty.

He tried the stage next, anxious but not alarmed yet. When the stage was empty too, his anxiety started to solidify into a rock in the bottom of his stomach, and he had to tell himself in no uncertain terms that Brad hadn't convinced both bands to pack up and leave altogether. He poked around the back of the stage, peering into the shadows and skirting the edges of the dressing room, when he heard Angel from outside, her voice unusually raised, shout, "You kidnapped us!" Kris wheeled around to follow the sound.

"You held us hostage like a bunch of thugs!"

"I'm sorry." A second voice, softer—Rikki. "They said— I didn't know how to stand up to them. They just want the Avatar back."

"It's a bird," Angel said flatly. "Get another one."

"That's not—"

"Nope. You telling me one bird is worth all our lives?"

Kris rounded the next tent, trying to figure out what the hell they were talking about.

"I'm getting security if I have to drag them here kicking and screaming, and this is all going to be over," Angel said. "No birds, no hostages—"

Kris caught sight of them by a tower of scaffolding between two empty stages a few yards off and veered toward them.

"You can't call the cops!" Rikki blurted. "We'll all get arrested."

"Yeah?"

"Please don't send me to jail." Rikki was still, his eyes downcast except to sneak glances up every now and then, shining and hopeful and full of regret. Angel opened her mouth to reply, but Kris interrupted before she got the chance.

"Angel!"

"You!" She smacked his arm as soon as he came into reach, then grabbed his hand and gave him a relieved squeeze.

"Me. Where is everybody? And did Rayne get a weird text from me earlier saying I quit the band?"

Angel narrowed her eyes. "He did. You've got some explaining to do, but it'll have to wait. The skinhead cult is holding the bands hostage in a tent and security's tied up dealing with some nutcase who started a fire on the far side. Apparently he's barricaded himself on a stage with a bunch of fireworks and is trying to incite a riot. Where's that damn peacock you stole the other day? The cult wants it back."

"Sorry, what part of that requires less explanation than a text?"

She took him by the arm and dragged him along through the tents, intent in her direction. "The peacock. They want it. Badly. They call themselves The Worshippers of His Serene Majesty, the Incandescent and All-Seeing God. That peacock? That's their god. And you went and stole the thing because you thought Rayne would think it was pretty. Which he did, and it is, but oh my god. And Rikki defected and helped me escape, which is the only reason I'm not throwing him to the wolves right now."

"Okay," Kris said. "Awesome. Hi, Rikki. And I didn't steal the peacock—I just picked him up and carried him around for a while. It's not like he was locked up on private property."

"He likes to wander," Rikki said. "Leif said it would be degrading to keep Him in a cage, since He's a god and everything."

"Uh," said Kris. "Do you believe he's a god?"

Rikki shuffled uncomfortably.

"He's still thinking about it," Angel supplied.

"I mean, I know He's not literally a god," Rikki said. "But Leif and the others were always really sure about it . . ."

"Crisis of faith later," Kris decided. "Where are they? It's three against three now, right? We can bust them out."

Angel looked skeptical, but nodded anyway.

"They'll have noticed we're missing by now," Rikki said, "but they can't do anything about it if they want to keep guarding the others. Do you have any weapons?"

"What? No, I don't have any weapons. Just— Take me to the tent, and we'll try to bluff them into giving up. Unless you think we can fight them," he added. He didn't know how to fight, but he could try.

"Let's try to avoid that, if possible," Angel said. "They've got knives."

"They have knives? This is insane. This is a terrible plan." Kris's voice pitched higher, and he tried to tamp down on it before it evolved into full-fledged hysterics. "Rikki, I'm sorry, but I'd rather you get arrested than anybody get stabbed."

"That's okay," Rikki said. "I have a knife too, if that helps."

"Rikki's right, though," Angel admitted grudgingly. "Cops aren't the best idea. They'll want to do things by the book: bring in backup and a hostage negotiator, the whole nine yards. That gives Leif and his friends too much time to get stabby if they panic. Besides which, the cops will take too damn long to get here."

Kris pushed both hands through his hair, aware he was exuding stress all the way into outer space. *We're not going to die at the hands of a bunch of stab-happy bird enthusiasts,* he told himself sternly. *Who even needs cops? Or backup?* Fuck. He took a deep breath. "Okay. Let's go. Aim for minimal bloodshed."

Angel led them through the festival to the tent in question. The cult's motorcycles were parked outside, hulking like shiny black beasts awaiting their masters' return. Boar stood outside the entrance, apparently watching for any passersby who strayed too near. Angel, Rikki, and Kris crept up from the side, ducking behind whatever cover they could find.

"We got out there," Rikki said, pointing to the slice in the side of the tent. "We can get back in that way, unless you want to fight Boar."

"His name is Boar?" Kris asked. "Jesus Christ. No, I'm not fighting a skinhead named Boar. Let's sneak in."

They slunk up to the side of the tent and Rikki crawled through first, his muscles bunching as he fought to keep quiet. Angel slipped through after him, with Kris following on her heels, wondering how the hell his life had come to this.

Red was waiting for them, arms crossed and a scowl on his face.

"Ah, shit," Kris said.

"Kris?" Rayne said. Kris couldn't see him around Red, but Passionfruit, The Chokecherries, and Cal were huddled around the center pole, sitting on the floor, tied up and looking so ridiculous that Kris did a double take.

"Hey, Rayne," he said. "Bad timing, but we have to talk later."

"No talking," Red growled.

Rikki pulled his knife.

"No!" Angel shouted. "Nope. No knives. Rikki, put it down."

"You little punk," Red said. "You think you can pull a knife on me? I'll take you apart with my bare hands."

Angel jerked Rikki's arm down. "Nope. Nobody's pulling any knives or fighting anybody. Rikki, stop it."

"But we have to—"

"No," she stressed.

Red smacked the knife out of Rikki's hand like a bear swatting a fly. "Traitor. You can join the others."

"Wait!" Kris shouted. Everyone stopped. "Wait. This is about the peacock, right? I'm the one who stole him; it's me you want. Let everyone else go and I'll get him back for you."

"That's not good enough," Red said. Boar lingered in the tent entrance, near enough to hear the conversation while still keeping a lookout. Leif watched them, weary looking and exasperated. "If you'd returned Him after an hour, maybe we could let this affront go, but it's been days. The All-Seeing God deserves a sacrifice to right this insult." Red glanced at Boar and Leif. Boar nodded enthusiastically; Leif very deliberately shut his eyes and pinched the bridge of his nose.

"What?" Cal cut in. "We've never sacrificed people!"

"We do now." Boar frowned. "The All-Seeing God needs to know these people are sorry."

"We're sorry!" Kris yelled. "Jesus, don't— It's just a fucking bird!"

That was, of course, the wrong thing to say, Kris reflected as Red dragged him to the pole and knotted his hands behind him. Diplomacy had never been his strongest suit, especially not when people were threatening to sacrifice him and all his friends to a glorified feather duster. Maybe that was something he should work on, now that he was living in the public eye.

"Hey, Rayne," he said glumly. He was tied up in between Rayne and Cal. It was sweltering in the tent, pressed up against so many other bodies, all of them sweating from stress and making the enclosed space more humid than the desert had any right to be.

"Hey, Kris," Rayne returned, his tone carefully unemotional. "You came back."

"I never left. My brother—"

"Stop talking," Leif ordered.

Kris obeyed, but leaned his shoulder against Rayne's in a silent bid for understanding. After a second, Rayne leaned back.

It was a start.

# CHAPTER NINETEEN
## A NEW GOD

There were few things worse, Kris decided, than listening to three giant skinheads discuss whether or not they were going to kill you, when you were tied up with no hope of escape. The prospect of dying without knowing how Rayne felt about him was one of those few things.

"We need to talk," Kris repeated under his breath, while the cultists argued back and forth about whether or not to kill them.

"I'm listening," Rayne said. "It's not like I have anywhere to be, after all."

"Whatever that text said, it wasn't me."

Rayne tilted his head. They were trying not to look at each other in case their conversation became obvious, but the tension between them was palpable.

"It said you regretted everything, you should have stopped me before we went so far, and you were leaving the band," Rayne said.

"That was Brad."

"Why was Brad texting me from your phone?" Rayne asked, his tone suspicious but his face bewildered.

"He stole it and kicked me out of the car. The point is, it's not true. Did you seriously think I was just going to run out on you guys like that?"

"No? But the things he said—"

"He made them up, because he's a lying bastard who lies!" Kris said, louder than he meant to. The cult paused in their conference and stared at them. "And you guys," Kris continued. "I thought my biggest challenge today was going to be stopping Brad from imploding my career, but you really blew it out of the park, didn't you?"

"Don't antagonize them," Cal muttered.

"Fuck antagonizing them! I've had a shitty day since I got up. I didn't need to be kidnapped on top of that. Fucking peacock cults, what the fuck? Why didn't you warn us when you saw I brought the bird back? You were all vague and unhelpful—how was I supposed to guess the peacock was from a goddamn cult? You never said a thing!"

"I didn't think they were going to do this!" Cal protested. "I couldn't know for sure about the peacock, and if it was a different one, I didn't want to cause trouble for no reason, not with the label already taking a chance on me—"

"Cults are more important than your music career! Jesus. I'm out. If they want a human sacrifice, fucking kill me already, man. Put me out of misery. I'm ready. I'm done."

Leif shifted uncomfortably. "It's not human sacrifice. It's—"

"Justice," Red cut in. "The All-Seeing God needs justice, so it's only right—"

"That we give Him an offering worthy of His Serene Majesty," Boar explained.

"And you're not," Red added.

Kris felt irrationally offended. "Then who is?"

The cult turned to Rayne.

The tent broke out in a cacophony of shouts from the hostages, all at once.

"You can't sacrifice him!" Kris shouted above the din, grappling desperately for any excuse, no matter how outlandish. "He's the chosen one!"

The tent fell silent like someone had pulled the power cord.

"That's why I took the bird," Kris said, talking slowly as he tried to invent a story out of thin air. "Because your god chose Rayne as the next . . . prophet."

Cal and Rikki stared at him with huge eyes.

"You're lying," Leif said.

"No, I'm not! Rayne, show them—show them the peacock tattoo!"

Rayne looked at him wildly. "Right. That's right, I have a peacock tattoo." He bent forward as far as the ropes would allow, not that anyone could see anything though his mane of hair.

Leif stepped forward, a frown marring his brow, to grab Rayne by the back of the neck and push his hair aside. The mandala was plain to see against his skin, even crisscrossed by the necklaces. Red and Boar crowded in to see, and all three of them stood there for a minute while Rayne, still bent double, waited, looking increasingly nervous.

"See?" Kris said. "That's a sign! You can't deny that's a sign."

"That doesn't mean—" Boar began.

"Yes, it does!" Kris shouted.

On cue, an eerie scream went up from outside the tent, and the cult froze like they'd been electrocuted.

"See?" Kris insisted.

Leif let go of Rayne's head and Rayne reared up just in time for Freddie Mercury to come flying into the tent like divine retribution, screaming the whole time and pushing the cultists aside to land in Rayne's lap in a whirlwind of feathers and talons.

"Look," Angel cut in. "Your god is beauty incarnate, right? So who's a better earthly incarnation of beauty than Rayne Bakshi?"

"He's literally perfect," Kris added. "The peacock knows it. Do you want to risk the wrath of the All-Seeing God by flouting his will like this?"

Leif, still frowning, stepped forward, flicking his knife out. Everyone on the floor flinched. The peacock flared his wings warningly, but Leif only knelt, reached around, and cut Rayne's rope. He drew Rayne to his feet—Rayne was shaky, but drew himself up tall—and studied him up and down as if examining a prime cut at the butcher's.

Rayne kicked Kris surreptitiously in the ankle in an obvious bid to know the plan. Kris winced and then shrugged. Freddie, devoid of lap in which to sit, began screaming again.

Like flipping a switch, Rayne cleared his throat and donned his stage persona like a robe.

"Your god is moving up in the world," he said, his voice low and smooth. It wasn't the voice of a hostage bargaining for his life: it was the voice of someone who held all the cards, and knew how to play them. "He wants to be admired by more than just four people. He wants to be adored by millions. That's why he chose me—I'm already loved the world over."

"But we've done everything He ever wanted," Red said plaintively. "Aren't we good enough anymore?"

"You did wonderfully," Rayne soothed, his voice like honey, "and you'll be rewarded for it. He's not dismissing you. This is just the next step of his plans."

"But He should have told us His plans," Boar protested. "We would have carried them out for Him."

Rayne straightened up another inch and glared. The cult took an involuntary step back.

"He *should* have?" Rayne demanded. "Maybe he thought you were getting too presumptuous; maybe that's why he left you. He's in me, now. I'm All-Seeing, and if you claim to worship me, prove it. Otherwise, I'll leave you here in the desert and find worthier acolytes." He glanced down at Kris, who nodded encouragingly. "I have the tattoo."

The cult nodded, slowly.

"You saw how Freddie—how the avatar came to me."

They murmured among themselves in quiet agreement.

"Have you ever seen anyone more beautiful than me?"

A frown and a ripple of debate.

"Have you?" Rayne demanded, steelier this time.

Kris was biased, but still, he couldn't see how they could deny it. From Rayne's dark complexion and the way his skin held the warmth of the sun like a jewel, to the sea-glass color of his eyes, to his curls—thick and silky, never a split end or a strand out of place—legs for miles and narrow hips—

Kris swallowed, distracted. Of course Rayne was the most beautiful man they'd ever seen. To think otherwise was blasphemy.

"I'll worship you," he said, over the cult's muttering.

Rayne and Cal both looked at him, startled.

"I will too," Angel said.

"And me," said Rikki.

"Fuck, sure," Jay agreed. "Why not."

"Good speech," Billie added.

"Stef will be furious they missed this," Maki said, "but I'll worship you."

"And me," Lenny sighed, regret plain in his words.

Hatchwork and Knocks chimed in, clearly lost, but amenable as long as it got them untied.

"Jesus Christ," Brian sighed. "Rayne—"

Rayne cleared his throat pointedly and tapped his foot.

"Your Serene Majesty," Brian corrected himself.

"And me," Cal said. "I'll worship you too." He glared at the cult before turning his gaze back to Rayne, who nodded to him.

"See?" Rayne said to the cult. "New acolytes."

The cult jostled one another for a second longer before reaching their decision and prostrating themselves, foreheads touching the floor. Rikki twitched but, being bound, couldn't join them. Cal closed his eyes for an instant with a wistful sigh. Rayne took a step back and looked around, shooting Kris a helpless glance before resuming his haughty stage character. Freddie walked between their prone forms, inspecting each one as they held quaveringly still, and everyone tied to the pole held their breath, waiting.

"Attention!" a voice blared from outside, crackling through a megaphone. Everyone jumped. The three cultists twitched and leaped to their feet, hands going to their knives. "We have you surrounded," the voice continued. "Come out with your hands up."

The cult glanced at one another. The megaphone screeched with static.

"You have until the count of three," the voice said. "On three, we're coming in, and we're not afraid to use force. One—"

Freddie shrieked and took wing, flying directly for Leif's face. Flinching, Leif ducked back with a shout as the bird drove him toward the tent entrance with beating wings and a tail that seemed far too heavy to fly. He fell through the opening, a scuffle sounded, and the megaphone blared again.

"Your compatriot has surrendered. I repeat, come out with your hands up."

Red and Boar exchanged a look and silently obeyed. As soon as they were out, the tent entrance flared open and the sun came streaming in, revealing Cassie, wearing a security guard's vest, and a very pleased Stef, who was wielding a megaphone. Butch headed an assortment of sooty-looking security personnel as cops and medics swarmed in the background, forcing the cultists into cuffs. The press, confused and overexcited, stood by with their cameras flashing.

"What's up?" Cassie asked. "You guys look like you had a fun afternoon."

"Please untie us," Kris said. "Now, please. Immediately."

"Sure, sure," she said easily, pulling a knife from god knew where. "So a cult, huh? An entire hostage scenario! And I missed the whole thing. I'm glad you're not dead, though; Mom and Dad would have had a fit. What happened with you, anyway? Brad said you weren't feeling good so he drove you back to the festival early—did you get your talk with Rayne?"

"I'm standing right here," Rayne said.

"Brad," Kris said. "Is he here? I'm going to kill him."

"Yeah, he'll probably be here in a sec," she said. "Why are you killing him?"

She finished sawing through his ropes and he rubbed the feeling back into his wrists before trying to stand. Rayne took his elbow and helped balance him, while fishing his phone from his pocket and handing it to Cass. "Read the last texts from Kris."

As Cass did, her eyebrows climbed higher and higher until they threatened to disappear into her hairline. "Brad sent these? What a dick. I missed a lot."

"What we get for sneaking off to make out," Stef said, cutting Passionfruit free. "Who wants a quickie when you can get kidnapped instead?"

"Seriously," Cass agreed. "And then there was that fire on that north-side stage! Most of security's still dealing with that. They caught the guy, though. See?"

She pointed to a couple of personnel who weren't manhandling the cultists: instead, they had in custody a skinny, twitchy-looking man who seemed to have been caught in an explosion. He was covered in ash from head to toe and littered with scratches, his hair standing on end and his eyebrows missing, but beaming manically. He shouted, squirming around in the security guard's grip as he tried to wave at Leif, who stoically ignored him.

"Huh," said Kris. "He's connected to the cult too?"

"Wild stuff." Cassie nodded. "You okay though, Kris?"

"Mentally?" Kris asked. Rayne still hadn't let go of his arm. His hand was warm, but he stood farther off than he normally did, like he wasn't sure he was allowed to touch. "We still need to talk," Kris said. "That's what I was coming to do before the fucking peacock cult got involved."

"Go," Cassie shooed. "Not far—the cops will want to talk to you. But go talk!"

Kris led Rayne through the side slit in the tent, ducking around the congregation of bemused but warily entertained law enforcement at the front, to stand a few yards back in an illusion of privacy, hidden by the tent's shadow.

"So," Kris said.

"I'm sorry," Rayne said immediately. "I never should have believed you would drop everything and run like that. I know you wouldn't, not for any reason, no matter how it looked. You're not Fink. You're nothing like him."

"I'm in love with you."

Rayne blinked, lips parted in shock. Kris doubled down and rolled with it.

"I've been in love with you this entire time." He forged on, speaking over the crazy pounding of his heart and the way his palms broke out in sweat. "Since way before we messed around. Maybe since you bought me that guitar and offered me a contract. And it wasn't messing around," he corrected himself. He needed to be completely transparent this time. "I needed to get drunk before I could make a move on you, but I didn't regret it, and I wasn't experimenting. I like guys too, Rayne. I've always liked guys, even when I was scared to say so back home. I'm bi, always have been, and I didn't need to get my hands on your dick to figure that out. But mostly I just like you. And I'm pretty sure you like me too. So, uh, anytime you want to say something, feel free to jump in. Please."

Rayne wet his lips. He looked lost, and like the sun coming through the clouds, radiant and hesitant and overwhelmed all at once. "Okay," he said. "I like you too. A lot. And I'm sorry for what I said this morning—I was scared of getting hurt, and I thought getting involved with you was going to hurt a lot. It usually does," he added, running his hand through his hair, "when straight boys are involved, and after Fink, I never wanted to take that chance again. I didn't want to risk the band, and I didn't think the sex would be worth the fallout." He dropped his gaze. "I didn't want to risk my heart again, either. Fink trampled it pretty ruthlessly, even if I was over him by the time he quit the band for good."

"Fink's a dick," Kris said bluntly, "and I'm sorry for everything I did that made you think I was like him. I should have told you I was bi sooner, but I'd never said it aloud before. I didn't want to complicate things, especially once Calloway showed up, but I still should have said something."

His heartbeat had calmed now that Rayne had heard him out, though as the adrenaline faded it left him weak-kneed and in need of a hug. Rayne made an aborted movement like he wanted to reach for him, but Kris shook his head. "Obviously I managed to complicate everything anyway. I wasn't planning on falling for you, if that helps."

"Complicate everything by encouraging me to do this stunt with Calloway, even though you liked me the entire time, for example?"

Kris's heart leaped at Rayne's cautiously teasing tone. "I was hoping that if you were off-limits, it would help me get my head on straight and I'd get over you," he admitted. "It kind of backfired."

"That night in the hotel, when I asked you whether I should do that stunt, I was hoping you'd tell me it was a dumb idea," Rayne said. "I was looking for some sign that you wanted me too."

Kris stared at him for a second before he started to laugh. "Oh man, did we ever fuck up. So, you and Cal . . . still just fake?"

"Yeah. We talked this morning, after you and I . . . after you left, but before Brad sent those texts. Cal said he wasn't ready for anything serious, but he didn't feel right about messing around when I was clearly hung up on someone else. And I'm not really into the whole casual-sex thing anyway." Rayne paused. "Of course, now he might be under arrest with the rest of the cult. I should go see about that."

"I'm sure you can convince the cops it wasn't his fault. Though you might have to fight Brian first. He's pissed."

"I can't blame him."

Kris shifted from one foot to the other. "So, are we okay?"

"Yeah. I should have seen this coming, though. I knew you'd be trouble the minute I saw you."

"The good kind of trouble?" Kris asked, daring to look Rayne in the eye.

"I think so. I hope so."

Rayne caught his wrist and tugged him near. Kris let Rayne reel him in, inch by inch, until they were standing a breath apart. Tipping his head back, he met Rayne's gaze, simultaneously shy and daring. His stomach flipped like it did when he'd first seen his own reflection after Angel had made him up, or when he'd walked out of the change room wearing girl's clothes for the first time, or when Rayne had come prowling up to him onstage and the crowd's roar swelled to a crescendo. He was going to kiss Rayne Bakshi—Rayne Bakshi was going to kiss him—in broad daylight, when they were both sober, and there was no audience to impress. He couldn't stop smiling as he leaned in. Rayne's hands hovered just above his shoulders, like he couldn't believe Kris was real, and—

"You!" a voice thundered.

They jumped apart.

Brad Golding stopped a yard away, glowering, one finger pointed accusingly, at which of them, Kris couldn't tell.

"You never learn, do you?" Brad demanded. "I thought I took care of this, but obviously—"

"Shut up," Kris interrupted. "What is even wrong with you? This is none of your business, man. Let it go."

"No. You—" Brad jabbed his finger at Rayne. "You're exploiting him for your sick gay exhibitionist fantasies, and he's going along with it because he thinks he needs the job. You messed with his head, and now he's confused, and he's dragging the rest of us down with him. I'm bringing him home to work in Dad's garage until he figures his shit out again, and we can go back to being a normal family!"

Kris punched him.

It wasn't a very good punch, as Kris had never had much practice, but it made a satisfying *thwack* when it connected, and the pain that shot up Kris's arm from his knuckles spoke of a job well done. Brad reeled away clutching his jaw.

"Oh, shit," Rayne said.

Kris shook out his hand. "I'm going to need an ice pack. You think the medics have one?"

"Yeah, probably."

Brad was bent double now, holding his face in obvious pain.

"Should we just . . . leave him?" Rayne asked.

"You just wait until Mom and Dad hear about this," Brad swore.

"What are you, five?" Kris said. "Get over yourself or I'll hit you again."

"I feel like I should be more offended about the exploitation comment," Rayne said, "but he's clearly nuts."

"Republican," Kris agreed. "If you want to fight him to defend your honor, I'll totally back you, though."

Brad, seething, walked up and shoved Rayne hard in the chest. Rayne staggered back a step, then shoved him in return. Shoving quickly turned to grappling, completely ineffectual on both sides, while Kris tried to figure out whether he should pull them apart or join in. Rayne was the taller of the two, and more fit, but Brad was clearly running on unadulterated anger, while Rayne had just escaped a hostage scenario and looked faintly baffled by the whole thing. When Brad resorted to hair-pulling, Kris intervened, wading into the fray to grab hold of Brad's ear—the only handhold he could manage—and yanking. Brad howled and pulled harder on Rayne's hair; Rayne yelped, and the police and medics, who were gathered at the front of the tent presumably straightening out the story behind the cult, finally took notice and poked their heads around.

"We're being attacked!" Kris yelled, pointing at Brad.

Brad finally let go, looked around wild-eyed, and booked it. He ran straight past the cops to the nearest motorcycle, which he leaped onto as if he had any idea how to ride the thing. He kicked the engine to life and made a bid for freedom. For a minute it seemed like he might succeed—Kris wasn't about to chase him down, and they'd run into each other at the next family gathering anyway—but the bike let out a shuddering cough and lurched to one side. At that precise moment Freddie Mercury, apparently seeing his own reflection in the shiny chrome of the motorcycle's body and deciding it was a threat, charged the thing head-on and latched on to Brad's scalp with an unearthly wail, louder and shriller than the engine. Brad yelled and drove straight into the nearest tent, which collapsed around him in a wave of canvas as the bike made a horrible noise and literally fell apart underneath him. The engine choked, sputtered, and went dead from under the wreck. Freddie fluttered out to land a few feet away, rearranging his wings and looking pleased with himself.

Kris and Rayne watched the tent settle. There was a conspicuous broken-motorcycle-shaped heap in the center of it, and it wasn't moving.

"Do you think he's all right?" Rayne asked eventually.

Kris couldn't muster any convincing amount of concern. "Let the medics figure him out," he said. "Let's go see how everybody else is doing."

Rayne slung his arm around Kris's shoulders like he'd done the day they first met, and Kris leaned into him, comfortable and warm, as the butterflies in his stomach finally settled into something hopeful rather than anxious, and together they walked back around to the front to rejoin the rest of their band.

# CHAPTER TWENTY
## NO ONE IS GETTING MARRIED IN VEGAS

In the end, the fallout went like this:

Brad ended up with a broken leg, some cracked ribs, and a colorful assortment of scrapes and bruises. He might have escaped unscathed had he not made the mistake of grabbing Rikki's half-dismantled bike instead of one of the other cultists' more functional ones, but Rayne said that was karma in action. Kris wondered if he should feel bad about not feeling bad, but if anyone deserved a hospital trip, it was Brad.

The cult was arrested on twelve counts of kidnapping and unlawful confinement—Travis, the fireworks arsonist, was likewise arrested and charged—though Rikki narrowly escaped thanks to having been tied up at the time of their rescue, and Angel's fierce insistence on vouching for him.

Calloway likewise avoided charges, though that wasn't to do with Angel, but with the label stepping in to smooth things over. Kris didn't hold a grudge, though Angel said she did, a little. Rayne seemed sympathetic, but not enough to resume their publicity stunt for the remainder of the festival—not that Brian would have let him anywhere near Cal following that whole debacle. Cassie was insufferably smug about the whole scenario, though Kris probably would have been too if he'd mounted a rescue mission like that while twelve people had let themselves be captured and tied up by three or four pseudo-religious skinheads.

Butch confessed that he spent the afternoon alternating between kicking himself for leaving them unguarded in their moment of need, and quietly laughing at them for being taken down so easily. He swore he would never take anything Rayne said at face value again, in case he was actually being coerced into sending his security away. Rayne apologized at great length and promised to negotiate a raise, which Butch said he would use to invest in a GPS tracker implanted under Rayne's skin so he couldn't get himself kidnapped again. Brian seemed uncomfortably keen on that idea, not that Kris could blame him.

Neither Passionfruit nor The Chokecherries were any worse for wear following their adventure, though Brian was verging on apoplectic as he conferred with the cops and made long-distance calls to lawyers, trying to cement the charges and get everyone's stories straight. Kris did his best to stay out of Brian's path, hoping that as long as Brian was preoccupied with those legal matters, he wouldn't have time to kick Kris out of the band for bringing the peacock to Rayne and starting the whole mess in the first place.

After giving their statements to the cops, the bands only had a minute to spare before stumbling onto the stage for their afternoon show. Passionfruit played a good set, their adrenaline giving way to giggles as they bounced off one another, reveling in their freedom. Kris watched the show from side stage, pressed up against Rayne, their hands entangled between them. They hadn't tried to kiss again. Kris knew they would during their show, and he'd love it as he always did, but after—when they left the stage, and the crowd finally went quiet—they were going to tuck themselves away somewhere dark and private, away from prying eyes. He could feel the promise in Rayne's heartbeat and the heat from his body, and the light that glinted in his eyes, and in the curl of his hair.

"Are you going to tell them you've been promoted to godhood?" Kris asked, standing on tiptoe to reach Rayne's ear and be heard above Passionfruit's din.

"I do like it," Rayne admitted. "I think I'd make a good god, don't you?"

"Like your ego needs any more stroking," Kris scoffed, but his heart still skipped a beat at the thought of worshipping Rayne like that, him laid out on an altar while Kris knelt for him, mouth watering.

Rayne squeezed Kris's hand tighter.

Kris didn't remember much of the show. The lights burned and the crowd screamed and Rayne was on fire, prowling to and fro like he couldn't keep his hands off Kris, and singing like he needed the whole world to sing with him. Kris sang too, away from any mike—he couldn't hear his own voice over the rush of blood and the screams from the audience and the pounding music, but he sang until his throat was raw and his head was spinning and he thought, *Yeah, I can see where the cult is coming from.* There was nothing like losing yourself in the oblivion of something beautiful, and Rayne—he was perfect. He demanded adoration, and the crowd was only too happy to give it to him.

Their stolen kisses came in rushes, hot and wet and all too brief, snuck in between verses. They were smiling too widely to do it properly, but Kris didn't care—he didn't care about a thousand people watching, either, because this time he knew it was for real. The kisses didn't taste any sweeter for it, not yet. They were still a shot of sweat and cologne, bumped noses and teeth, but with every one Rayne reinforced the promise that soon—as soon as they got offstage—he was going to take Kris apart atom by atom, and Kris was going to love every second of it.

Kris finished the show in a daze, drunk on possibility. They didn't stay for an encore—"Tomorrow," Rayne said, "for the last show, but not now"—and Kris handed his guitar to Cassie without a word, not even stopping to get changed, as Rayne grabbed his hand and dragged him back to their bus, while the rest of the bands whooped and wolf-whistled behind them.

"What happened to the no-fucking-on-the-bus rule?" Kris asked.

Rayne paused, one foot on the step. "Is that what we're doing right now?"

Kris wanted to do everything and then some. In lieu of answering, he climbed the last step of the bus and reached up to wrap his arms around Rayne's neck and kissed him on the mouth.

It was better than kissing drunk or kissing onstage. Kris waited for the screams, or fireworks, or for the earth to tilt off its axis. None of it came. All he felt was warmth, starting in his lips like the burn from eating too many peppermints, and traveling down his body to burst around his heart and pool in his stomach, low and burning, until every inch of his body was transfused with it. He felt like he was glowing, but he didn't want to open his eyes to look.

Rayne was solid against him, his hands running up Kris's shoulders to tangle in his hair, teeth tugging at Kris's bottom lip like he wanted to eat him alive. Kris would have let him.

"Can we—" Rayne began.

"Yes."

Rayne laughed and backed Kris farther into the bus, toward the bunks. They stopped only when the backs of Kris's knees hit the edge of his mattress. Rayne met his gaze, a question in his eyes, before pushing Kris down to sit. "I thought about this," he confessed, "a lot more than I meant to. I imagined a hotel where I could spread you out on a real bed and take my time with you. Show you how good it can be."

"Yeah?"

"Really draw it out," Rayne promised. "Make it last for days."

Kris blushed hard and his mouth went dry. He could practically feel his pupils blowing out, and he straightened, reaching for Rayne. There was little room in the bus, and as soon as they both tried to cram into Kris's bunk there would be even less, but he was up for the challenge. He didn't need to take up much space.

Rayne laughed. "God, I can't believe I ever thought— 'Historically straight,' as if you were ever—"

"Stop talking," Kris ordered, grabbing Rayne's wrists. "Either kiss me or take your shirt off, I don't care which."

Rayne pulled his wrists free and unbuttoned his shirt one hole at a time, teasingly slow. The silk shifted, revealing his skin in glimpses, and Kris's heart beat faster with every inch Rayne exposed.

"Tell me what you want," Rayne said. "Tell me what you thought about." He finally let his shirt fall open, and dropped it behind him on the bus floor. Kris shuffled forward until he was sitting on the very edge of the mattress, his feet on the floor, with Rayne standing between his knees, the opposite wall of bunks within touching distance of Rayne's back. Kris put his hands on Rayne's hips, his thumbs brushing the skin just above his belt.

"Get down here."

Rayne ducked and crawled into the bunk beside Kris, all warm skin and still too many clothes.

"I need to memorize every single one of your tattoos now," Kris told him.

"Okay," Rayne said, breathlessly. "Sounds good."

Kris started at Rayne's throat, on the side of his neck where the wild roses were. He kissed his way down to their leaves on Rayne's shoulder, leaving tiny lipstick marks like petals as he went. His lipstick was purple this time, so dark it was nearly black. He couldn't tell the difference between the ink and the plain skin by taste alone—it was all sweet and salty—but he was diligent in tracing every line, either with his tongue or his fingers. He kissed his way across the key under Rayne's collarbone. He kissed the two birds on his chest. His breath ghosted over the snake that curled down Rayne's arm; the last of the scab had since fallen away, but it was still so fresh in Kris's memory that he was scared to touch it. He ran his fingers over the mandala on the back of Rayne's neck and the sun between his shoulder blades, slow and deliberate, while Rayne panted and shivered under him. Kris was in no rush. Their last time had been so hurried—he didn't regret it, not for a second—but now, he wanted to take his time.

He nipped Rayne's skin, and Rayne tightened his grip in Kris's hair, warningly. Kris laughed, his breath huffing over Rayne's chest. "You can tell me to stop," he pointed out, "if you have a better idea."

"I might," Rayne said.

"Does it involve taking off your pants?" Kris dipped lower, down past Rayne's ribs to follow the faint line of his abs, then over to bite at the jut of his hip bones. He traced the veins in Rayne's stomach down to where they disappeared under his belt. "You hiding any more ink down there?"

"No."

Kris sat up. "Guess I'm done, then."

"You're the actual worst," Rayne informed him, and pulled him into a kiss. Whatever was left of Kris's lipstick smeared between them, and he moaned into Rayne's mouth. When they pulled apart, Rayne looked fucked and all they'd done was make out; Kris couldn't imagine how he appeared, with his makeup trashed and his hair mussed. *Debauched* might be the word for it.

He could always get more debauched.

"You, sit," he said, and climbed over Rayne and out of the bunk to kneel on the bus floor, manhandling Rayne into the position he wanted: upright, with his feet on the floor and knees spread wide. Rayne went obediently, and soon Kris was sitting between his thighs, at eye level with his belt buckle. Kris wet his lips, his insides turning somersaults.

"I don't really know how to do this, so you don't get to complain about technique, okay?"

"Baby, you could bite it off and I'd probably thank you," Rayne said. "I mean, try not to, but the bar is low."

"Personally, I'm just going to try not to choke." Kris took a deep breath. He was shaky, but the expression on Rayne's face—like Kris was awe-inspiring, down on his knees like this—was exhilarating. He reached for Rayne's belt. "Okay, rock star. Let's see what you've got."

Rayne threaded his fingers through Kris's hair and tugged to get Kris to look up again. "Hey," Rayne said. "Love you."

Kris's butterflies flipped over and he grinned. "Love you too." He slid Rayne's belt from its buckle and smoothed his hands over Rayne's hips. "Okay. Here we go."

After, they lay side by side, crammed in the narrow bunk, sweaty and glowing.

"I still owe you dinner and roses," Rayne commented, dragging his fingers up and down Kris's side like he was petting a giant cat.

Kris hummed and stretched, tangling their legs together in the sheets. "We're pretty close to Vegas. We could do a stopover before we head to LA. Hit the strip, find a little neon chapel, and get hitched on the down-low . . ."

Rayne flicked him in the ear, and Kris laughed and squirmed away.

"Can you imagine what Brian would say?" Rayne asked. "He wouldn't let us out of his sight for the rest of our contracts. Maybe never."

"Okay, no shotgun wedding." Kris shuffled over to lie on his side, propped up on one elbow to look Rayne in the eye. Rayne gazed up at him, blissed out and adoring. "Roses and dinner for sure, though. No cop-outs this time."

Rayne caught Kris's hand and brought it to his mouth, pressing kisses over Kris's knuckles. "No cop-outs this time," he promised. "Like I said in New York—whatever you want, I'll get you. Anything in the whole world, babe, it's yours."

"Well, I want to stay in the band," Kris said. "After my contract's up, I want to sign on for good, if Brian's not out for my head."

Rayne nodded. "He likes you, really. He'll let you stay."

Kris smiled, relieved. "And I want to do this again. Or something like this."

"I wasn't joking about the hotel," Rayne said immediately. "Or if you don't want a hotel—anywhere. Anytime. Whatever you want, that's what I want."

"Will you still take me to India and show me around? With or without the band, I'd really like that."

"Yes, absolutely. I'll take you everywhere and show you everything. What else?"

Kris bit his lip. "Mostly I just want you, any way I can get you."

Rayne kissed him softly. "I'm sorry I didn't believe you the first time you told me. I panicked. I thought you were too good to be true."

Kris rested his head on Rayne's chest and let Rayne play with his hair. "I'm pretty sure I've fucked up my fair share in this. Let's call it even." He dropped a kiss to the nearest bird tattoo.

Rayne laughed and tugged his hair. "So we're good?"

"We're good." Kris kissed the underside of Rayne's jaw and flung an arm around his ribs, nestling in close. "We're perfect."

# CHAPTER TWENTY-ONE
## THE BEGINNING

The next morning, Kris, Angel, and Rikki sat side by side in the shade of the bus, their legs stretched out in the sand, watching the clouds drift by. They were white and fluffy like cotton candy, and Kris wanted to remember the image forever: the bright-blue sky and the fierce orange desert sand, cacti on the horizon, and the endless highway winding through it all. Angel's thigh was warm where it pressed against his, casual and unobtrusive. Rikki sat on her far side, and Kris shut his eyes, breathing in the hot, dry air, and took a moment to enjoy the company. They were a million miles from Rayne's penthouse where he and Angel had first met, and Kris couldn't imagine life without her now—her or Rayne.

"You and Rayne are a sure thing now, for real?" she asked.

"For sure for real," he confirmed.

"Finally. It was driving me crazy trying to get you two on the same page, you know. Like you were both determined to make things as hard as possible."

"Sorry. Next time I'll listen to you from the start."

"Smarten up and there won't need to be a next time," she suggested.

"That's fair." He couldn't speak for Rayne, but now that he had him, Kris had no intention of letting this relationship slip through his fingers. He poked Angel in the shoulder. "Thanks for not giving up on us."

She rolled her eyes and swatted him away, but she was smiling.

"What will you do after the festival?" Rikki asked Angel.

"I'll finish the tour, then head back home to my club for a while. What about you? You've got no gang anymore."

Rikki watched the sky for a minute, his expression contemplative. "I think that's good, though. I don't know what I'll do, but I'll figure something out. Like a fresh start." He dropped his gaze and turned his hands over in his lap, knotting his fingers together before asking softly, like it had been bothering him for a while: "How come you took a chance on me?" He kept his head down like he was afraid of what he might see in their faces.

"Did you not want us to?" Angel asked.

He shrugged.

She touched his chin and raised his head. His gaze flickered before settling on hers, his eyes wide and cautious. "I'm a black trans girl living in America: I have to believe in the good in people. If I weren't an optimist, I might as well be dead. I'll help you figure things out, if you want."

When Rikki leaned in to kiss her, he did it slowly, like he expected her to move away or shove him back, but she did neither. Kris cleared his throat and got to his feet.

"I'll leave you to it," he said. They ignored him, so he ambled out of the shadow, scuffing the dust with his sneakers as he walked. It was a beautiful day, and cults notwithstanding, he'd be sorry to leave the desert. Still, he expected LA would be just as breathtaking, if in a different way. Hopefully with less kidnapping.

He returned ten or fifteen minutes later and dropped back down beside them like he'd never left. They both seemed bonelessly content, their fingers tangled together in the dust between their legs, shy smiles on their faces, eyes downcast. Kris thought back to his night on MDMA, when every touch sparked like electricity. Angel and Rikki were practically glowing; was that how Kris had seemed when he looked at Rayne? He elected not to comment apart from jostling Angel with his shoulder as he got comfortable.

"So?" he asked.

"He said he'd come back to the White Rabbit with me. Help out with repairs, that kind of stuff."

Rikki nodded, something reverent in his gaze. "Anywhere. Anything, as long as it's with her."

Kris decided to trust Angel's judge of character. "Well, good. I'm happy for you."

The clouds had long since drifted past, leaving the sky bright blue and blue alone. Rikki curled up against Angel, leaning his head to rest on her shoulder, and traced shapes on the back of her hand with his thumb.

"You see that blond guy over there?" Kris asked, nodding to Tom, who was wandering the grounds, seemingly elated by his surroundings, and possibly high. "He's going to be a priest someday. If you still have questions about finding a new god, you should talk to him sometime."

"I don't know if I want a new god," Rikki said.

The way he looked at Angel, he might have already found one.

Tom paused in his walk and glanced over. He brightened and waved. Kris and Angel waved back.

"I'll introduce you," Angel said. "Never too early for him to start practicing sermons, right?"

"Oh, I gave him a head start on that already," Kris said.

"Okay," Rikki said, turning so he was nestled more securely against Angel's shoulder, her hair brushing his face. "I'd like that. Anything you want."

Angel hummed and held him close.

"So, back to the White Rabbit, huh?" Kris said. "You're done with the music industry?"

"Not until this tour is over," Angel said. "I'll get Rayne set up with a new makeup artist long before I call it quits. The Chokecherries will get by fine without me. I miss my club; it deserves some undivided attention for a time."

"Course it does. It's your baby."

"And we'll still see each other," she added. "Hell, Rayne will probably book you to play there before the year is up. We'll be just fine."

Kris wasn't worried. He felt on top of the world, like he had everything he'd ever wanted. It was hard to worry in that state.

"Tell me about your club?" Rikki asked.

Angel smiled and tipped her head back to look up at the sky. "It's a burlesque club. You know anything about burlesque?"

Their parents came to say goodbye that afternoon, whisking Kris and Cassie out for lunch one last time before they parted ways. Brad had been left behind at the hotel, apparently sulking like a toddler but unwilling to start another fight with his leg in a cast and his ribs bruised to hell and back, in almost as bad shape as his dignity—that, and the fact that Freddie Mercury was still roaming the grounds as part of Rayne's ensemble.

"The doctors say he'll recover just fine," their mom said as they sat around the diner table, "though he'll be sore awhile."

"As soon as he's come down from his painkillers, we'll be giving him a talking to, you believe me," their dad added. "It's not how we raised him—not how we raised any of you—and we won't stand for it any longer, not as long as he calls himself a Golding."

"I'm sure that'll go over great," Kris said. "Rayne's offering to help pay the medical bills, by the way."

"Oh, dear—no, we couldn't possibly accept that," their mom said, visibly flustered. "Tell him thank you, but we'll get by."

Kris shrugged. He had protested the idea too at first, but Rayne was as stubborn as he was loaded, and the battle had been short-lived.

*"I'm not a saint,"* Rayne had said. *"I'm not offering because I think he deserves a second chance. I just want to see his face when he realizes he owes me his life, and I won't let him pay me back to settle the score. Anyway, your parents shouldn't have to shoulder his bills all by themselves."*

Kris was confident Rayne could win his parents over as well.

"You and Rayne, though," his mom said.

"Us," Kris agreed.

"The young man he was seeing earlier wasn't serious?"

"That's a funny story, but no. They're not together. They never were."

"But you two are? Should we expect him for Christmas?"

"I think so, and . . . I don't know? But it's good. I'm happy." He let his grin burst out. "I'm really happy."

His parents beamed back at him as Cassie leaned over for a fist bump.

"So, Knocks is getting his cast off in a couple of weeks," Cassie said, smoothly changing the subject as she chased her waffles through a sea of syrup, "but the guys have been talking."

"Knocks has been playing rhythm guitar in the meantime," Kris supplied for their parents.

"He likes it," Cassie said. "A lot. So much, actually, that they asked if I wanted to stick around for the rest of the tour."

"Is that something you want?" their mom asked.

"Hell yes, absolutely. This is the best thing I've ever done. I was thinking..."

Their parents looked at each other in trepidation.

"About what happens after the tour. Assuming I stay on as their drummer, of course." She speared a waffle piece with a strawberry on it and popped it in her mouth. "Because they said they like playing with me, and if Knocks wants to keep playing guitar, well, after the tour they're going to start work on their next album."

"You want to join the band for real," Kris said.

"Obviously."

"You've got your last year of college starting in September," their dad pointed out, in a careful, nonjudgmental voice.

"That's the part I was thinking about," Cassie said. "I can put school on hold and go back next year if this doesn't work out, but I won't get another chance to join a band like this. Not without starting from scratch and forming my own, you know?" She looked back and forth between them.

"This isn't something you should jump into," their dad began.

"Like I jumped into drumming for them?"

He held up his hands. "It's your future, Cassie, and your education on the line. You've only known them a week."

"We're not saying don't do it," their mom added. "We're saying sleep on it a little longer."

"These are all hypotheticals," Cassie said. "We have to finish the tour first. Hell, we have to get Knocks's cast off first. I just... I think it would be really cool. I'm happy here. I feel like I could do it forever."

Their parents softened.

"Both my babies growing up and joining bands," their mom said. "Touring the world. What a turn."

"I'm twenty-five," Kris said, without much rancor. "I've been grown-up for a while."

"You look like you're going through a second puberty, though," Cassie pointed out cheerfully. "You're wearing more makeup than I did in high school."

Kris kicked her under the table and she kicked back, grinning.

"As long as you're happy," their mom said again.

"We are," they chorused together, and Kris had never felt anything truer in his life.

When they returned to the festival, he called Brad. He was still angry; Brad getting thrown through the wringer hadn't changed that.

"Hey, listen: we're heading to LA in a day and then we're going for the international leg of the tour, so we won't see each other again for a while. I wanted to make sure you knew something, before I left."

"What?" Brad croaked. He sounded terrible, but if the doctors said he was going to be fine, Kris wasn't going to worry about it.

"We hooked up, me and Rayne. I sucked him off and he told me I was pretty, and we had a really good time. And in another day or two, after we're back on the road, we're going to book a hotel and I'm going to ask him to fuck me, for real."

Brad sputtered incredulously over the line.

"And I'm going to fucking love it, Brad, and there's nothing you can do about it."

He ended the call before Brad could respond and turned off his phone with a smile. Though his heart was racing, he felt insurmountable.

"Are you going to be okay?" Kris asked.

He and Calloway stood by The Chokecherries' bus. Passionfruit was wrapping up their final show, and he was due to take the stage in a few minutes. The last show of Purple Sage.

"I feel like I owe everyone an apology, though I'm not sure what to say," Cal said. "I'm grateful Rayne's not pressing charges."

"He's good like that."

"I should have spoken up as soon as I saw you with the bird. But I was scared the label was going to drop me if I caused the slightest problem, and I hoped . . . you know. I hoped I was wrong about the cult and everything. I hoped the whole thing would blow over before it could come to a head." Cal rubbed the back of his neck. "I fucked up on that one, and I'm sorry for it."

"No lasting damage done," Kris said amiably, "but yeah, an earlier heads-up would have been nice."

Cal nodded. "I feel like I should apologize on behalf of the label, as well, for that whole publicity stunt. I suppose I got in the way a bit, didn't I?"

"The stunt definitely wasn't your fault. I fucked that part up on my own. We all made our fair share of mistakes the past week or two."

"I suppose we did. Granted, some were bigger than others." Cal shook his head with a wry smile. "But you and Rayne are an item now, I hear? That's good. He was fucking pining for you, man, as sure as you were for him. Absolutely painful to watch, I'm telling you." He tentatively touched Kris's shoulder. "I'm glad you got it sorted. Sorry I wasn't much help."

"Sorry your stunt got cut short," Kris said sincerely. "I guess you never got enough press coverage to really boost your career like you wanted, huh? Now all people are talking about is the hostage-cult thing."

"Ah, it's for the best, I think. I'm not sure I'm ready for the sort of fame Rayne has. I'll take a few years to grow into it." Cal tipped his head back to squint at the sun. "Actually, I thought I might take a break once this bit of touring is over, see a counselor, maybe. Talk about the whole cult scenario, get it off my chest."

"Yeah?"

Butch hollered at them from the stage, beckoning Kris over.

Kris clapped Cal on the arm. "Listen, it was cool meeting you, despite everything. Good luck with the band and the counseling, if you go that route. I think it'd be good for you."

Cal smiled widely, the same smile from that picture Kris had seen way back before he'd met him. "Good luck to you too. We should keep in touch—Rayne Bakshi's fake love interests. Though of course you're the real thing now."

"We should. We will," Kris promised as Butch yelled again, this time with greater insistence.

"Go on," Cal said, laughing. "Give him one last kiss from me, will you?"

Kris grinned and shivered—he could kiss Rayne now, he was allowed, and there was no one to stop him. Waving goodbye to Calloway, he broke into a run, heading to the stage for their last show as his heart tripped with excitement in the best way possible.

He arrived backstage just as Lenny drummed out his cue. Slinging his guitar strap over his shoulder, he ran to take his place in front of the crowd. Rayne caught him before he went out, pressing close to drop a kiss to Kris's cheek. Kris twisted around to kiss him back—mostly teeth, he couldn't stop smiling—before slipping out onto the stage.

Their intro song flared up around him as he shouted a hello to the crowd, which roared back at him in adulation. Standing there, soaking up the noise and the heat and the love, he felt like he was flying. He got to kiss Rayne again and mean it, and keep meaning it, for as long as they were together. He couldn't think of anything better.

When Rayne took the stage, Kris could feel the crowd's excitement all the way down to his bones. He kept pace with the rest of The Chokecherries as they careened through their intro song, and then everything dropped off, music and screaming cheers alike, as Rayne slunk up to the mike.

"This is our last show of the festival," Rayne said. The crowd cheered. "But these kinds of things stay wild right to the end. Did everybody have a good time?" Screams. "Yeah? It got crazy there for a minute, let me tell you. But as long as it turns out all right in the end, that's what matters. You have to remember that." He turned to look at Kris. "Now, this show—I want to dedicate it to all the lovers out there. I don't care if you're fifteen or fifty or ninety-three, if it's your first love or if you met an hour ago or if you've been married for thirty years. All the lovers, and everybody who's still looking: this show is for you." He paused for Lenny to tap out a beat. "So let's get started. You know how it goes. You going to show me you love me?"

The crowd screamed and stomped and flung their hands up in worship, and Kris closed his eyes and let it all wash over him. When he opened them, Rayne was watching the crowd, leaning on his mike stand with both hands as he basked in their attention, the stage lights casting a halo down around his curls. He was larger than life, his skin shimmering with glitter, and Kris had never seen anything more beautiful in his life.

"Yeah, just like that," Rayne said. "Okay. Let's roll."

Dear Reader,

Thank you for reading Arden Powell's *A Summer Soundtrack for Falling in Love*!

We know your time is precious and you have many, many entertainment options, so it means a lot that you've chosen to spend your time reading. We really hope you enjoyed it.

We'd be honored if you'd consider posting a review—good or bad—on sites like **Amazon, Barnes & Noble, Kobo, Goodreads, Twitter, Facebook, Tumblr,** and your blog or website. We'd also be honored if you told your friends and family about this book. Word of mouth is a book's lifeblood!

For more information on upcoming releases, author interviews, blog tours, contests, giveaways, and more, please sign up for our weekly, spam-free newsletter and visit us around the web:

**Newsletter**: riptidepublishing.com/newsletter
**Twitter**: twitter.com/RiptideBooks
**Facebook**: facebook.com/RiptidePublishing
**Goodreads**: tinyurl.com/RiptideOnGoodreads
**Tumblr**: riptidepublishing.tumblr.com

Thank you so much for Reading the Rainbow!

RiptidePublishing.com

# ♪ACKNOWLEDGMENTS♪

Thank you first and foremost to my beta readers: Lin, for reading my very first draft and telling me about New York; Neurtsy, for assuring me it was funny and fact-checking my drug scenes; and K.D., for general encouragement and positivity, even when I'm sure I was driving her mad.

Thanks to my parents, Earla and Jamie, for listening to me ramble on about writing and rewriting for months on end, and promising to buy a copy (or ten) when it was done.

Thank you to my entire publishing team at Riptide, who made my book beautiful, but most specifically my editor: for pulling me from the purgatory of the slush pile, for excising my draft of errant semicolons, and for helping shape this book into something much better than I could have done on my own.

## ALSO BY ARDEN POWELL

Reset to Zero
The Botanist's Apprentice

# ABOUT THE AUTHOR

Arden graduated from St. Francis Xavier University with an Honours degree in English literature and the realization that essay writing is just another form of making up stories. They also came away with an overriding and all-abiding love of semicolons, to the general dismay of their editors. Arden lives in Ontario with a dog, a fellow human, and an unnecessary number of houseplants.

Website: ardenpowell.wordpress.com
Twitter: twitter.com/ArdenPowell
Goodreads:
goodreads.com/author/show/8053059.Arden_Powell